LOKi

KEIRA MONTCLAIR

DEDICATION

To all my readers of the Clan Grant Series:

This is for you! You loved the Grant and Ramsay families, so here are the stories of their bairns several years later.

For all new readers to my novels:

This is a stand-alone series that began in Scotland about twenty years after the Clan Grant series.

Hope you all enjoy!

THE GRANTS AND RAMSAYS IN 1280

Grants

1. Laird Alexander Grant, and wife, Maddie (Book #1)
a. Twin lads-James (Jamie) and John (Jake)
b. Kyla
c. Connor
d. Elizabeth

2. Brenna Grant and husband, Quade Ramsay (Book #2)
a. Torrian (Quade's son from first marriage)
b. Lily (Quade's daughter from first marriage)
c. Bethia
d. Gregor
e. Jennet

3. Robbie Grant and wife, Caralyn (Book #4)
a. Ashlyn (Caralyn's daughter from a previous relationship)
b. Gracie (Caralyn's daughter from a previous relationship)
c. Rodric (Roddy)
d. Padraig

4. Brodie Grant and wife, Celestina (Book #3)
a. Loki (adopted)
b. Braden
c. Catriona
d. Alison

5. Jennie Grant and husband, Aedan Cameron(Book #7)
a. Riley
b. Tara
c. Brin

Ramsays

1. Quade Ramsay and wife, Brenna Grant (see above)

2. Logan Ramsay and wife, Gwyneth (Book #5)
a. Molly (adopted)
b. Maggie (adopted)
c. Sorcha
d. Gavin
e. Brigid

3. Micheil Ramsay and wife, Diana (Book #6)
a. David
b. Daniel

4. Avelina Ramsay and Drew Menzie(Book #8)
a. Elyse
b. Tad
c. Tomag
d. Maitland

PROLOGUE

From THE BRIGHTEST STAR IN THE HIGHLANDS
1267, Clan Grant Castle, Highlands of Scotland

Loki Grant knew he would never be good enough.

What a fool he'd been to think Jennie Grant would ever be interested in him. He stood on the periphery of the great hall of the Clan Grant keep after the ceremony in which he'd been given a special crest by Aedan Cameron for saving his new wife, Jennie Grant.

Jennie, the lass Loki had thought he loved, stood not far from him, laughing next to her husband, their love apparent to anyone who glanced their way. The Cameron chieftain was a proper match for someone as fair and kind and wise as Jennie. Loki, of course, was not. He had spent much of his early life tucked inside an old crate in the royal burgh, begging for scraps of food, running the many paths of Ayr to work for coin, doing anything to keep from going hungry. But then God had sent him Brodie and Celestina Grant, who had brought him to the Highlands and adopted him as their son.

That had been the best day of Loki's life. He'd finally felt a sense of belonging. With time, he'd fallen for the brown-haired, brown-eyed lass standing in front of him.

But he'd known all along his feelings for Jennie were wrong. She was too old for him, and besides, she was his adopted aunt, the baby sister of his adopted sire, Brodie Grant, and Laird Alexander Grant, the best swordsman in the land. How could he have ever imagined a match between them was possible?

Because he'd always been a dreamer. Otherwise, how would he have ever survived living outdoors with the rats and other critters of the world, fending for himself at the tender age of six summers?

Now he understood. Jennie was his aunt, and that relationship would last a lifetime. He was young, and someday, he'd find another lass to wed. He walked over to her once her husband moved to talk to another, feeling the need to explain himself so she wouldn't think too poorly of him.

"Aye, Loki?" Jennie gave him her warmest smile.

He struggled for words, but finally said, "I want you to know… I want to say…you were correct before. I did have feelings for you, but no longer. Well, now I have different feelings. I realize our ties as family are much more important, and I also want you to know that I followed you because you are like my sister, not for any other reason." He had saved her from a man intent on killing her. It was one of the best things he had ever done.

Jennie smiled. "I know. We are family, Loki."

"I like the Cameron. I will miss you, but I think you chose well, and I wish you much happiness."

She hugged him and said, "My thanks."

Directly behind him, three young lassies about his age stood gazing at him. Jennie took a step back, giving him a clear view of the girls. Loki scowled a little, puzzled by their attention.

The first lass said, "Loki, you are such a strong guard."

The second lass said, "Loki, you are so handsome."

The first two lasses ran away, giggling.

The third lass, a girl with reddish-gold curls and a spattering of freckles across her nose, stepped up to him, took a deep breath, and declared, "Loki Grant, you are the handsomest, most braw warrior I have ever seen. Someday, I'm going to marry you." She leaned toward him, closed her eyes, and pressed her lips against his.

Her lips were warm and soft, and she smelled nice, different from any other lass.

When she ended the kiss, she whispered, "My name is Arabella, and I promise to love you forever." She twirled around and ran away.

Loki turned to look at Jennie, blushing a deep red.

"Verra nice, Loki," Jennie said, her eyebrows raised. "I think she's quite bonny."

Loki couldn't help but grin. He'd never met Arabella before, but she liked him, she really liked *him*, Loki Grant—a lad who'd lived in a crate under the stars for longer than he cared to remember. She had a smile on her face that made him feel extra special, as if he were the only one that mattered in the world.

"I like her. Someday, I'll make her my wife."

He nodded to Jennie standing next to him.

Arabella would be his, forever.

CHAPTER ONE

Late autumn, 1280, Scotland

Loki Grant opened one eye and the first thought that passed through his mind was: *Who am I?* The strangest thing about that was it was the one question he could not answer. He knew his name, but what else did he know?

He closed his eyes again as pain from his head rippled through him. He reached up with one hand to feel the swelling by his eye and the giant egg on his head. Rolling onto his side, he placed his hands on the cold, hard ground beneath him and pushed up with a roar loud enough to send the few birds left in the Highlands squawking off to another tree.

A voice came from off to his side, a voice he knew and trusted but couldn't quite place yet.

"How's the head feel? Like you are daft and have no sense? If so, then you have the right of it. You have no sense at all. How many, or do you not remember?" Logan Ramsay, his uncle, chuckled at him. Actually, Logan wasn't truly his uncle, but his Aunt Brenna had married into the Ramsay family, and the bonds between the two families were so strong that he considered the man an uncle. Loki managed to turn his head to stare at Logan, who was seated on the log next to him.

Logan held his hand out, offering him a bit of ale from a skin.

Loki took it, groaning again. "Arseholes. Every one of them."

"How many?"

"Five."

"When the hell are you going to stop trying to get yourself killed, fool? I've taught you better than that. You're interested in working for the Scottish crown like I do, and I'm happy to teach you. I'd like you to take over some of my jobs so I can spend more time at home with my Gwynie before I die. I'm not getting any younger, but you are not getting any smarter, are you?"

Loki took another slug of the ale before handing it back to his uncle. "How did you know where to find me?"

"People talk. Even reivers. They all talked about the tall fool who thought he could take on five men. When will you learn?"

"The news we heard about my sire was wrong. There was no information to be found about him anywhere near Ayr. The lad who gave us that information must have been daft. I was about to return to the Highlands when the reivers set upon me. I'm practicing everything you've taught me, Uncle."

"Apparently not. I've taught you that the most valuable weapon you have is your head, yet you keep getting it beaten. You'll have no brains left if you keep going on in this manner."

When a rustling from the forest reached his ears, he jumped up and grabbed for his dagger, though he came up with naught. Logan's wife, Gwyneth, emerged from the trees a moment later, her boots crunching on the thin layer of snow on the ground. "Leave off, Logan. He'll have enough pain without you making it worse. Loki, where are you hurt besides your head?"

Loki paced in a circle, moving about awkwardly at first, but then settling into a limp.

"How old are you, lad?" Logan asked, his green eyes narrowing.

"How in hell would I know the answer to that?"

"Dinna rail at me. How old did your mother and father decide you were when they found you and took you in?"

"Seven or eight summers. Would make me twenty and four or five."

"Well, you look and act like you're an auld man. You better start using that quick mind of yours or you'll soon be in trouble. There is no call to lose your head because you could not find your sire. You knew 'twould not be easy."

"Enough, Logan. Let him get his bearings before you chew his arse out." Gwynie made her way over to Loki, carrying a wet linen she'd presumably brought from the creek.

"I do not need it. My thanks." Loki Grant had two goals in life—to find his true parents and to marry Arabella Lewis. At this point, he faced failure on both fronts. Despite his best efforts, he could not find his sire. Thus he could not prove his worth to Bella's father, who would not allow his daughter to marry a man of uncertain blood. This trip had been intended for a dual purpose—to begin training to work for the Scottish crown and to search for his sire. This most recent experience had forced him to concede to the impossible. Since he could not measure up to Bella's father's standards, he might as well leave the clan and work for the Scottish crown as his aunt and uncle had done for years. But he knew Bella, the love of his life, would not be happy about his decision even though he'd attempted to get her ready for the possibility by telling her this trip was to train for work with the crown.

The truth was he didn't wish to tell her he'd failed again on obtaining the information necessary to make their marriage possible.

Gwyneth held out the cloth and charged toward him. "I'm cleaning it, whether or not you wish it. You're not thinking clearly yet. Now hold still." Gwyneth set to work on him, not speaking during her ministrations. His aunt had the magic intuition of knowing when to speak and when to keep quiet. Her dark leggings and forest green tunic, her favorite colors, almost made her melt into their surroundings. Still as thin as a young lass, she was agile and tough. Whereas most lasses he knew were proficient at needlework, his aunt was a renowned archer and hunter.

Loki did as he was told. He loved his aunt and uncle as much as he loved the rest of his adopted family. His real mother or father had left his life, for whatever reason, too early for him to recollect either one of them. Brodie Grant, his adopted sire, had found him living in a crate behind a tavern, and the two had worked together to save Brodie's new wife, Celestina. Afterwards, the young couple had brought him back to the Highlands and accepted him as their son. Loki adored them both for all they had done for him, and someday, he hoped to be able to tell them how much, especially his mama, but not yet. He didn't know why, but whenever he tried to express his love and gratitude, it was as if he turned mute.

But while his adopted family never made him feel less than accepted, other members of the clan liked to remind him that he was not truly of Grant blood. Now it was his job to prove himself to everyone, but he was still making a fool of himself. When Gwyneth finished cleaning the dried blood off his face and placed some salve on him, she said, "You know, you do not have to do this. You'd be happier if you stayed at the Grant castle in the Highlands. 'Tis where you belong. We all know it but you."

Loki nodded his thanks for her ministrations, then stalked off into the woods to relieve himself. Once finished, he found a nearby creek and knelt down to throw some ice cold water on his face, pausing to wash his hands and neck as well. He had few memories of the battle, only that five men on horseback had stolen all his weapons and his horse and knocked him out.

He'd failed again. Mayhap his aunt was right, and it was finally time to head back home to the Highlands—only to leave forever. He returned to the clearing and shrugged his shoulders at Logan. "My decision is made. I'll return to inform my parents that I'll be working for the crown from here on out. Then I'll meet you wherever you would like to complete my training. I'll not go searching for my sire again."

"Loki," Gwyneth said, "I think you're making the right choice about your sire. You have two adoptive parents who love you. Give up on your true parents. You may never know, and there's no point in allowing it to ruin your life. But are you sure you do not wish to reconsider and marry Bella?"

"I cannot, Gwyneth. Her father will not allow it. So I'd rather leave and work for the crown than see her marry another. Will you train me?" He glanced from Gwyneth to Logan, feeling the defeat weigh down his entire body. All his sword work, all the careful training and eating he'd done to increase his size and his muscles, suddenly taunted him. As a young lad, all he'd desired had been to train as a Grant warrior, to live in the Highlands and fight like the renowned Alexander Grant, his uncle, and now that he was close to accomplishing that goal, it had lost all its power over him. Perhaps he should have done something entirely different with his time.

Logan nodded his head. "Aye, we'll train you. Gwynie can ride with me. We'll go with you to your keep."

"Mayhap we can stop at Drummond or Cameron land and get a horse. That way you can have a shorter journey home."

"Nay," Logan snorted. "We'll travel with you all the way home. Your father would have my arse if I let you ride alone, looking like a lad with no brain to use his brawn. Then, when you're ready, we'll leave together. You'll just have to stop at Clan Ramsay for a bit afterwards."

Rather than argue, Loki climbed onto one of the horses and flicked the reins.

Logan helped Gwynie mount and climbed up behind her, wrapping his plaid around the both of them. Silently, Loki cursed himself for having made them come out in such cold weather. It was not quite winter yet, so they could still navigate, but it would not be the best of treks through the Highlands at this time of year. He'd try to talk them out of following him the entire way later. He didn't have the energy right now.

"Did you find out anything at all about your true sire?" Gwyneth asked.

"Nay." Loki frowned. "I really do not care any longer. I've ended my search."

"Whenever you change your mind," Gwyneth said, giving him a knowing look, "we'll be glad to help again."

"My thanks," Loki muttered. It was hopeless. He'd never find out who he truly was and why he'd been living in a crate at seven summers in the royal burgh of Ayr.

His interest in his past had finally been beaten out of him.

Arabella Lewis trudged down the hill from the Grant keep kitchens to her father's cottage, carrying a loaf of fresh bread and a trencher of stew. When she reached the hut near the stables, she opened the door and walked straight to the table to set the food down in front of her sire along with some mead.

"What took you so long? You've been playing around with the lads again?" Her sire's narrowed gaze told her exactly how much he trusted her.

"Nay, Papa, I do not play with the lads." Bella had to admit her interest was limited to one lad in particular—and had been since the first day she met Loki Grant. He was the strongest, most loyal, and cleverest lad she had ever met, and she liked how his brown hair had a glint of gold in it. Her mind filled with a vision of him all muscle from working hard in the lists. A sigh escaped her lips as she remembered all the times she had sneaked out to watch him work at his sword-fighting skills, usually taking off his tunic to practice. Her favorite part of Loki was his eyes, strictly because they did not match, something that made him unique. But now Loki was busy training to be a tracker for the Scottish crown, something that would take him away for long periods of time, and Bella was stuck in her role as a kitchen maid.

Her sister, Morna, piped up. "Papa, she's not interested. She's sworn off all lads after you refused Loki Grant as her husband."

"Aye, well, 'tis a good thing I did," her sire barked. "He's not good enough for my lassie, and he ran away, besides."

She glanced at the ceiling to keep herself from shrieking at her father. His repeated refusal of Loki's request to marry her made her want to tear down the walls around them. "Papa, that is ridiculous. He's the nephew of our laird, Alexander Grant. Who is good enough for me in your eyes, the King of England?" She wished to scream to the rafters over her father's foolishness, but he was too stubborn for that to do any good.

Her father snorted, "Aye, he would suit. I know you all favor Loki, but I promised your dear mama you would marry a lad born in our clan, and I will not go back on my word. Loki grew up in a crate until Lady Celestina brought him here. You know I tire of this conversation, daughter. You will not marry him."

"Why do you hate him so? You know all he has done to protect his clan. There have been many, many times when his ingenuity has saved others, especially his mother and his Aunt Jennie." She made her way around the small hut, picking up after her father and her sister as the two of them shared the stew she had brought in from the keep.

"Aye, you mean his adopted mother and his adopted aunt," Morna added.

Arabella bumped into her sister as she passed by, intending on giving her a not-so-subtle message of what she thought of her disloyalty. "They consider him their true kin, so why can you not see it? The two of you drive me daft." Bella wanted to punch something. No matter how often they discussed the same topic, neither would budge.

Her father barked, "I do not hate the lad as I can see he is a hard worker, but he is not a true member of our clan. Who knows what blood runs through his veins?"

"According to everyone but you, he's a Grant."

A bony finger pointed at her. "You need to watch that sassy mouth of yours, lass. You'll get yourself in trouble. There are plenty of other lads you can marry, or you could stay here and take care of me once your sister marries."

"Papa, I'd like a family of my own. You know that, and I'm sure Mama would want the same for me."

"Mayhap one day, but for now you can help your sister get ready for her marriage. I may even send you with her for the wedding, then you can return shortly after. She must keep her hands pretty for her husband. He is a cousin to noble blood, so she will not be working once she's married." Her father slurped up the last bite of stew in the trencher, glancing up at her with veiled innocence once he was done. "Sorry, but you did not want any stew, now did you? You've probably had plenty working in the kitchens and all."

"Nay, Papa. I do not need any. I'm tired. I'm going to sleep."

Bella ignored her rumbling stomach and moved over to her small pallet behind the partition in the corner.

"Bella, you need to wash the dishes from the day," her sire shouted.

"Morna could not wash them?" Exasperated and exhausted, she flounced down on her pallet.

"Nay, all that water would ruin the tender skin on her hands."

Bella glanced at the red skin on her own hands, calloused from carrying heavy pots in and out of the great hall.

"I'll take care of it in the morn, Papa. I'm too tired." She leaned back onto her pallet and covered herself with the threadbare plaid, dreaming of a lad with one blue eye and one green eye.

CHAPTER TWO

Once inside the Grant castle gates, Loki thanked Logan and Gwyneth, dropped his horse off at the stables, and headed straight for the great hall. Jake and Jamie, his twin cousins who were younger than him by five summers, ran to his side from an unknown location.

"Loki, you're back. What tales have you for us today?" Jake asked.

Jamie added, "Must be at least one good one. Look at the scars and wounds he's wearing this time. Tell us how you beat the devil out of the whoresons who attacked you." His eyes widened in anticipation.

Not bothering to lift his head, Loki continued on his way. "I have naught to tell you, lads. I'm off to see my mother. I'm sure my sire is in the lists."

"Aye, 'tis where we're going, to train. We'll let him know you've arrived. But at least tell us where the black eye came from? Please? We'll tell the others!"

He quickened his pace, but shouted back over his shoulder at them. "Uncle Logan and Aunt Gwyneth are on their way. They'll be happy to tell all. I need sleep."

He stepped inside the door to a large chorus of greetings. He waved to all the friends and family gathered in the great hall, then turned to the right to head toward the corner passageway that led to the tower rooms, the place where his parents lived. His uncle had continued to expand the keep, eventually adding another building of chambers due to the swelling size of their immediate clan, but his parents had remained in the towers—the most comforting place in the world as far as Loki was concerned, mostly because of his mother. He continued down the passageway, wondering how his parents had been. He grimaced and reminded himself that he was thinking of his *adopted* parents.

He'd been so fortunate to be adopted by Brodie and Celestina Grant, no one knew it better than he did. So why had he risked hurting them by seeking out his true parents? Even though they had never said so, he could tell how much it wounded his mother by the look that came into her eyes every time he mentioned searching for his real parents. He could not tolerate that look. In fact, every time he saw it, he turned away, feeling so guilty he wanted to run in the opposite direction. If not for Arabella's foolish sire, he would never have tried to seek out his true sire. He believed he was a lad of value, but there was no way of proving his lineage.

Celestina's English father had kept her locked up in their house as a young lass. Loki had first set eyes on her as she sobbed from the balcony of her home, basically her prison. Being wee at the time, he could sneak anywhere without being seen. So he had followed Celestina, his 'missy angel,' as he had referred to her, wherever life took her. It was this sneakiness that had earned him the admiration of Brodie Grant, the youngest brother to Laird Alexander Grant, for it had helped Brodie to find her after she was kidnapped, right before the Battle of Largs.

After the conflict ended, Brodie and Celestina were reunited in the Highlands, and it was then they had adopted Loki and brought him into their home. He still counted the day he became Loki Grant as the happiest—and luckiest—day in his life.

He opened the doorway to the tower chambers and stepped inside.

A chorus of "Loki!" greeted him. His mother sat with her needlework in her lap, but she stood as soon as she laid eyes on him, dropping her sewing onto a nearby stool. Her expression had gone from sadness to excitement in an instant. His two sisters, Catriona and Alison, twelve and five summers, ran up and hugged him. His brother, Braden, would be in the lists with his father.

His mother waited for him to come to her, as she always did— a relic of her proper English manners. With a still trim figure and long yellow hair threaded with only a few strands of silver, Celestina Grant was still a beauty. Some of his aunts had widened at the hips after carrying bairns, but not his mother. She was still the most beautiful woman in the Highlands.

But that wasn't really what he saw. To him, she was simply the woman with the biggest heart he had ever known. She held her arms wide and he stepped into her embrace, towering over the wee woman.

"Loki, how I have missed you." She patted his shoulders. "I am so glad to see you." She stepped back and cupped his cheek. "How do you fare? Did you find your true parents?"

And that look of excitement in her gaze changed to one of worry as fast as could be. Just the mention of the identity of his true parents was enough to send heartache through his adopted mother. Loki chastised himself, as he'd already done countless times already. He could never love his birth mother as he loved Celestina. Someday, he promised himself, he would tell this woman how much her love had meant to him.

It had all been for Bella—to prove to her father that he was not some worthless orphan. True, his uncle could force the marriage, but it would feel wrong to allow his powerful adoptive relatives to fight his battles for him. Since he'd been so long without parents, he wanted Bella's relationship with her sire to be strong. He had no desire to cause any discord between the two. Someday, he hoped he and Bella would have their own bairns, and bairns needed their grandparents, just as he had needed parents of his own.

But he had searched and searched, turning up naught. Now it was time to give up.

Or was it?

"Nay, Mama, I have not found them. I believe I'll stop searching. There is no way to determine who they are or were."

Celestina took his hand and ushered him over to the table. "Catriona, find your brother some mead. He must be thirsty."

Five-year-old Alison stood next to him and said, "Loki, my friend said you are not really a Grant. 'Tis not true, is it? I told her that you are truly my brother, and she said you are not and you are a phony." She turned to her mother. "Mama, she's wrong and I'm right, do you not agree?"

"Shush, child. You are not to bother your brother with such foolishness when he has only just arrived home. Of course, he is a Grant. Now apologize to him."

Alison hung her head, clasped her hands behind her back, and whispered, "My apologies, Loki."

Loki smiled at her and ran his fingers through the golden strands that were just like her mother's. "Do not worry, wee one. They cannot hurt my feelings."

How he wished that statement were true. Aye, it was this incessant need for others' approval that niggled at him. He wished to prove he was of value, that he deserved to be a Grant, that he was intelligent, braw, and strong of his own right.

He wanted to prove that he deserved his adopted name—and that he deserved Arabella.

But how was he to do that if not by finding his birth parents?

"Catriona, if you please, after you have gotten the mead, I would like for you and Alison to go to the kitchens and find something for your brother to eat."

As soon as the girls left the chamber, his mother drew his attention again. "Loki, will you speak to Arabella while you're home? Will you be staying for a while?" His mother settled on a stool across the table from him, her back straight and her hands on her lap as she'd been taught. The beautiful woman in front of him had been brought up by a brute. How Loki wished he had gotten his hands on her father before Brodie Grant had killed him. His mother was as prim and proper as anyone Loki had ever met. Loki would do anything to keep from disappointing her.

"Mama, I have just arrived. I do not think Bella's sire has changed his mind."

"Oh, but Loki, I think Bella missed you terribly. I do believe you make a lovely pair. But you do not?"

"Her sire believes I am not good enough for his daughter. There is no point in pursuing the lass."

"Loki, can you truly dismiss your feelings so easily? I know in my heart how you feel about her, and I know she reciprocates your feelings. Why not marry her and start a family? You'll make such a wonderful father. Uncle Alex would speak to her father on your behalf. As laird of the clan, Uncle Alex can force the marriage if you truly wish it."

Loki did not know how to answer her. "I've actually decided to work with Uncle Logan for the Scottish Crown. I've come home to tell you my decision, then we'll be leaving again. I think I'll head out to the lists to speak to Da. Do you need anything?"

Celestina's face fell. "Nay, go as you wish." She stood up to embrace her son again.

The door opened and Arabella entered carrying a trencher of stew for Loki. "Lady Madeline instructed me to bring this for you, Loki."

Celestina hurried over to the door. "I'll just go check on the lassies."

Once she left, silence echoed throughout the tower chamber. He did not doubt that his mother had intended to leave him alone with Bella.

"Is there aught else I could get ye?" Arabella lifted her chin to stare off over Loki's head, her pinched lips telling him exactly what she thought of him at the moment.

Loki sighed as he stared at her luscious pink lips and soft curves. True, Bella was a wee thing, but it did not stop her from having beautiful rounded hips and an enticing pair of breasts that was presently level with his eyes. Hellfire, what he loved most about her was her feistiness. Never shy, she let everyone know her feelings, including her feelings about him.

Aye, he'd promised himself that he would give up on her—on them—after his failure, but that was akin to asking a Highlander not to carry his sword. He rubbed his hands on her saucy hips, then grabbed her by the waist and plopped her onto his lap. Her scent set him afire in a way that no other lass could do. "Och, my Belle," he whispered close to her ear. "It has been a long time. Both the scent and sight of you reminds me of how I've missed you."

She feigned disinterest and shoved against his chest. "Leave off, you brute. You left me."

Loki could tell her efforts were minimal, so he cupped her cheeks to force her gaze to meet his. "Do you truly wish me to leave off, or would you rather I kiss you senseless, lass?"

Bella threw her head back and giggled, then wrapped her arms around him. "Loki, why must you work for the crown? Stay here on Grant land. I missed you so."

Loki's mouth descended on hers and she leaned close to him, moaning that sweet sound he so loved to hear. He angled his lips over hers, parting her mouth to tease her with his tongue. When she responded, he groaned and tugged her closer, deepening the kiss and threading his hands through her hair. When he ended the kiss, he leaned his head against her forehead and whispered, "You're mine, my Bella. We belong together."

Bella fussed with her skirts and mumbled, "'Tis no use, Loki. My sire would never allow us to marry. No matter how I reason with him, he stays the same, saying my mother insisted I marry someone born into the Grant clan. He wants me to help Morna get ready for her marriage. You know how I feel, do you not?"

"Aye, I know you love me, lass, as I love you." She'd snagged his attention with that comment. "What? And exactly what does he expect you to do to help Morna?"

"I do not know, nor do I care." She rubbed her hands up and down his arm, squeezing his biceps.

Loki tugged on her hair, lifting the fine strands that had escaped her plait. "Is your hair golden or red? Sometimes I cannot tell. It seems to depend on the light."

She shoved at his hands, forcing him to release her hair and bring his gaze back to hers. "Why can we not marry as we wish? Is that not what you wish?"

The failure of his recent venture found its way back to the forefront of his mind. "Aye," Loki sighed. "Say no more. I know I will never be good enough for your father. I'll leave you be. My thanks for the meal."

Sounds of wee feet in the passageway brought Loki back to his senses enough to set her away from him. The door flew open and Catriona and Alison ran in and stopped in front of Loki, wee Alison staring at him wide-eyed. "Look, Aunt Madeline sent two sweet tarts for you. May we share one with you?"

Loki smiled at them, then glanced over his shoulder as Bella walked out the door, unable to tear his gaze from the enticement of her bottom. "You can eat them all, lassies. I'll eat the stew. My taste for something sweet is leaving me."

Bella turned to grin at him, and Loki winked at her.

He ate the food Bella had brought, trying to figure out a way to convince her father that he was a fit husband for his daughter.

At the moment, he could think of naught that he hadn't already tried.

Just for a moment, he imagined what it would be like to tell Bella's father that he, Loki Grant, truly did have noble blood in him. Being of noble birth would change everything. If he could just find his true sire, he'd know. What had his father been like? Was his mother as sweet as Celestina? How had he ended up living alone behind an inn in the royal burgh of Ayr? He'd tried so hard, but now he would never have the answer to his questions. Perhaps it was better to just leave it all alone.

He'd also understood he could discover the complete opposite to be the truth. Was his father a thief or a murderer who had been condemned or sent away? He'd never know, and perhaps it would prove a blessing.

Nay, coming home had been the right thing to do. Unfortunately, Bella could soon leave Grant land to assist her sister. This news told him he was doing the right thing. He'd never have a chance with her, so his decision to leave with his aunt and uncle was the right decision. Everything here would merely remind him of his love and his loss.

He loved Bella, but some things just could never be.

CHAPTER THREE

Loki paced in the great hall after dinner. Alex and Madeline had insisted on a special meal for the clan once a week, with everyone invited inside for meat pies, bread, cheese, and fruit tarts. The men would hunt boar, deer, or wild pigs for the meal— even a pheasant if they could. They'd had a good summer this year, so the food stores were well-stocked with apples, pears, beans, and peas. They had music and dancing as well, and the minstrels stopped in whenever they came this far into the mountains. Two were here tonight, but once heavy winter set in, they would be gone.

Highland weather was another reason he needed to leave soon. Once the heavy snows came, there would be no departing Grant land. Loki sat at the dais with his mother and sire, along with his other aunts and uncles, Alex and Maddie, and Robbie and Caralyn. Most of his younger cousins sat at a nearby table, but he had finally been given a seat at the dais, along with Alex's eldest lads, Jamie and Jake.

Jamie leaned over to address Loki. "Who have you chosen to warm your bed tonight, Loki?"

Loki scowled at his cousin. "You will not speak in such a way at the same table as my mother."

Jake gave him a look that was probably intended to convey maturity. "Why are you so sensitive?"

"Because 'tis my mother. You two have the sweetest mother on the face of the earth, and you do not respect her enough. That, then, is your choice. But if you do not respect *my* mother, I'll take the two of you outside and explain it to you with my fists," he whispered.

His mother gave him a sweet smile. Hellfire, but he would miss her. His sire Brodie wrapped an arm around Celestina's shoulder and hugged her close. Watching the two together was much like a fist in his gut. *This* was what married life should be—loving and supportive. It was undeniable that the sight of their happiness often made him wonder what had happened to his true parents— sickness, an animal attack, reivers, what? What could make two parents desert their child? He knew his adoptive parents would never do such a thing.

He scanned the room automatically, though it would only cause him pain when Bella crossed his line of vision. Shite, she was a beauty tonight. He caught her gaze once in a while, though she sat with her disapproving sire, a man with a permanent frown on his face because he was in the same room as Loki. Loki glanced at Brodie, who was laughing as he spoke to his brother, Robbie, also laughing. Aye, he had been blessed to find himself in such a family.

He should probably tell his sire how much he appreciated him. Rolling the stem of his goblet in a circle on top of the table, he wondered why he found it so difficult to put words to his feelings for them.

The music had started and a few of the younger clan members started to dance. His cousin, Ashlyn, soon appeared in front of him, her eyes cast downward. "Loki would you dance with me, please?"

"Ashlyn, you are close to my age. Are you sure there is not a lad here you would rather dance with?" His cousin was the daughter of Robbie's wife Caralyn and his uncle had adopted her.

"Nay, you know I'll never marry. 'Tis not for me."

Loki sighed, then got to his feet and held his hand out to Ashlyn. Her face lit up, so they strolled over to the dancing area and joined the group. Ashlyn was someone he could never refuse. He and Ashlyn shared a special bond—both of them had been adopted by the Grant clan after difficult childhoods. To this day, she spent most of her time protecting her younger sister Gracie, and now she had two brothers to protect as well.

Loki was a natural protector, too. He was completely devoted to his adoptive mother and father, his brother, Braden, and his two sisters. He loved every one of his aunts, uncles, and cousins. Bella was also on that list, though he knew he did not have any right to be her protector. He would never let aught happen to any of them. "Someday, you'll find a lad and change your mind."

"Nay, I will not. And you know why. I do not trust men." As she twirled in a circle, laughter erupted from her normally serious face and her brown hair swung in a curtain behind her.

Loki said, "Ashlyn, you've become a beautiful lass. You must marry."

"Do I? And what about you? You're older and not married." She smirked as her chin jutted out another notch.

Loki had no answer for her. He decided to let her win this argument, so he focused on dancing instead. Of course, he did not fail to notice that Bella had just moved into the dancing area. His gaze honed in on her and her partner. The lad who was chatting with her was not very big, and not very smooth either, but he was having a laugh with her.

"Your scowl is telling everyone what you think of Bella dancing, cousin."

Loki jerked his gaze back to Ashlyn. "I've no scowl on my face." He tried to smile, but failed.

Ashlyn giggled. "I can see you are trying. You're almost there, though I know better than to believe it. 'Tis making you daft to watch her with another."

The music ended, so they walked back to the table, but Loki purposefully altered their path so he could swing a sharp elbow at Bella's dance partner in passing. He could feel the emotion churning in his gut as he headed back to the dais.

His sire moved to the stool across from him. "Jealousy is a wicked emotion."

"I do not know of what you speak, Da."

"Nay? I think you do, and if it bothers you so, say the word and we'll see you married to her. You know your laird can order it."

"As I've said before, I do not want it ordered. I want Bella to want to marry me, and I want her sire to believe I'm deserving of her." He plunked onto the bench, frustration seeping from his pores. He would never survive Bella marrying another.

"That will not happen if you run away." Brodie spoke to him

quietly, but Loki was sure his mother could overhear.

"Aye, well, her da does not accept me, so there's no reason for me to stay any longer."

"Why is that? I think your mother," he tipped his head toward Celestina, "would say otherwise."

Hellfire, why did his sire always do that to him? He could not bear to look at his mother now. "Bella may be sent with her sister to assist her upon her marriage."

Brodie appeared surprised. "We were not aware of that."

Loki clenched his fists on top of the table. "There is no chance of our marriage."

"There is, you're just insisting that it happens on your terms."

"And if it were up to you, Da, would you do the same or have your laird force it?" Loki knew the answer to this question, but he did not know if his sire would admit it.

Brodie turned to gaze at his wife, who was deep in conversation with her sisters-in-law. His father's hair had flecks of gray in it and he kept it longer than he had years ago, but one thing about him that had never changed was the deep love he felt for his wife. "At your age, I'd have done the same. But knowing what I know now, I would allow my laird to force the issue. I could not imagine life without your mother." Brodie reached for Celestina's hand and held it cocooned in his two while she continued to talk to Maddie and Caralyn. "Pride is not always worth it, Loki. Love is. But I'll not interfere. 'Tis your decision to make."

Alison came over and tugged on her father's sleeve. "Papa, may I sit with you?"

Brodie let go of his wife's hand and turned to his youngest daughter with a smile. "Of course you may, lassie." He swung her up in the air and then plopped her down in his lap with a shriek. He then kissed her cheek and growled, "There'll be no lads dancing with my sweet lass." Alison laughed and wrapped her arms around her father. "I love you, Papa." She had the look of her mother, while Catriona more closely resembled the Grants.

Loki couldn't help but feel a little envious of Alison. Why was it so easy for his sisters to admit to their feelings?

Another giggling voice caught his notice, and he glanced up in time to see another lad pulling Bella onto the dance floor. He knew why the lads all wished to dance with her, so it did not surprise him. Bella wasn't just beautiful, she was also as nimble on her feet as his Aunt Gwyneth. Still, it released an ache in him that traveled all the way to his soul.

His sire stood up and grabbed his mother's hand, and with Alison in his arms, the three of them headed to the dance floor. Loki's adoptive parents tickled Alison and played with her until she was quite hysterical. There they were for all to see—the perfect example of a loving family. *His* family. Soon, Catriona ran over to partake in their revelry. Braden was busy with his friends in the corner, eyeing up the lassies.

Where did he fit in? Did he? He ran his hand down his face and closed his eyes to rid himself of the vision of Bella with another lad. *Of course* he belonged. The Grants had been his clan for over fifteen years. The area near the musicians was full, but not so full that he did not notice when Bella was tugged out the front door by some lad he didn't know.

He bolted out of his chair so fast, he almost knocked it over. He made his way through the crowd, trying to get outside as soon as possible without being too pushy. It was already dark outside and the cool air hit his face as he searched the immediate area for Bella. He blew on his fingers to warm them up, allowing his eyes to adjust to the darkness. They were not in the courtyard, but a light sound from Aunt Maddie's garden caught his ears. He turned toward the sound, just in time to hear Bella shout out a loud, "Nay! Leave me be, Evan."

His feet carried him in the direction of her voice, and when he came upon them, he could see she was struggling with the lad who had led her outside.

"Please, Bella. I just want a wee kiss. You've kissed the outsider before. If you do not kiss me, too, I'll tell all the lads you showed me all you've got." Evan tugged her closer as she tried to push him away.

"Leave me be, you big lout." She shoved at him as hard as she could and tried to kick him, but it was no use. He would not release her.

That was all it took for Loki's temper to explode. He rushed forward and grabbed the lad by the neck, then tossed him through the air. Moments later, he landed on top of him and started pummeling him with his fists.

"She's mine, you rat bastard. You'll never touch her again." He punched the lad's face again and split his lip, sending blood flying through the air.

Bella screamed and tried to grab his arm. "Get off him, Loki. Stop! You'll kill him. Stop, please!"

Loki heard her, but an unknown force had stolen over him as soon as the words, "Leave me be," had left her mouth. Hellfire, but someone had to show this Evan that Bella was off limits to him and every other lad on Grant land. What her sire wanted did not matter.

Other noises approached in the background—footsteps and shouts—but he still did not stop. Suddenly, he was grabbed from behind and tossed in front of a nearby tree with enough force that he went flying through the air and hit the ground hard as if he were a wee lad. Grunting as he landed, he was all set to fight back until he saw who had tossed him like he weighed no more than a feather.

Uncle Alex had grabbed him, and Brodie and Robbie were standing right behind him.

Bella's father followed. "If either lad touched my daughter, I want him whipped. Nay, I'll whip him myself."

"Papa, please. Loki was trying to protect me." Bella slipped over to Loki's side and grabbed his hand to rub the dirt out of the scraped skin on his knuckles.

Loki lifted his finger to point at Evan, but Alex stopped him. "You'll say naught until I speak to you."

Loki snapped his jaw closed, knowing better than to argue with his uncle. He'd heard the stories about how the laird had killed a man in the middle of the courtyard with the entire clan watching. The man had dared to hurt Maddie, and he had not lived to regret it.

Alex turned to face Bella's father and said, "'Twas not my nephew at fault. Take your daughter and go home, Nevin. I'll deal with the situation."

Loki could see the old man wished to argue, but instead he grabbed Bella by the hand and yanked her down the pathway.

Bella turned to shout over her shoulder, "Many thanks, Loki, for protecting me."

Loki pushed himself up and brushed the leaves and dirt off his hands, watching as the lass he loved was dragged away from him. Aye, her father would probably rather she married someone like Evan who mauled her and treated her like a wench.

CHAPTER FOUR

The next day, Loki stood in the middle of the solar, tapping his foot as he waited for the inquisition…or whatever this would turn out to be. He'd rather be back in the forest trying to fight off five reivers than standing in front of these five people.

His da stood at one end of the room with Laird Alex Grant and Uncle Robbie, while Uncle Logan and Aunt Gwyneth stood on the other. These were five of the people he admired most. He'd do anything rather than disappoint them.

Was the day finally here? Had his welcome faded from Clan Grant? It was what he had always feared.

Loki's mother had tried to nurse his wounds before he was called into the solar, but he'd just pushed her away. He could not allow himself to be coddled anymore.

He kneaded his hands in front of him to try to hide the slight tremors.

Alex, still the tallest and most braw warrior in the clan, spoke first. "If you want the lass as your wife, lad, just say the word."

Loki stared at the floor and clasped his hands behind his back. "My thanks, my laird, but her sire does not consider me an acceptable husband."

"I do not care what her sire wants. I'll see that it happens if 'tis what you and Arabella want."

Loki gritted his teeth. "I wish to earn her sire's respect, and if I cannot, then we shall not marry."

A voice came over his shoulder from someone he had not seen enter the solar. His mother. "Loki, I know you have felt the need to prove your worth to your clanmates over the last few years, but you do not need to prove it to us. We all know your worth."

Brodie added, "None know your worth more than we do, lad. They've not seen you in action. We have. Everyone in this chamber has seen what you can do. You are deserving of the lass, but if you do not act soon, she will probably seek another."

Loki didn't answer, mostly because he couldn't. He wished to say so many things about how unfair and unreasonable Bella's sire was, but it was impossible to do so with his mother in the room. He would never, ever disrespect her. When he had nicknamed her missy angel in his youth, he'd had no idea how close to an angel she was.

Now he did.

"Do you have feelings for her?" Alex asked. "Or is there another?"

Another? Shite, nay. Remembering his mother was near, he replied, "Nay, there is no other."

His sire asked again, "So your feelings are for Bella?"

Feelings? How the hell could he answer that? Of course, he knew what his uncle meant, but a part of Loki was not sure what to say. He'd spent the first seven years of his life with no feelings at all. The only thing he'd ever felt was hunger. He recalled almost every moment of his life in that wicked crate. He'd lived with rats and mice and bugs, and dug through the trash thrown out of tavern windows... But Bella, Bella made him wish for all the things he wasn't quite certain he deserved.

"Loki?"

Not knowing how to express himself, he mumbled, "I do not have feelings..."

Alex made his pronouncement. "Then it's settled. We'll not question you anymore about this. But you are to stay away from Bella. Understood? She's free to choose another. You've had your chance and you've turned it away." Immediately, he heard the door close behind him. His mother had left. His sire soon followed. Loki stayed rooted to the floor. He had no wish to see his mother cry.

Logan moved over to his side of the room. "Then we'll take him in training for the crown if you are agreeable, Laird."

Alex's narrowed gaze focused on Loki. "Aye, take him. His

hot head will get him in trouble. Loki, before you go…" Alex tipped his head toward the door. "You know how you've hurt your mother. I expect you to mend this. I recall how foolish young lads are. 'Tis why I'm ordering you to say goodbye to your parents before you leave."

Loki frowned. "I'd be happy to pen her a note."

"Loki, you did not hear me. You will speak to her before you leave. Lad, I know you've not had the easiest life, but no one could care for you more than Brodie and Celestina do." His voice softened. "I believe you know that, but you're young, and my guess is you must work through this in your own way. I'm forcing you not to be too heartless along the way. You'll speak kindly to your mother before you leave, or I swear, I'll hunt you down. Understood?"

Loki swallowed before answering. "Aye, my laird. My thanks for all you've done." His uncle was the last man he wished to anger.

"Do not thank me, thank your parents. They are the ones who brought you home. And this *is* your home, lad. I trust you'll discover that in your own way. There will always be a place for you in Clan Grant."

Logan turned to Loki. "Go see your parents. We'll be leaving before first light on the morrow."

Loki nodded and trudged out the door to make his way into the great hall. Bella was there serving the midday meal, so he turned away and headed toward the tower rooms. Though every ounce of his being warned him to run in the opposite direction, he would do as he had been ordered. He stepped inside the tower, but the vision he saw there halted him in his tracks.

Brodie stood with his arms wrapped around his wife, her tears drenching his shoulder. As soon as Loki closed the door behind him, Celestina stepped back, but Brodie kept his arm around her shoulder.

"Oh, Loki," Celestina whispered, the tremor in her voice squeezing his insides.

Loki closed his eyes, not wanting to see this sadness in his mother. How could she understand what he was going through? He could hardly even understand it.

"Loki, I know how it is to feel like you do not matter to anyone, but it saddens me to think you believe that about your da and me. You know we love you as much as if I had birthed you from my own womb."

"I know you love me, Mama."

"Then why do you wish to leave? Why will you not allow your uncle to help with Arabella?"

He turned his gaze away, unable to bear the pain he was causing her. "Mama, it's not that. It's..." How could he explain that his worth had always been based on his cleverness? That the only reason the Grants had fallen in love with him was because he thought quickly and responded to situations with unparalleled instincts.

All the tales had been told over and over again—how Loki had saved his mother, how he had helped with Gracie and Caralyn, how he alone had saved his Aunt Jennie after she was kidnapped. But what had he accomplished since then?

Naught. And that meant he had no value. At least he would be using his quick wit if he went to work with his uncle.

As if reading his thoughts, his father replied, "Son, your value is not based on saving people, but on being part of a loving family. You are good to your sisters and all your cousins. You've always helped where needed. You've shown yourself to be honest, hard-working, and dependable. That's what tells us your worth."

Celestina spanned the room until she was standing directly in front of Loki. "I believe I know what you are thinking. You are questioning whether you truly have feelings for others because you cannot express them. But you do. I know you love me. Aye...you love me, your da, your brother and sisters, your cousins, your aunts and uncles, *and* Bella. We see it in you every day. Why must you run from us? I do not understand. Help me to understand, please, Loki. Why must you leave us? Will you not marry Bella and live the life you deserve? You so deserve a life of happiness."

Did he? If he did, why had his true parents deserted him? He must have been bad, really bad. Who would leave a good child, one they adored, out in the burgh alone to fend for himself? A part of him felt he deserved the rejection of Bella's father.

He could feel it creeping around inside of him. There was some knowledge there, and he was afraid of it.

Desperately afraid.

Bella had spent all day slowing her feet as much as possible, dragging her feet around the kitchen, hoping Loki would find his way to the great hall. She'd heard he was leaving on the morrow, and she just had to see him one more time. It was late, but there was still no sign of Loki. She grabbed her mantle and headed out the back door, closing it with a heavy sigh.

She was almost to the courtyard when a familiar voice reached her ears. "Lass, I thought you'd never leave. Is Cook working your fingers until they fall off?"

She spun around to find Loki leaning against a tree, barely visible in the moonlight.

"Loki, I was waiting for you," she said, letting her exasperation leak into her voice. "Where have you been? I heard you're leaving on the morrow forever."

Loki shoved away from the tree and tugged her close, wrapping his arms around her to give her his warmth. "Bella, Bella, what shall I do without you? Ever since that day many moons ago when you kissed me and swore to love me forever, you've had my heart."

"Then why are you leaving me?" She grabbed his plaid in her fists, not wanting to ever let go.

"Your sire will not have me, so I must leave. Besides, Bella, you know there are…other things pulling me away. I've told you before how I feel tugged in two directions." He leaned in and nuzzled her neck.

"Loki, you are good hearted. We all love you—your *clan* loves you. Do not be so thick-skulled. You are quick and bright, and you have the biggest heart of anyone. I know that to be true, why can you not see that you belong here?"

"I made myself useful once, but many moons have passed since then. I do not want to be a burden on my clan."

"They do not see you that way, and never would. You've done too much for the Grants."

His fingers caressed the back of her neck as he held her close. "Mayhap your sire has the right of it. Mayhap I'm still naught more than an orphan living in a box, of no worth to anyone."

"Loki Grant—and your name is Grant, remember?—you'll

never say that to me again. You are worth more than any of the foolish louts practicing in the lists who know not which end of the sword to grab. You can teach us all something. You're brave and smart and quick, but most of all, you are verra loving whether you will it admit it to yourself or nay. You're just blind to yourself. But I can see it, and so can your mother."

Loki cupped her face and kissed her, their tongues dueling together until she made a sound deep in her throat, telling him just how much she loved him. She savored the taste of him, and just the thought that this could be their last kiss made tears roll down her cheeks.

He jerked back in surprise. "Bella, my kiss makes you cry."

"Nay, you make me cry," she said, sniffling. "The thought of you leaving me, never to return, makes me cry. The thought that this could be our last kiss makes me cry. Do you not know we belong together, you big brute?" Bella grabbed his arms, pinching him as if she needed to wake him up somehow. "You keep working yourself until your muscles are bigger than all. You've grown almost as tall as my laird, and you are still not happy. Loki, stay with me, please. I do not care what my sire thinks. I love my da, and I know what he says is because of my mama, but he is being unreasonable. We can just marry and he will adjust to it, I'm sure. It may take time, but we have time." Tears rolled down her cheeks. She couldn't stop them now. "But if you leave me, what will become of us?"

"Lass," he kissed the salt on her cheeks. "You know I must go. But someday, I'll do something to make your sire proud of me. I'll find some way to make them all proud of me. Will you promise not to marry another, to wait for me?"

Her breath hitched. "Loki, I love you. You big lout, there is no other for me. I promise I'll wait for you." She smacked his arm lightly. "Do not make me wait verra long or my heart will be broken." She gave him her most fierce scowl.

He smirked at her and brushed a tear from her cheek. "You have always believed in me, Bella, and I thank you for it. I shall return, but I know not when, and this time, I promise to bring good news."

"The only good news I want is that you're well and you are staying the next time. And that you'll marry me no matter what anyone thinks." She rested her head on his shoulder and he ran his hand along the strands of hair that had loosed themselves from her plait. "And you know I want a daughter of ours to have your eyes."

"What?" Loki stared at her-wide-eyed.

"I want a lass with one eye blue and the other green, just like you. I've never seen another like you." She kissed him and ran her tongue across his bottom lip before she plunged it inside his mouth.

Two voices echoed in the distance, coming closer, putting an end to their play. "Bella, I must go. Those are my uncles coming."

He kissed her soundly, then stole off into the night.

She sobbed in the dark, no longer interested in heading home.

CHAPTER FIVE

The snow had started when they left Clan Grant, but it only lasted long enough to slightly slow their travels from deep in the Highlands to the Ramsay castle on the edge of the Highlands. Loki loved this time of the year, when the leaves were still falling from the trees, whipping around in the cold wind before they tumbled to the ground in the wet snow. The sun came out occasionally to melt the snow in some areas, but the land stayed white in the darkest glades and valleys.

Once they'd come out of the deepest of the mountains, Logan met up with a messenger and spent quite a bit of time chatting with the lad, which gave Loki plenty of time to think about his circumstances. He turned his horse around to stare at the beauty of the mountains behind him, dusted with white, their peaks proud and strong pointing to the heavens. The Highlands were heavenly, 'twas the only word for them.

Loki hadn't wanted to leave the Grant keep. Having Bella in his arms for one short moment had brought all his desire for her back with a fury. Hell, but he wanted the saucy lass. He grinned when he recalled how she'd slapped his arm and told him not to break her heart. Och, he hoped she'd be able to do as she promised and wait for him. If he could not find his sire, he could at least do something important for the Scottish crown—something important enough for Bella's sire to finally accept him.

Once on Ramsay land, they headed to the great hall to greet all the Ramsay cousins. Torrian, son of the laird, greeted them first. Loki and Torrian were of an age, and though they hailed from very different backgrounds, they were the best of friends. Torrian was not as colorful as Uncle Logan—he was more solid and steadfast like his father, qualities that would make him a great leader someday. Loki trusted him completely.

"Glad to see you, Torrian," Logan said. "I was hoping to take you along with us."

Torrian didn't mask his surprise—he only glanced at his sire, Quade Ramsay, to see how his father would respond to his uncle's statement.

Quade jerked his head toward his brother. "You wish to take my son where?"

Logan replied, "A messenger caught up with us not far from here. He delivered a request for my presence in Ayr. Seems there is something new they'd like me to assist with so I thought I'd take Loki and Torrian with me to Ayr and leave Gwynie behind. I thought 'twould be a good time for your son to meet King Alexander."

"Is he in residence?"

"I believe he is." Logan winked at Loki and Torrian as soon as his brother looked away.

Gwyneth had left his side to head to their chambers, and she returned with their bairns running alongside her. Though she and Logan had a lovely cottage deep in the forest, the children stayed in a chamber in the castle when the two of them were gone.

"Papa!" cried out two of Logan's daughters as they raced to greet him—Maggie, almost Loki's age, and Sorcha, now six and ten. Molly trailed along behind, holding the hand of the youngest—Brigid, now five summers—and gave her da a kiss on his cheek. Then she let go of the wee one's hand so she could launch herself into her father's arms. Logan and Gwyneth had adopted Molly and Maggie, and Sorcha, Gavin, and Brigid were their natural children.

Gavin and Gregor came tearing inside, running to the dais to greet the newcomers. Now five and ten summers, they were as inseparable as they had been as wee laddies.

"Too much, too much!" Logan yelled as he moved away from the table so he could swing into the air each of the youngsters who had come to greet them.

Quade headed out of the hall, and Torrian and Loki followed

behind him to give the family some time alone for their reunion. "Meet me in my solar after the midday meal, Logan. You have a few hours to come up with a good reason to take the laird's heir off of my land and decide how many guards you'll take along."

Logan, Loki, and Torrian set out the next day with several guards. Gwyneth had chosen to stay home with the bairns since she had been journeying across the Highlands for a time. They arrived at the outskirts of the village toward the end of the day. As they paid the toll to enter into the royal burgh of Ayr, chills ran down Loki's spine. This was where his sire had found him. He had not been in Ayr proper since the Battle of Largs in the 1260s, when the Scots had gained the Western Isles back from Norway. Exhausted, he glanced at Torrian, who seemed awed by the place. He was surprised his Uncle Quade had allowed Torrian on this excursion, but Logan had pressured his brother into agreeing, arguing that it would not only be an opportunity for Torrian to meet King Alexander, but for him to learn some basic survival skills.

Loki was so exhausted that he was starting to have strange flashes in his brain. Visions of past experiences that he could not quite identify popped into his mind. People without faces in unfamiliar settings called to him, but naught and no one was recognizable. As soon as they rode past a certain spot at the edge of the burgh, he stopped his horse and called out to his uncle and cousin, asking them to give him a minute.

He dismounted in front of a dingy inn, one for the travelers with few coins. He stood in front of it and stared. The inn his father had found him behind was a place much like this one. Bits and pieces came back to him, memories he had chosen to forget. Logan asked him a question, but he ignored it. Driven by an unknown force, he stepped to the back of the building and found what he'd been seeking.

A crate.

He nudged the crate with his foot, and it moved just a touch, enough for him to see there were items inside the crate.

It was exactly like the crate he'd lived under in Ayr. Something told him that as impossible as it seemed, this *was* his create. He'd lived in it for many moons before he was invited to come to Grant land in the Highlands. He glanced over his shoulder, taking in all the familiar surroundings, smells, and sounds, which reminded him of what it had been like to live on the roads of Ayr, hungry and alone and cold.

He'd begged for most of what he ate at the time, though he'd found a nearby inn that used to save scraps for him once the travelers moved on.

The sound of running feet came from behind him.

"Leave off, you surly brute. Those are my belongings you're wantin' to steal."

Loki spun around to see a laddie running toward him, a furious expression on his face. Dark disheveled locks that hadn't seen a comb in days hung to his collar. A dirty face stared up at him with sharp eyes and a fierce scowl, a jutted chin daring Loki to challenge him. He looked to be the same age or just a wee bit younger than Loki had been whilst living in his crate.

"Bugger off, you auld man. Why'd you want my stuff? You'll no' get my crates either. I've taken good care of all three of them."

Loki stared about the area, only then noticing that this lad's home was larger than his own had been. He'd found two more crates and arranged them as additional protection against the approaching cold weather.

"Problem, Loki?" Logan stood at the end of the alley next to the inn, both hands on his hips.

"Nay, no problem, Uncle. I was just leaving." Loki stared at the lad.

"Aye, he was just leaving. So bugger off, auld man." His chin lifted another notch and he gave Loki his most aggressive expression, one he'd clearly practiced well.

Loki recalled how often he'd had to keep others from stealing his goods—his crate, his moth-eaten gloves, the one plaid he'd found for warmth, even the pan on which he'd carved his initials with a dagger. Instinct and memory told him that pan sat directly in front of him.

Loki leaned down and picked up the pan, but not before the urchin took a swing at him with his dagger. Catching the lad's arm just in time, Loki said, "Calm down. I'll not steal it. I'd just like to take a look at it."

"That pan is mine, no' yours. It belonged to somebody

special." The lad continued to grab for the pan, but Loki held him at bay. Logan continued to stand there at the end of the alley, watching and listening.

"Aye, it did, lad." He turned the pan over and smiled. There they were, his initials—LL for Lucky Loki.

"How would you know? It belonged to a lad named Lucky Loki, and those are his initials he carved in it himself. He was so good with a sling, he became a hero in the battle with the Norse at Largs."

Loki smiled and peered down at the lad. "Is that so? How did you hear about Lucky Loki?"

"Everyone knows about Lucky Loki. He's a hero. He fought so hard that Laird Alexander Grant, the Highlander with the horse in chain mail that scart the Norse away, took him to the Highlands to be his son."

"Truly?" Loki could not help but grin. He had a reputation he'd known nothing about. A hero? Had the lad truly called him a hero?

"You canno' have it, 'tis mine. If you try to steal it, I'll hunt you down." The cheeky lad bounced up and down, trying to reach his invaluable pan.

Loki didn't know what to say. Not that long ago, he had stood in this lad's place, hoping everyday for some meat and enough rainwater to drink. "I'll not steal it from you, lad." He handed it back to the boy.

"Nay, 'tis valuable and 'tis mine. I'll sell it someday. Mayhap he'll come back."

"Who?"

"Lucky Loki, o' course. Mayhap he'll come back and adopt me."

Loki stared at him in shock. Aye, he should. He should do for this lad just what his uncle had done for him—adopt him and take him back to Grant land. He stared into the hopeful eyes, but it would not do. Not now. He was not in the same place his sire had been.

"We need to move on, lad," Logan yelled.

"Aye," he answered. He then turned his gaze back to the urchin. "I hope you meet Lucky Loki some day."

His eyes lit up. "Or mayhap Laird Alexander Grant will adopt me, too."

"What's your name?" Loki asked.

"Kenzie. Sometimes I call myself Lucky Kenzie, but no one else will. Will ye?"

"Aye, Lucky Kenzie it is. Where are your parents?"

"They both died of the fever, so I came to the burgh."

Loki turned away and headed back to the street, but halfway there, he stopped and glanced over his shoulder. "You're wrong, lad."

"About what?" Kenzie gave him a puzzled look, clearly believing he knew all.

"Alex Grant did not adopt him. His brother Brodie did." He tossed the lad a silver coin, enough to buy him food for a couple of days.

The lad caught it and yelled, "My thanks," his eyes lighting up.

Loki caught up with Logan. "My apologies."

"Something you wish to share? You know this area?"

"Aye, I do. I lived here for a time." Loki mounted his horse, not willing to talk about it any further. Fortunately, Logan mounted and left him alone with his thoughts.

His first consideration was whether or not his birth parents could have died of fever, too. Nay, he didn't think it was possible because Kenzie remembered his parents. Loki did not. Though he'd tried scores of times to force himself to remember aught about them—a face, a name, a piece of clothing—naught had ever come to him.

Logan led the way through the burgh to another inn near Doongait.

Loki pushed himself to get past the guilt for leaving the lad on the streets. Mayhap he could ask his father or his uncle to adopt him. Logan and Gwyneth already had adopted two lassies, so they would surely take him in. Because even though he fancied the idea of giving the lad a home, what would he do with him? It would be different if he were married to Bella. He smiled as he pictured sharing a home and a family with Arabella. He knew she would cook for the skinny lad until his belly was full. First they had to marry.

He would need to prove himself worthy of Bella before they could consider adopting Kenzie. He'd done the best he could by giving the lad enough to buy food for a couple of days. He wondered what Kenzie would buy himself first, a meat pie or a pastry. Brodie's friend Nicol had bought Loki the biggest pastry he'd ever seen for giving them information about missy angel, his mother.

The inn on Doongait actually had a stable for the horses, something the other one lacked, but that was why Loki had lived near the inn in Woodgait. Sometimes he would earn a coin by grabbing a man's horse and tying it up for him. Unfortunately, the travelers with coin were more likely to stay at the nicer inn.

He followed Logan and Torrian inside, where they were led to a large chamber outfitted with four pallets on the floor, a table and chairs, and a washstand. Loki washed his face and hands and lingered in the room while Logan headed to the inn. "I'll get us some food after I meet with Hamilton's man. Meet me in the tavern room in an hour."

Hamilton was Logan's contact with the Scottish crown—the man with the information and the man with instructions. If all went according to plan, he would soon be *Loki's* contact. His uncle would be gone for a while, so Loki settled on the pallet and closed his eyes, his mind focused on a thin lad who lived in a crate.

CHAPTER SIX

Three hours later, they sat in a private chamber in the inn, enjoying pottage, thick brown bread, and cheese. Loki wished there was a certain young lad seated beside him, enjoying the stew, but he knew it couldn't happen at this time.

Logan Ramsay had worked for the Scottish crown ever since the Battle of Largs. The confidentiality of the work varied depending on the mission. It warmed Loki's heart to know his uncle wished to work with him.

Unfortunately, Loki couldn't make up his mind, especially when reddish gold curls and luscious lips popped into his mind. Part of him wished to run from the Grants and part of him wished to never leave them. They'd given him more than anyone else. But something was missing from his life, and he had to discover it or go mad.

Logan spoke in a level tone, cutting himself off whenever the servants entered the room. "Lord Hamilton's instructions are simple. We are to find out whatever information we can on the royal jewels. The jewels disappeared from the last time the king was in residence, and he has no idea where they are."

"What kind of jewels?" Torrian asked.

"Rubies, sapphires, emeralds, and one ring. We are to glean what we can at the feast at King Alexander's Royal Castle on the morrow's eve. We'll find appropriate clothing for both of you at the weaveries before then. Any questions?"

Torrian set his knife down. "They do not have any idea who stole them? Has something happened we should be aware of?"

Logan shook his head. "Sometimes, Hamilton gets a sense, a feeling, that something is not right. He's received information that something is about to happen, and he believes the jewels are about to surface in the hopes of being sold. I'll remind you that oft times you will receive no explanation for your duties, you must simply do as ordered."

Loki's heartbeat sped up. This was it. He would be helping the legendary Logan Ramsay with his covert work, and this assignment involved the royal jewels. Mayhap if he could uncover them, he'd be deemed a hero. Mayhap this would be his long-awaited opportunity to prove himself. He could not wait until the next day.

Loki stared at Torrian, beaming with excitement. Torrian looked a mite green.

"Plans before then, lads?" Logan quirked his brow at the two of them. "If not, I suggest you practice with your dagger and your sword."

"You know I prefer archery, Uncle Logan. But mayhap I'll practice all three." Torrian gulped down the rest of his ale in one swallow and stood. "Let's carry on, cousin."

That eve, Loki and Torrian mounted their horses and headed toward the royal castle, Logan riding ahead of them quite a distance. He didn't wish to be seen with them initially. Loki glanced at Torrian. Torrian was the first son of his father, so he would be laird one day. A youthful illness had left him weak and sickly, and he had lost his mother at a tender age. Loki thought it was this shared difficulty in their youth that made them understand each other so well. His cousin's father had since remarried Loki's aunt, Brenna Grant, who had discovered the source of Torrian and his sister's illness: wheat. Their recovery had been remarkable, or so he had heard.

"We'll learn much today, Torrian."

Torrian nodded in response, but his coloring was still a wee bit green, and his hands still showed a fine tremor when he wiped the sweat from his brow. Once at the castle, the stable lads took care of their horses, and they made their way through the cobblestoned courtyard and up the entryway to the great hall. The royal castle was impressive, and the bailey was full.

Torrian looked quite spectacular in his white *leine* and his *breacan feil,* the Scottish belted plaid he wore over his linen shirt and braies. He didn't wear his clan crest or anything else to identify himself as the laird's son, as this would work against their ultimate goal of gathering information without attracting notice. Logan had promised to introduce both lads to King Alexander on the morrow. They'd agreed to separate and then meet outside in a few hours for updates.

Loki wore his red Grant *breacan feil,* but he could not help wondering what his true colors should be. His first impression once inside the hall was that it was not larger than the Grant great hall, but tonight it was filled to capacity. Clasping Torrian's shoulder, Loki led the way around the long chamber, stopping to speak to a few people here and there, but also recognizing that this was not the time to be questioning people about the missing royal jewels. It would be easier to gather information after the meal, after much whisky had loosened tongues and ale had been passed around to all who were attending.

Torrian whispered, "What are we to do now?"

"I'll tell you my plan. I expect to get to know the layout of the castle, move myself down the passageways to find the garderobes, the kitchens, and all the storage. I want to know where the wine and whisky are kept, for that is where the scum of Ayr are most likely to be found. The only place I am not going to visit is the king's chambers. His wife is here, and I have no intention of meeting her near her chambers." Loki tipped his head toward the far passageway. "I'll head that way. You make your way around the hall, see who you recognize, and look for certain types of characters. I'll return before the meal is served."

Loki made his way to a corner of the room, only to be waylaid by a beautiful redhead, a fine wench who grasped his arm and pressed her breasts against him as she whispered in his ear, "I'm afraid we've never met. Introduce yourself."

Loki's gaze ran down the length of her fine pastel blue gown and back up again. "You first, my lady."

She snickered. "I've not seen you here before. I'm certain I'd remember you if I had. My name is Tessa. Would you like to sneak into an alcove with me before supper is served?" She waggled her brows at him and thrust her breasts toward him.

Loki was not interested in any woman other than Bella, though Tessa was certainly pretty. Besides, something told him that he could not trust her. "Are you here often, lass?"

"Aye, I am often at court."

"Well, I'm headed to the garderobe, so you must excuse me, but I hope to see you later. Come find me after the meal." Loki rubbed her backside, making her squeal and run off toward the hall, peeking at him over her shoulder all the way. He didn't wish to question her yet, but she could know something useful. If she was a loose wench, she might have heard all kinds of tales in a lord's bedchamber.

He continued down the way and turned a corner, only to nearly run into a gentleman. "Pardon me, my lord." He had no way of knowing the gent, so he felt it best to consider him nobility.

The man had unkempt wavy brown hair and wore a patch over his right eye. He took an alarmed step back as soon as he set sights on Loki. "Who the devil are you?"

"My lord?"

"I've never seen you at the castle before. Who are you?" the man barked at Loki. The haughty expression on his face implied he was used to getting his way.

"I'm Loki Grant of Dulnain Valley. And you?" Loki's gut told him not to trust the man.

"You're of no import, so get out of my way." The man shoved Loki aside so he could move around him.

Loki's gaze followed him, memorizing every detail he could.

The rest of his excursion was uneventful, though the castle had a maze of passageways, chambers, and alcoves. He ran into a few couples, but did not bother them. Most were clearly on their way to the hall for food, so he turned around and headed in the same direction.

Once he was back inside the hall, his gaze immediately searched out Torrian. Fortunately, they both towered over most of the men in the hall, though Loki was taller than Torrian. Loki indicated for him to find them seats at one of the trestle tables since the serving women had started to bring out food. Every tray or trencher that passed by him smelled wonderful, setting his stomach to grumbling.

He found himself hoping Kenzie had saved enough of his coin

to eat again this eve.

The meal was uneventful except for the constant attention Tessa gave him from across the room. She'd found a friend and they sat together amongst a group of young lads who were doing their best to entertain the two lasses, but that didn't stop her gaze from finding Loki's again and again.

"Torrian, we're going to meet with two lasses after dinner. Can you accept that?"

Torrian's gaze widened, but he nodded, apparently willing to go along with him. "Aye, I've not much experience with lasses, and mayhap 'tis best to gain some here, away from my clan."

Loki couldn't disagree with his reasoning. "As soon as the minstrels and the fiddlers start, we'll get up and move toward that passageway. I'm quite sure we'll be stopped along the way."

Later, once the music got underway, they moved toward the outside of the hall. Just as Loki had predicted, they had only taken two steps into the passageway when high-pitched giggles sounded behind them. Sure enough, Tessa came toward him, her arm intertwined with her friend's.

Loki whirled around and flashed a grin at the ladies, stopping them both in their tracks. "Evening, Lady Tessa. Have you met my friend, Torrian?"

Tessa gave Torrian a lingering look and then sidled up to him and rubbed her body against his. In a husky voice, just loud enough for Loki to hear, she whispered, "Nay, we have not met, but I'd sure like to get to know him better. This is my friend, Dona."

Loki bowed to Dona. "Good eve to you, lass." Giggling and lowering her dark lashes, she slipped her hand around Loki's elbow.

Tessa grabbed Torrian's arm and said, "Follow me." She led them through the torch-lit maze to a small chamber.

Just as Loki was about to step into the chamber, he recognized the man he'd seen earlier. He was headed directly toward them, so Loki motioned to Torrian. "Go on in, I'll be right there." Loki and Torrian had discussed how to go about ferreting information from the lasses, but he did not trust the man with the eye patch. Addressing Dona, he said, "I'll return in a moment." He hurried down the corridor, but suddenly the man with the patch increased his pace. Loki caught up with him, but the two collided, and the man fell to the floor. He cursed fluently, and when Loki offered him a helping hand, he shrugged it off and headed back toward the great hall.

Loki shouted, "My apologies." Patch man ignored him. Loki's gaze searched his clothing for any indication of who he was or what he was about. Giving up, he hurried back to Dona's side and held the door for her to enter the chamber. Inside, there were two small pallets and a small table surrounded by four chairs in front of the hearth. Goblets of wine sat atop the table. Torrian and Tessa had already started to drink wine.

Tessa said, "This is much better than the ale. You should try it." She glanced at Loki and fluttered her eyelashes, implying that her flirtation with his friend had changed nothing between them.

Loki sat on the corner of the table. "Nay, mayhap in a few minutes. Tell me about Ayr. We have not been here in a while. We're from the Highlands."

"What do you wish to know?" Tessa asked.

"Who's the most powerful man in the area, besides the king?"

"I do not know. Why do you ask?" Tessa answered, a subtle movement in her lower jaw.

Loki was quite sure Tessa did not like the direction of the conversation, but he didn't allow her body language to stop him. If anything, it made him more intrigued. "Is there a certain earl or viscount that is the primary vassal to the king?"

"Alexander of Dundonald is still his favorite, but there are others." Tessa took a sip of her wine, a suspicious look in her eyes.

Loki tired of her game, for he knew it *was* a game. He decided to move things along. "Just wondering who would be powerful enough to steal the king's jewels."

"What do you know about the jewels?" Dona asked, her back straightening.

"I know naught. I heard the missing jewels mentioned in the great hall. As I explained, we just got here from the Highlands. Do you know what happened to them?" Loki caught the glance exchanged by Dona and Tessa, and a sour feeling crept into his gut.

"Nay," Dona replied. "But I'd sure be appreciative of anyone who gave me gemstones like the royal jewels."

Loki tipped his head toward Torrian. "I'll return in a moment. Need the garderobe."

"Again?" Tessa asked.

Loki winked at her, "Aye, I drank quite a bit of ale with my meal. I promise to return post haste." He crept out of the chamber, looking both ways before he stepped into the passageway. His intuition was not telling him anything good. As he made his way to the garderobe, he listened for any strange sounds, checking every nook of the mazelike corridors before making his way back.

When he entered the chamber, the first thing he heard was a gurgling noise.

A bald muscular man was holding a dagger to Torrian's throat.

Loki's gaze searched the room. The two girls stood in opposite corners, as far from the mischief as possible. The man was of rather large proportions, and it was clear he was waiting for Loki to act. There was noticeable sweat across Torrian's brown, but Loki was pleased to see there was also fury there.

Humph. This would be easy.

Loki took a few steps toward his cousin.

"Halt. Do not take another step or your friend dies."

Loki did as he was told and froze in place. "No reason to hurt anyone. What is the problem? Why are you here? We've done naught wrong, we're just two traveling Highlanders looking for some entertainment." He smiled, hoping to give the impression that they were two foolish young lads.

The brute's dark gaze skewered into Loki. "Why are you asking about the jewels?"

Loki shrugged his shoulders. "Because we heard about them and hoped to uncover them and become heroes. No other reason. Why do you not release my friend?"

"I ask the questions, not you." He tightened his hold on Torrian, who turned a darker shade of red. "My assistant will be here soon to tie you up."

"Why must you tie us up? We've done naught wrong. Tessa and Dona promised us a sweet eve of pleasure. 'Tis all we were seeking. Let us go and we'll be on our way." Loki managed to move himself to the exact spot he needed for good aim.

The door opened and the man with the eye patch stepped inside and closed the door behind him.

"Where have you been, Egan?" Clyde asked. "Get control of him. Find your dagger. 'Tis the only way he'll talk."

Egan reached into his hidden belt, but he came out with naught besides a puzzled expression. "Clyde? Where's my…"

"That could be a problem," Loki announced, both hands on his hips.

Clyde smirked, "And why is that?"

Loki winked at him as Egan reached into his boot for another weapon. "Seems I have Egan's weapons." Loki flung one dagger straight into Clyde's thigh, then pulled out a second dagger and twisted Egan around until he had the dagger pressed to the man's throat.

As soon as the dagger was embedded in Clyde's thigh, Torrian swung the man around and pointed his dagger at his throat, though the stronger warrior was a little harder to restrain than Egan had been.

Loki said, "Not bad, cousin. Nice job, especially with one his size. I didn't know you had those kinds of moves." Clyde only growled in response.

Torrian said, "He is my uncle, you'll remember, and he has taught me a few things. How'd you get his weapons?"

Loki laughed. "Didn't trust the fellow, so I knocked him down in the passageway and stole his weapons."

Torrian grinned. "Nice strategy. I have much to learn."

Squeezing the dagger against Egan's throat, Loki said, "Now, would you mind telling us what you know about the missing jewels and why you're after us?"

Neither Egan nor Clyde responded. Loki squeezed again.

"All right, I'll tell," Egan spewed. "And this has naught to do with the missing jewels."

"You wee fool! Blackett will whip you."

"I do not care, Clyde. I've had enough. We have naught to do with the jewels. We've been hired by another to follow you both."

Loki squeezed again.

"Nay! I'll talk…"

Loki gave him a moment to catch his breath before squeezing again.

"Are you not Loki Grant of the Highlands?"

"Who wants to know?" Loki ground out.

"Your father," Egan spit out. "The Earl of Cliffnock is your sire."

CHAPTER SEVEN

Bella stood in shock in the middle of her father's cottage. "What did you just say, Papa?"

"I said to make sure you have everything ready. You'll be leaving with your sister in less than a fortnight." Her sire continued shoveling stew into his mouth, ignoring his daughter's reaction to his proclamation.

"I am? But I asked you the other day if I could stay and take care of you, and you promised I could." She had asked him to stay after telling Loki she would wait for him. She could not break that promise. Not for anyone.

Her sire set his utensils down with a clatter and stared at her. "Arabella, I think it would be best if you went away for a short time. Why not travel with your sister, see her wedding, then return after another sennight? I think 'twould be good for you. I'll be going for the wedding as you must, but I'll be returning immediately after the ceremony. I'd like you to stay for a while. 'Twill help you get over that lad you pine for."

Morna said, "Bella, you may as well go with me since Loki is gone and he's not returning. He's working for the crown. 'Tis time for you to find another. Think on it. I'll be running my own keep. You can help me get started running the kitchens since you have much more experience than I do. Besides, I'll need to focus on my husband. And the only other chores you'll have is to help me with are dressing and bathing. I'll see that you have your own chamber, something you've always wanted. Mayhap my betrothed will match you with someone. Then we could live there together."

Bella could not believe what her own sister had just said. "Morna, I do not wish to spend my life in the kitchens. I wish to marry and have bairns." She pivoted toward her sire. "Papa, I do not wish to go with her. Besides, I thought you wished for me to marry a Grant lad. Is that not what you promised Mama?" Desperation took over as she searched her mind for anything she could use to reason with her father. She'd promised Loki she'd wait for him.

"I believe it will be good for you to travel with your sister. When you return we'll find another for you. Morna, she will marry a Grant so cease your matchmaking. You have less than a fortnight, Bella, and you will obey me." Her father stood up and moved to the chair in front of the hearth. "Now, pick up the dishes and see that they're cleaned while your sister and I warm ourselves in front of the hearth."

Bella spun on her heel and ran out the door. But then she tore back inside, ran over to her pallet, and packed a satchel before she took off again, slamming the door behind her, ignoring her sire's comments yelled at her as she raced back out the door, tears blurring her vision. She loved her father, but she hated him for this, for refusing to accept the lad she loved and the life they deserved together. He was right, she had to get away, but from him, not the Grants.

She did not care where she went—she just had to leave. Morna was not so bad, but her father acted like he hated her. Where would she go? She slowed her movements once she was far enough away to let her tears fall. The only place she belonged was in Loki Grant's arms, but he was not here.

She trudged through the courtyard and headed around the back to the kitchens, tears flowing freely down her cheeks. Her vision was so blurred, she almost walked straight into Lady Celestina.

"Oh, my lady, please forgive me." Her breath hitched as she tried to stop her tears.

"Arabella, are you crying? What is it, my dear? Why are you so upset this eve?" Celestina carried a basket of fruit and walked with wee Alison.

She tried to respond, but her chest hurt so much she couldn't speak.

"Oh, Arabella, why do you not come and sit by the fire with

us?"

Bella nodded and followed Celestina back toward the keep. Where else could she go?

Once inside their tower chambers, she greeted Brodie, Braden, and Catriona. Brodie asked, "Is there aught I can do, Arabella?"

Standing just inside the door, Bella swiped at her tears and shook her head.

Celestina took her satchel from her, setting it aside, and led her to a chair in front of the hearth. The three bairns were staring at her, so Brodie ushered them over to the table in their quarters.

"When you are ready, tell me what is wrong, Arabella," Celestina said gently, covering her with a blanket.

Bella glanced at her and the entire story tumbled out of her. "My sire wishes to send me away when my sister marries—" her breath hitched, "—and I wish to stay here and wait for Loki. I love him." Her sobbing increased no matter how she tried to stop it. Still, it felt good to confide in Celestina, who was the most kind-hearted woman she'd ever met. Celestina and Maddie, the laird's wife, were much alike, and the entire clan adored them both.

She noticed Celestina and Brodie exchange a glance, and then he left his chair to sit beside her.

"Arabella, if you do not wish to go, I'll speak to your laird and see if we cannot insist you stay to help us in the kitchens. I know Loki would not want you to leave, and it heartens me that you are staying true to him. Celestina and I believe he is confused right now, but he needs to sort out who he is on his own. None of us can begin to understand how his early life was or how it feels to not know your true parents. We must let him deal with this in his own way. We are comforted by the fact that he is still with family members, but we will need a great deal of patience."

She hiccupped three times before she managed to speak. "You would speak to our laird for me?"

"Aye, we do not wish to lose you to your sister's new clan. Rest assured, I'll speak to our laird on the morrow. You may sleep in the bed with the lassies this eve and we'll settle this matter later. How does that sound?"

Arabella nodded, trying to catch her breath and stop her tears. "My thanks."

Celestina hugged her and whispered in her ear, "I know our

son loves you. He's just a bit confused right now."

Bella hugged her tight, not wanting to ever let go.

Loki rode his horse next to Logan, and their guards followed directly behind them. At the king's request, Logan had left Torrian with Alexander for the day. The king understood the importance of getting to know all of his vassals and chieftains-to-be.

Together, Loki and Logan approached the small castle where the Earl of Cliffnock resided.

"Are you sure you wish to do this?" Logan asked.

"Aye." He glanced at Logan. "As we discussed, if this proves I'm of noble blood, Bella's sire will have little excuse not to accept me as her husband. Morna is marrying one of noble blood so he would have to allow Arabella the same."

"You do not think you'll wish to stay here, mayhap live your life here? If you are his first born son, you could inherit all that is here, including the title."

"Aye, possibly, but is it not more likely that I will prove to be a bastard? 'Twas not the friendliest way to greet his son, either way."

Logan shook his head. "I shall have to speak to King Alexander about this. Why weren't we told long ago?"

"Mayhap Cliffnock kept it to himself for whatever reason." Loki slowed his horse to give him the chance to take in everything about the land and the castle. It was not a large building, and there were only parapets on the gates, not on the walls. The cottages in the village outside were sparse and not well kept. A few clan members came out of their huts to stare, but none offered greetings. There was an odd feeling to the area.

Logan said, "My hunch is that Hamilton is right, and the something that is off centers around the earl, but I know how important this is to you, lad. Keep that clever mind of yours open at all times. I'd thought to leave you here for a fortnight to get to know your sire better, but mayhap not that long. My gut tells me nay. We'll see if he offers us a place to stay for a night or two."

Loki nodded, then brought his horse to a canter. They arrived at the gate when it was near dusk. A strange feeling of anticipation fluttered through Loki. This could answer so many questions. The first one he would ask was why the earl had allowed his son to live in a crate behind an inn.

The guard at the gate said, "Your business, lads?"

Loki cleared his throat and spoke loud enough for all to hear. "Loki Grant of the Highlands to see my sire, Edward Blackett, the Earl of Cliffnock." He had to admit it had a nice sound to it. Wait until Bella heard he was the son of an earl. Even if he was a bastard, his noble blood would have to count for something.

His palms turned clammy as the gates opened, allowing them inside. Would his sire be kind? Would he get the opportunity to meet his mother? Did he have any siblings? One question popped into his mind after another. How he hoped he would finally get some answers.

Logan, as if able to read his mind, said, "Now remember to take it slow. I know you have many questions. We'll get to them all in due time."

A couple of lads emerged from the stables to take care of their horses. From there, they moved through the bailey, small but functional, and on to the steps leading to the great hall. A man came out and addressed them.

"My name is Hamish and I'm your sire's second, Loki. I'm pleased to see you again after all these years." He smiled and clasped his shoulder. "Do you remember me at all, lad?"

A flicker of something flashed through Loki's mind, but not enough. The man seemed pleasant and kind, but Loki had no recollection of him. He shook his head. "Nay, sorry."

"No bother. We'll get to know each other all over again." He led them inside the hall and over to the dais. The man in the center stood as soon as they entered the vast space. His gaze followed Loki as he made his way over. There was no lass beside him, Loki noticed.

"Come, come, I cannot wait to see you again, son. Please, come closer." Once they were near, the man smiled and introduced himself. "Edward Blackett, the Earl of Cliffnock. I've waited a long time for this day." He stepped down from the dais to be closer to Loki, gazing into his eyes, probably searching his face for some sign that he was truly his son.

Hamish said, "'Tis him, Blackett. Do you not agree?"

The earl replied, "Aye, 'tis my son."

Loki was looking at the earl just as intently as the earl was staring at him. He did not see many similarities except the earl was almost as tall and thin as Loki, though the man was not muscular. "How can you be so sure?"

"Actually, 'tis quite simple. You have your mother's eyes, one blue and one green. Have you ever seen another with the same?"

Loki had to admit, he never had. His eye color had always been a curiosity to others. "My mother? Is she here? I'd like to meet her."

Blackett motioned for them to sit. "And your friend?"

"My apologies. This is my uncle, Logan Ramsay."

Blackett stared at Logan. "My compliments, Ramsay. I've heard of you and your wife by reputation, of course. You'll have to tell me about her someday. But for the moment I'd like to talk with my son."

He motioned for Loki to sit next to him and sent the servants for ale and meat pies.

After the servants left to do his bidding, the earl said, "I'm sorry, Loki, but your mother passed on a long time ago." He paused. "She died giving birth, which upset you so much you ran away. I searched and searched for you...I had my guards comb the entire countryside, but we never located you. Where did you go?"

Loki stared into this father's eyes, wondering if he was telling the truth. Without knowing the man, it was impossible to tell. "I lived in Ayr in a crate behind an inn near Woodgait for many years. I had no recollection of aught but my name, but I was fortunate to meet Brodie Grant. He eventually adopted me and took me to the Highlands to live with him and his wife. I've been there ever since."

"You do not remember aught about me? About where we lived?"

"Nay, I do not. This castle is not familiar to me."

"We lived in a small cottage when you were a bairn. I was given this land after the battle with the Norse. You do not recall your home or your mother?"

Loki shook his head, sad that he would never know his mother, but after all these years, his sire sat in front of him. He would do better to focus his attention on the present.

The servants brought out the food and drink, and once they

were gone, Blackett asked, "How long ago did you move to the Highlands?" The flat expression on his face was puzzling. If he had been happy about meeting his long-lost son, wouldn't there be a bit more of a spark in his gaze? "I moved after we battled the Norse."

The earl paused and stared at Loki for an uncomfortably long time. "So you lived alone on the road, behind an inn for many years. How can I forgive myself? How could you forgive me? I'd understand if you did not."

"Why did you not follow me right away?" Loki knew it was a harsh question, but he thought it fair.

"Och, lad, I did not have a group of guards at my command then as I do now. Hamish was a friend, but not many others lived nearby. We lost both your mother and the babe in one eve. I was so upset, I never noticed you were gone until 'twas too late. 'Tis all my fault, I know that. I should have kept a better eye on you, but I was distraught from losing your mother."

"Do I have any other siblings?"

"Nay, lad, just the one sister who passed on with your mother. I never named her. Hamish buried her with your mother."

The group ate in silence for a bit. So many questions had been running through Loki's head, but suddenly he did not know what to ask.

"How many men do you train here, Cliffnock?" Logan asked.

"Not as many as I'd like. We've managed to draw a few new men, but not many. All total, mayhap three score. Not as large as the Ramsays or the Grants. 'Tis true that Clan Grant has a mighty guard?"

"Aye," Logan said. "The laird lives a distance north in the Highlands, but he's always drawing more. He's good to his men and their families. He has over five hundred guards, I'd wager."

Blackett whistled. "I had no idea there was such a clan in the Highlands. And the Ramsays?"

"We're not as many, but we have close to three hundred. Both our families have connections throughout the Highlands. My sister married the Menzie, Jennie Grant married the Cameron, and my youngest brother married the Drummond. We have many close ties."

The Earl of Cliffnock was not quite as tall as Loki, and his brown eyes seemed to always be strategizing. He was mostly bald, which made Loki reach up to run his hand through his thick hair. Seemed most of the Grants and Ramsays had kept their hair, though some had thinner hairlines than others. Brodie's hair was still the same with little gray, and though Uncle Alex's dark hair was peppered with gray, it was still long and thick. Uncle Robbie's hair had thinned a bit around his crown, but he kept it short.

So what qualities had he gained from his sire? He was not sure yet, but he'd pay attention.

"So you're connected to the Camerons, as well? I hear they have wealthy coffers sitting on their land in Lochluin Abbey." His eyes seemed to take on a life of their own at the mention of wealthy coffers.

"I do not keep track of Cameron wealth." Logan gave Blackett a more calculating gaze, one that Loki could not quite interpret. What did Uncle Logan think of the man?

The earl's hand reached up to clasp Loki's shoulder. "Son, I'm so pleased to have you home where you belong. You plan on staying, aye? This is your home now, no need to return to the Highlands."

Loki glanced at Logan. Stay here? Never return to the Grants? Nay, he would never move away from his true family or his Bella. But should he stay a bit to learn more of his sire?

"What say you? You'll stay for a couple of moons, at least, will you not?" The earl glanced at Logan before turning his gaze on Loki, as if the act of staring could force compliance.

Loki gave the proposal careful consideration before he answered. "I will not promise a couple of moons, but I would like to stay for a couple of nights to get to know you better, if you are agreeable."

The earl smiled and pushed his chair back. "I cannot ask for more at this point. I'm pleased you've decided to stay."

Logan turned to Loki. "Is this what you want? If you like, I will return to the royal castle, then return here in a sennight to see what you've decided. Is that acceptable?"

"Aye. I'll stay, but you can leave today if you would like. Half a sennight should suit me fine." Loki turned to Logan, hoping he understood his hesitancy. There was just something about this man he didn't trust. "Come back in a few days and see how I fare then."

"Sounds reasonable," Logan said. "I'll leave after the meal."

Loki glanced at his father and nodded, happy to have some time alone with his sire. At the same time, there was a strange glint in his father's eyes that made him appear far more sinister than when they had first arrived.

An uneasy feeling crept up his spine. What would he discover about his real father?

It didn't take Loki long to discover his father's true nature.

The next morn, after most of the clan had left to do their daily chores, Loki sat at the dais with his father. His father passed him another goblet of mead.

"Try this one. It comes from my special stores."

Loki had to ask one more time. "Are you sure I just ran away? And you searched far and wide for me?" For some reason, he'd hoped for a more satisfying answer—one that would tell him his parents had loved him, that they had suffered from losing him.

His father smiled. "Och, you did run away, but I can see you are searching for a different answer, so I'll give you one. See if it's what you want."

A sick feeling settled in Loki's gut as he took a sip of the mead. His vision blurred, and his knees turned to butter. He attempted to stand, but needed to grab the edge of the table to keep his balance.

"I did not follow you. I did not care a bit about you, lad. 'Struth is I was glad you were gone. One less mouth to feed."

Loki whispered the only word he could get out. "Nay…"

He'd been drugged. It was the last thought he had before he crumpled to the ground.

CHAPTER EIGHT

The first thing that popped into his mind when he awoke was that he'd finally found his sire, and the man was a bastard—a rat bastard. He held in his groan as he opened one eye to see where he was, only to discover he was behind bars in some type of dungeon. His own father had drugged him and locked him up. But for what purpose?

He pushed himself to a sitting position and glanced around the small area. The entire chamber at the base of a winding staircase was small with half of the area encased in bars, then divided. He sat on the dirt floor in one cell, only an urn of water next to him, the other was empty. There were two stools outside the cells, presently unoccupied, and a table. One small window allowed the light in. Loki had no idea what time of day it was or how long he'd been out. Thank goodness Uncle Logan would be here in a few days. He could survive until then.

A short time later, the door leading to the dungeon opened and his father came down the stairs with Hamish and another guard. His sire chuckled and crossed his arms, leaning up against the stone wall while Hamish stood to one side. "Aye, as I said, Loki, 'struth is I never missed you, but at least your trip to see me won't leave me empty-handed."

Loki snorted. "And just what do you expect to get from me? I have naught to give you."

"I noticed you had little in your sporran, but you came from a place with coin, and besides, you know many others from whom I can squeeze coin, so 'tis exactly what I'll do."

"And who are you planning to squeeze?" Loki stood up, no longer willing to allow this evil man to look down at him.

"The Grants, the Ramsays, and the Camerons and their rich Lochluin Abbey. I'll get coin for you from somewhere. You'll see."

His father's cold beady eyes told him he would not be stopped easily.

Loki ran his hand down his face, shocked to find himself in such a situation. "Sorry to disappoint you, dearest Papa, but you'll get naught for me. I'm of no value to any of them. I would appreciate something to eat while I'm here and you're waiting for your coin."

"Come now, lad. I recall how clever you were as a bairn. You were traveling with Logan Ramsay, one of the fiercest of all the Scots. He'll give good coin for your return, I'm sure of it. In fact, I've sent a messenger to the Ramsays, Grants, and the Camerons. Now I'll just sit back and wait."

Loki couldn't believe the bastard was that ignorant. "And you did not think better of sending a messenger to Logan Ramsay at the royal castle? Are you not the least bit concerned about getting caught by the king, losing your land and your title?"

"Nay, I sent the message to the Ramsay keep. I'll keep Logan Ramsay at bay for a few days. Mayhap I'll have my men take care of him. As for the king, once I get my coin, I'll be leaving. Do you think this hole is fair compensation for all I did for him in the war? I smuggled many goods for him. I deserve better, and I'll find better once I am paid my just due. "

Loki laughed.

"You think 'tis funny that I plan to kill Logan Ramsay, lad?"

Loki sauntered over to the metal bars where his sire stood, looking down on the older man. He'd never thought he would be disgusted by the sight of his own father, but the truth stood right in front of him. "Aye, 'tis funny and foolish if you think you can kill Logan Ramsay. I'll be having the last laugh on that one. The man's invincible. And if it did come to pass that something happened to him, his wife would hang you upside down by your ballocks."

Blackett chuckled as he moved closer to his son, close enough to whisper. He stared down at the old rushes on the dirt floor.

"Lad, I raised you to be wiser than that. No one is invincible, least of all a Ramsay."

Loki took advantage of the moment. As soon as his sire took his eyes off him, he reached through the bars and grabbed ahold of the rotten scum, grasping him behind the neck and slamming his head against the metal bars, sending blood spurting everywhere. He didn't stop the attack until the guard stuck him in the arm with his dagger.

His sire stepped back, holding his bleeding head, dazed by the beating, but not so much that he could not give orders to his second. "Teach him a lesson and then chain him to the wall. He deserves to be treated like the animal he is." He moved out of the doorway and up the stairs.

"Thanks, Da. Your feelings warm my heart." Loki stared at Hamish, hoping Hamish would decide to go easy on him if he did indeed remember him as a wee laddie, but there was naught but excitement in his gaze. The door opened again and two more guards ran down the steps.

His sire yelled down the staircase, "Do not kill him. I want him alive, and I want him able to talk."

One of the other guards opened the door to the tiny cell and three of them came in after him. Hamish smiled at him as he punched him in the face, "Sorry, lad, but you shouldn't have done that."

Loki caught Hamish by surprise when he lifted him and threw him back toward the iron bars of the cell door. He managed to bring down the next two men with his fists and his kicks, but there was no way to hold up against all three of them. His last thoughts were of Bella, many years ago, saying, "I promise to love you forever."

Several days later, Bella was in the kitchens when one of the other maids came into the room and whispered, "You'll never guess." Then her shoulders hunched up and she held her hand in front of her mouth as if she were about to be caught and whipped at any moment.

Bella glared at the lass. "What is it?"

"I just heard something terrible, and you'll want to know."

Bella grabbed the girl's wrist. "Tell me." When the girl did not answer, she stood on her tip-toes and wrenched the lass forward. "Now!"

"A messenger came in and spoke to our laird. Brodie was at the table, too. He spoke to both of them. Loki has met his sire." The look on her face did not match the news.

"And? That is not terrible."

The lass scowled at her. "His real sire holds him prisoner. He wants coin for Loki's life."

Bella jerked as if the news had physically struck her. Had she heard correctly? Loki's life was in danger? Saints above, what was she to do now? "Are you sure you heard correctly?"

"Aye. 'Tis what they said. Brodie Grant jumped out of his chair when he heard the news." She nodded.

For a long moment, Bella stood there, frozen with fear. Then said a quick prayer and ran into the great hall, but she was too late. The Grants had already departed and reconvened in the laird's solar. She stood at the staircase, wondering what to do.

After completing her chores in the kitchen as soon as possible, she spoke to Cook. "Please, Cook, may I go home to speak to my sire? Then I promise to return."

Cook frowned, but then she nodded to Bella. "Ah, Bella, your heart is lost to the boy, is it not? Well, I hope for your sake that they pay the coin and get him back. Loki is a fine lad, though your father has yet to see it. Go…go see your sire and return after the midday meal. I'll do without you for a bit."

Bella ran to the tower room and grabbed her things. Brodie and Celestina were speaking privately in their chamber, so Bella sneaked into the main room, trying not to disturb them. She could not help but overhear their conversation.

"Brodie, where is he?" She could almost hear the tremor in Celestina's voice.

"Do not worry, love, they'll find our son. His sire, or the man that claims to be his sire, is a fool. How long can he expect to keep him locked up with the Grants, the Ramsays, the Camerons, the Drummonds, and the Menzies all set to battle, if necessary?"

"But how far away is he? I'm so worried."

"He was in Ayr, but his sire's castle is northeast of the town, not far from where Bella's sister will be living once she marries. The castle is between Morna's betrothed's castle and Cameron land. 'Tis part of the reason the man is bartering for coin. He knows how much wealth is housed in Lochluin Abbey."

"Please save him, Brodie. You must go as soon as you can."

Arabella's mind was spinning with all the possibilities. Now that Loki had promised to return to her, she knew there was only one path in life for her. She would do whatever she could to ensure that she married Loki Grant. She hugged Catriona, then said, "Please tell your mama that I must go home."

She raced out the door, down the steps, and through the courtyard. Ignoring most everyone, she continued without speaking, though it wasn't hard to notice that most of the clan was in a turmoil. The news about Loki was traveling quickly. Everyone loved him here, everyone except her sire.

As soon as she made it to her cottage, she tore through the doorway and stopped, attempting to catch her breath. Panting, she surveyed her home to see if her sister had left.

Her father barked at her from his chair at the center table. "I wondered how long it would take you to return. 'Tis about time, your sister needs help, and I certainly cannot assist her. Now do your chores and help her pack. Her back is nearly broken from all the work she's had to do without you. She'll be leaving soon and I'll be following her for the wedding. You can start my packing, also."

Ignoring her sire, Bella rushed over to Morna's side. She noticed right away that her sister was in the midst of packing for her trip.

"Here, allow me to help you. I do not mind."

"Where have you been?" Morna scowled at her.

"I had to get away from Papa. 'Tis just the way of it sometimes. Now, do you wish to have my assistance or not?" She gave her sister a pointed look that ended her scowl.

"Aye. Look at all I must squeeze into this trunk. 'Tis the only one I'm allowed to take, so I must fit everything inside. Please help me. I am lost."

Bella took over for her sister, pulling everything out of the trunk before refolding the items and rolling them to make room for more. Morna watched her as she repacked it, then set her hands on her hips and stared at Bella.

"How did you know how to do that?"

"It just made sense to pack them differently. Now what else must go?"

"Why are you being so agreeable all of a sudden?" Morna asked, as she refolded some linen squares and tucked them neatly into the trunk.

"Because I've decided I will go with you after all. I realize 'twill be better for me to be with you than to be with Papa." Bella couldn't look her sister in the eye. She did not want her to guess it was a boldfaced lie.

"Papa's thinking of getting married," Morna reminded her. "I think 'tis a dream. I do not think he's found anyone yet."

"And if he finds someone, I'd be happy for him, but what would there be for me here? 'Twould be time for me to move on. Loki is gone, Papa will be remarried and my only sister is leaving. It makes sense for me to go with you." She picked up Morna's slippers and folded them, packing them at the edges of the trunk.

"So you have finally realized you have no future with Loki?"

Bella's instinct was to slap her sister, but she controlled it. This would go easier if she pretended to be agreeable. "Aye, I'll leave with you and hope to find another at your new keep."

"Mayhap we will find you a nice lad there, Bella. You know I only want what is best for you." Morna leaned over to give her a quick hug.

"I know. When do we leave?" In her mind, she checked off everything she would need to pack into the one small satchel she could carry. Once she arrived at her sister's destination, she would be off on her own to find her true love. That meant she would not be able to carry much.

"We leave on the morrow. You'll be busy this eve."

Bella sighed. "Perfect. I cannot wait to leave."

Morna glanced at her sister, a perplexed expression on her face. "Why the sudden change of heart? You did not wish to go before, and now you cannot wait."

"Of course, I'll go for your wedding, Morna. No change of heart, only that I'll stay a wee bit longer. Loki's gone and will probably never return. I need to live my life without him, and I'd prefer to be with you over da." Bella continued to pack, hoping her sister would cease her questions. She would do whatever necessary to make sure her betrothed was safe. Well, perhaps they were not quite betrothed, but she was certain they would be soon.

Their father walked over to stand and stare at the two of them together. Bella halted her work, unsure of what he was about to do. He had an unsettled expression on his face, something she hadn't seen before.

He let out a big sigh before setting his hands on his hips. "My wee lassies have grown, have you not?"

Morna replied, "Aye, Da. We have. 'Tis time for us to start our own families."

He rubbed the corners of his eyes. "Morna, I hate to see you go. 'Tis a good thing Bella will return to me so I will not lose you both at the same time."

Morna hugged her sire while Bella just stared. She'd never seen her father like this. Was it true? Was there a slim possibility that he only turned Loki away because he couldn't handle losing both his daughters at once? The thought had never occurred to Bella before, and it gave her a bit of hope.

The next morn, the Grant guards arrived to escort them to their destination, and Bella breathed a sigh of relief. She'd gone back to the kitchens herself to speak to Cook and to find a bit more food for her satchel, only to discover that Brodie Grant planned on traveling to Ayr himself in a couple of days.

Mayhap she would see Brodie in Perthshire or Ayr. At first, she had considered requesting to go along with him, but she knew she'd be turned down since it was expected she'd attend the small wedding. There were lads' clothes tied up in her satchel, so she could switch into them once she got to Perthshire. She had also packed the small dagger Loki had taught her how to use.

Aye, she would find Loki Grant if it killed her.

CHAPTER NINE

When Loki awakened, the first thing he noticed was that only one eye opened. The right one was swollen shut. Fortunately, he appeared to be alone in the dungeon. He reached to feel his head, hoping to determine how badly he was injured, only to discover he had iron shackles around his wrists. Squelching his need to bellow to the rooftops, he decided his best course of action was to keep his mouth closed.

When he attempted to sit up, the pain that rippled through his body told him exactly how much damage the fools had done. He remembered the look of sheer enjoyment in Hamish's eyes as the man delivered punch after punch. Apparently, that enjoyment had continued well after the scum had knocked him unconscious. Hellfire, he'd just been through this not long ago with the reivers. Mayhap it was finally time to change the way he lived. One thing would definitely change—he was done seeking out his parents.

He could only imagine what his life would have been like if he'd stayed with his sire instead of running away to Ayr. Fleeing had been the best decision he'd ever made, for it had led him to Brodie and Celestina Grant. Now that he knew his sire's true nature, he had to wonder at the veracity of his story. Had Loki truly run away in fear?

He shoved his back against the cold stone, the only possible position that would allow him to sit up and move his arms. Dried blood stuck to his chin and caked over his injured eye. A large swelling was also on the back of his head—likely from falling— and it was probably the primary reason for his raging headache.

Noticing a container full of water nearby, he grabbed it and took a drink of the cool liquid, then poured it over the blood on his hands. Every inch of his body screamed in pain.

He wondered how long he had been out, and how much more time would pass before Logan returned. He had to survive until then, he just had to… He was more driven than ever to return to marry his Bella. The hell with her sire, they'd marry and be happy together. His adoptive father was right—some things in life were too important to lose.

The door slammed open at the top of the stairs, and his sire came down the stairs, chuckling all the way. "Well, I see my son has awakened. I'm glad they didn't kill you yet."

"You have a strange sense of loyalty." Loki spit blood out of his mouth, feeling for all his teeth to make sure he hadn't lost any. "Amazing you could treat your own son this way."

"I tried to talk you into staying here where you belong for a couple of months, but you were not interested. I had to convince you to stay. I'll get some coin for you, it's my just due."

"What? Why would the Grants owe you anything? They took in your own kin when you treated me like dirt. You owe them; they owe you naught."

"The Scots owe me. The king should have given me a much larger castle than this one. I made him piles of coin during the war with the Norse. I knew how to send the right goods out and smuggle others in to keep the money flowing to build ships, only I didn't get just compensation for all I did."

"Sounds like the Lowlanders owe you and your king, not the Highlanders. Leave them out of this. Just let me go and all will be forgotten. I'll be certain never to come within your sights again."

Loki stared at the earl, sad to see that all his searching, all his desires had come to this. If Bella's father would be appeased by learning Loki was the heir to this man, then he had all his priorities wrong.

His sire tossed him a couple of oatcakes through the bars. "Here's your dinner, lad. I'll see you on the morrow."

Loki managed to catch one oatcake, but the other rolled out of his reach. No matter, he had work to do. This was not the first seemingly impossible challenge he had faced and bested. Staring at the iron manacles attached to the wall, he reviewed each small detail about his prison, until finally the answer clicked…

He just couldn't wait for Logan Ramsay. He knew what to do to get himself out of this predicament.

As soon as they reached Perthshire, Bella's insides started to do flip-flops in anticipation. Thank goodness she'd thought to ask Catriona to pen a note for her. She knew all the Grant bairns could read and write, and she did not want to leave her sister without any explanation. Her sister would be upset, but at least she would know where Bella had gone. It would save her from fretting unnecessarily or attempting to send guards after her.

Shocked that she had the gumption to attempt such a daring plan, she had to continuously take deep breaths to keep focused on her path. Nothing would stop her from pursuing Loki and finding out what had happened to him. They were meant to be together forever, and she was ready to handle any test they were given. True love would prevail, and her true love was the strongest, most clever warrior out there. He would find a way to escape.

Once they arrived at the castle, Bella dismounted quickly. Morna's betrothed came out to greet them, but as soon as he saw her on horseback, he rushed forward to help her dismount. "Why are you riding, my lady? You should be atop pillows on a cart." He snapped at the head of her guards. "Have you no sense? She is of tender sensibilities and should be treated as such."

Bella had to look away from her sister's smile. All her life, she would be fussed over and taken care of by others. Bella was so different from her sister, though she did love her. Bella wished for nothing more than to be free to live her life as she wished, either in her own cottage or under the stars. She did not care where she was so long as Loki was with her. If he wished to travel and work for the Scottish crown, then she'd be happy to travel with him.

Morna's betrothed helped her to her feet, and they put on quite a show—Morna almost fell, but the baron held her steady with both his arms. Bella rolled her eyes, grabbed her satchel, and moved ahead of the lovebirds.

She glanced back at the baron. He was quite a bit older than Morna, and his red hair had thinned in spots, but he was neither particularly handsome nor homely. Plain—that was the best description she could muster. Of average height and well dressed, he took care of his appearance.

They came up behind her chatting. "And how was your journey, my lady?"

Morna replied, "It was quite pleasant, with little rain or snow to cause any problems. The horses had trouble with part of the rocky descent, so we were forced to walk at times, but I managed to keep from turning my ankle with Arabella's help."

"Arabella? Who is Arabella? Is this your maid you brought to attend you?"

"Nay, Arabella is my sister. She's just ahead of us carrying the satchel. Bella's talented in so many ways. She helped me pack all my things because I could just not find a way to fit what I needed in the small trunk. She's quite talented as a maid."

Bella glared at Morna over her shoulder. Maid, indeed. True, she did not mind helping her sister when she was in need, but that did not make her a maid.

"If there are more things you need from home, do not worry your pretty head about it. I'll send someone to retrieve them later. I'll do whatever you wish, my dear."

Morna clutched his elbow, acting as if she needed help to keep from falling, but Bella was quite sure she was just looking for an excuse to lean her breasts against the baron. "Oh, my lord, you are so kind."

"I'm committed to making your stay before our marriage as agreeable as possible." He lowered his voice, "I do so look forward to our wedding night."

Bella swung her head around again to see if the baron was jesting. The baron was quite serious, it seemed, and there was even a glint of excitement in his gaze. Bella felt a bit sorry for missing her sister's wedding, but it could not be helped. She hoped Morna would forgive her and understand that Loki's life was at stake. She'd be leaving in the middle of the night, which was only a few hours away. Thank goodness she had a plan in place. She had to get to Ayr to find her love and help him escape.

Loki, I'm coming!

"I'd like to see my sire." Loki issued his request as soon as Hamish and one of the guards descended the curved staircase.

"I'm sure you'd like a good many things, don't you think, Hector?" Hamish asked.

Hector laughed, "I'm sure he would, too. Can we get you a nice wench to pass your time with? Or mayhap you'd like a meal of lamb, meat pies, and sweetmeats."

Hamish leaned against the stone wall directly in front of Loki, crossing his arms. "Mayhap you'd like a dagger and a sword, or a nice bath. Hector, did you bring the tub with you?"

"Apparently, the lad does not know the meaning of prisoner."

"So why are you here?" Loki sat without moving a muscle, not wanting to allow them more entertainment at his expense.

"You've got a few moves in you, Grant. You did more damage to my two guards than I would have expected. I always knew you'd be something special." Hamish's eyes carried some secret knowledge Loki wasn't sure he wanted to know.

"When I first arrived, you acted as if you missed me, Hamish. Care to tell me what that was about? And since I have naught else to do, I'd love to hear your version of my life and the reason why I left. I think I deserve that much." Loki lowered his voice to remove any threat or anger from it, hoping to get some honest explanation. He knew he'd never be back to see his sire again—and he never wanted to admit to being related to anyone other than the Grants—but he was still curious about many things.

A slow smile crept across Hamish's face as he lifted his shoulders and sighed. "Aye, those were the good days. I do remember you well, lad. You see, I was the one who administered your sire's punishments, just as I do now. You were a hard one to break, even at the tender age of three summers. You are much like your father."

"I am naught like my sire. We have naught in common except the color of our hair."

"Nay? You do not agree? Your father would never speak unless he had something verra important to say. Why, he never expressed his opinions about anything, and I think you are the same. When you were a wee laddie, you would always take a beating without uttering a sound, and now you are careful to hide your true thoughts and any indication of the pain I know you're in. You hide everything well. Aye, just like your father."

Loki paused to give Hamish's words some consideration. Aye,

he had a very high pain tolerance, but so did many. Maddie Grant had the highest pain threshold of any person he had ever met. It did not mean he and the earl were true kin.

"You were adopted, but you've never thanked anyone for doing it. You never ask for aught, and you never give aught. 'Tis exactly what your mother worried about. She was afraid you'd become just like your father, never expressing any consideration for aught but yourself. Course, your mother called it feelings, like lasses do." Hamish nodded. "I see you're realizing the truth of my words."

Loki hadn't thought any of this man's words could hurt him, but Hamish's words sliced deep into his belly, more so than he wanted to admit. Was that why he'd never been able to thank Brodie and Celestina? Or thank Alex Grant for giving him the name of Loki Grant? Or why he had such difficulty admitting that he loved Bella more than anything in the world? If Hamish's words about his sire were true, then mayhap he had more in common with him than he would ever care to admit.

"Your sire's a heartless man, Loki, and you are the same. Cold and calculating, always looking for ways to outsmart others. You were a clever lad, always outthinking your sire. I believe his fear of your talents was the true reason he…"

"He what?" Loki wanted to grab the bastard by the throat and choke the words out of him. "Finish it, you piece of scum."

Hamish's eyes glittered with mischief. "Nay, I've said all I care to say."

"You've told me what I got from my sire, then what did I get from my mother?" Loki locked his gaze on the dirt floor in front of him, not wanting to give Hamish a chance to see how much the answer to this question mattered to him.

"Your mother? Hmmm…what did you get from your mother. She was a comely thing, but she was too soft-hearted to survive life with your sire. If the bairn hadn't taken her, your sire would have sucked the life from her. Naught…you got naught from her that I can tell."

"You have me chained to the wall. Why can I not speak to my sire? I'd like to see if some of my memories are true. Will you not ask him to come down? You know it will be some time before the message arrives in the Highlands." Loki decided the only thing that could bring his father down was the threat of his memory returning. Of course, naught had returned to him, but it would interest him to know if his father was threatened by that possibility—and if so, why.

Hamish shoved himself away from the wall. "We'll pass the word on to your father. See if he'll consider blessing you with his presence. Glad to see you're enjoying your chains." He winked over his shoulder on his way out.

The irony of all that had transpired was not lost on him. He remembered telling everyone in Ayr that his mother had died birthing him, and he'd never known his father. The truth had been that he had no recollection about his past. He realized that faulty memory had served to be a blessing. Remembering his true sire would have made him ill and angry.

Loki would see that Hamish got what he deserved someday.

CHAPTER TEN

A few hours later, the door opened and one set of footsteps crept down the stairs. Whoever it was carried a torch in his hand since night had fallen. Loki opened one eye to look at the visitor. The earl.

"Hamish said you have questions for me. At first, I was determined not to answer, but then I decided there was no harm in it. I'll not see you again, so 'tis of no concern of mine if I answer your questions." He stood outside the locked door after he set the torch in the wall holder. "You have big questions, mayhap I'll give you big answers."

"They are not the most revealing questions. I'd just like to know more about my mother. I have no memories of her. What was she like?"

"Your mother? That wee bitch?"

"You did not get along?" Loki knew this could be his only chance for freedom. Who knew if his sire intended to let him go if his ransom was paid? Mayhap his own father would kill him at the end of this ordeal. Escape was the only way he could guarantee his survival.

Edward Blackett sat on the stool by the staircase, settling his elbows on his knees and clasping his hands together in thought. "Aye, we got along well enough, at least 'afore she carried your sister. Then she didn't want aught to do with me. I didn't take kindly to that, so I let her know."

Loki didn't wish to hear about this man beating his mother, but he needed to keep him talking. "You let her know?"

"Aye, if she could not keep her mouth closed, I closed it for her."

His sire's hard gaze caught his, daring him to pass judgment on him, daring him to say aught at all about his mother. Loki could see this was not the direction he needed to go. If he wanted to accomplish anything at all, he had to use a different tactic. "I've been in Lochluin Abbey."

"And why would that matter?"

"You are trying to get coin for me, and they probably are not willing to part with it. You're wasting your time with my adopted family. I'm naught to them, but I can tell you where the riches are hidden in the abbey."

"Then speak up, lad. Speak up and I'll let you go."

"I'll not yell it to you for all to hear. There are guards outside the door, are there not?"

"Aye. But they'll not listen."

"And you expect me to believe that just because you say it? I'll not give the secret entrance away to everyone."

Silence settled between the two. Loki held his breath, hoping his sire would bite the bait so he could reel him in.

"Then come closer and they'll not hear you." The earl grinned, an evil grin if Loki had ever seen one.

"If you recall, I'm manacled to the wall. 'Twould be impossible."

"Fine. I'll come in so you can whisper it to me. You are a bit stronger than your auld man, so I cannot set you free. But I'll get close enough for you to speak in a low voice."

Loki heard the key in the lock, the scraping of the metal as sweet a sound as the finest fiddle playing he'd ever heard. His palms dampened in anticipation as his sire fussed with the lock. Finally, the door released with an outward swing, and the squeak of the metal set Loki's gut to churning. His father took two steps toward him and said, "All right. Where's the secret entrance? Which side of the abbey? Make sure you tell me where to find it in the building. I know enough about the abbey to know if you're lying, lad."

Loki coughed first, but then whispered his response. "It's on the north side, next to..." He shuffled his feet to muffle his last words.

"What?" The earl kicked Loki's boot.

"I said, 'tis next to the..." As soon as he started the sentence, his sire leaned in toward him.

"I cannot hear you." His lips formed a surly line that looked familiar to Loki.

Loki lifted his head to get closer, hoping it would subconsciously cause his father to lean forward. When he mumbled an answer, his sire turned his head to lean in close to Loki's lips, just as he'd hoped.

Loki's boot tripped the man, forcing him to fall forward directly toward him. Freeing his hands from the broken manacles he'd worked on for the last two hours, he flipped his father face down and an arm around his neck, twisting the man's head back and his throat forward.

"Now, you're going to walk out of here with me." Loki located the man's dagger and held it against his back. It was an awkward maneuver, but he managed to stand and pull the earl up in front of him, though the stiffness in his legs was almost keen enough to make him go down again. "We understand each other? You say I'm naught to you, well, you're naught to me. I'm walking out of here, and as we walk, you'll instruct your men to stand back, else I'll stick a knife in your kidney, fast and simple."

Blackett chuckled. "Shite, you're my son, I can tell for sure. You always were smarter than me and quicker, too. All right, I will not fight you on this. You've won fair and square. You can let me go. I promise to tell my guards to allow you to walk free. You've proven your worth to me."

"You're right about one thing, I'm not a fool, so I'll not take your word for it. I'll take you with me to the stables to find a horse, and then we'll walk it outside the portcullis."

Loki shoved his sire up the staircase, hesitating when they reached the door. "Instruct your guards to stand back and let us pass." Fortunately, it was dark so his eyes would not have trouble adjusting to light.

The door opened just as his father's first words came out. "Take ten steps back and let us pass. He's got a dagger at my back and he's capable of snapping my neck." The door flew open and two guards grabbed their swords from their sheaths as they stepped back into the night. "Put your weapons down. I gave my word he could pass. The lad outsmarted me fairly."

"Aye." Loki recognized the guard who had spoken as Hector. A slight smirk reached the corners of the man's mouth. "He's proven he's your true son then." He returned his sword to its sheath and allowed them to pass, but followed along at a short distance.

The earl finally ordered, "Stay back. We'll go alone. Tell the others to stay back as well."

A pathway opened up for them in the courtyard—the few men who were still outside in the night stayed back as ordered. Loki's eyes darted back and forth, not willing to trust his sire's men. Aye, the earl had issued an order, but it did not mean that some fool would not try to save his master. Sweat dripped down his brow, threatening to run into his eyes and blur his vision, but he managed to keep going.

Hamish stood to one side, Loki noticed, arms crossed. When he dropped his arms to his sides, Loki expected the man's sword arm to swing toward him, but naught happened. His heart was pounding loud enough to explode out of his chest as they continued on their way. If he failed, he'd be a dead man, and he knew it. Lack of food and movement caused his steps to be a bit unsteady—each one of them sending pain flowing through his body—but he did his best to hide his weaknesses. If he could just make it outside the gate on horseback, he could use the dark of night to escape.

Once out of range of his men, Blackett whispered, "I hope you have no one you care deeply about, Loki, because if you do, I'll find out. I know your heart is like mine, hard and cold, but a lass can sneak inside when you least expect it."

"Nay. 'Tis impossible. I'm as cold-hearted as you raised me to be."

"Best keep it that way, or I'll find her and you'll regret it. I want my just due, and I'll get it one way or another. You're my best chance for coin now."

Rather than speak, Loki continued on toward the stables. Once outside, he yelled, "Lad, bring out one saddled horse."

A stable lad raced out and stared at him, unsure whether to take instructions from the stranger in front of him. Loki pressed the point of his knife into Blackett's back. "Do what he says, lad," the earl ordered.

The lad disappeared into the building and returned a few moments later with a horse. Three other men from the stables came with him.

"Do not fret. As soon as he's free, he'll let me go. True, son?" Loki nodded.

"You see. 'Tis all right. Do not follow us."

"I'll set you free once I'm outside the portcullis," Loki whispered in his ear. Then he addressed the lad. "You bring the horse, just you. Walk ahead of us."

The lad took the reins of the horse and moved toward the portcullis. At the gate, the earl spoke again. "Let us pass. Do not do aught or he'll kill me."

Four guards stood with their hands on the hilts of their swords. "Tell them to raise their hands in the air. They are to leave me be once I'm on the horse."

The earl gave crisp instructions and they passed through the gates. Loki moved a safe distance away and halted. "Let the horse go, lad, and run back to the stables."

The boy did as he was instructed. Loki shoved the earl away and mounted the horse, flicking the reins to spur him into a gallop.

The last thing he heard was his sire's voice saying, "This is not over, lad. You'll see me again."

Arabella shivered and tugged her mantle around her shoulders. Even in lad's clothing, she was absolutely frigid after having ridden in the wind and the cold of the night.

Her sister's betrothed owned a large horse farm, so it had been a simple matter to steal a horse without anyone noticing. Someday she would return it to her sister. She only hoped Morna would forgive her one day. Her father would never forgive her, but she was not concerned about that in the least. Had he supported their marriage, this would never have happened.

She reached the edge of the royal burgh, surprised to find that she needed to pay a toll. Praying she would pass as a lad, she tucked her mantle around her as tight as she could.

"We need a coin to allow you to pass, lad."

Bella's hands shook as she reached into her sporran and pulled out a coin. The man frowned and gave her a glance, but he was swaying on his feet. Fortunately, he appeared to be half-sotted. "Do not know where you're headed, but be careful. The roads of Ayr are not always safe for a young lad. Travel carefully, but be on with you." He waved his hand into the air, so Bella flicked her reins and moved forward.

Where did she go from here? She headed down the path at a canter, hoping to find somewhere to sleep for an hour or two. A thin sheet of ice covered the stones, probably due to the cold rain that had started about an hour ago. Would she dare try the stables in the middle of the night? Mayhap if she asked at the town stable, she could find information about Logan Ramsay or Loki. Logan had to be known here since he worked for the crown.

Shivering in the rain, she huddled closer to her beautiful horse, hoping to gain some heat from the beast. When that did not warm her enough, she tugged her hood up and rested her head down for just a moment, closing her eyes against the wind that had whipped up out of nowhere. If she could just sleep for a wee bit, she'd be sure to find Logan in the morning. Loki had been kidnapped, so she would not find him, but she must find Logan Ramsay. He was her only chance.

If she could just close her eyes for a wee moment…the scent of the horse reminded her of Loki, such a soothing aroma…

The next thing she knew, she was sliding off her horse, headed straight for the ground. She squealed and grasped for her horse's mane, but to no avail. The air whooshed out of her when she landed on her back, stealing away her breath. Frantic, she glanced around for someone to help her, but no one was there.

A young laddie appeared in front of her, cursing under his breath. "Devil take it, have you lost your mind, lad? You cannot ride until you fall off."

She reached for him, still unable to speak, desperate for air in her lungs. "I cannot…I cannot…" She could get no more words out.

The boy tugged on the hood from her mantle and slid her across the layer of ice on the path. When he stopped, she noticed they were behind a tavern under two old oak trees, the thick branches protecting them from the sheeting rain. She glanced at her young savior in surprise. "Many thanks." Still gasping for air, she noticed her breathing had improved. "My horse? My satchel?"

The lad said, "I'll tie it up and get your satchel, but you'll owe me a coin, come morning."

She nodded as the lad took off around the tavern. Pushing herself to a sitting position, she glanced around at the items connected beneath the tree. A tarp had been arranged beneath the branches to protect them from the rain. The three crates that sat nearby had to be where the lad slept. Leaning back against the tree, she fought the liquid welling in her eyes, feeling quite foolish at what she had attempted. How the devil would she ever find Logan Ramsay when she had no idea where to go?

The lad returned and stood in front of her, his hands on his hips now. "Hey, you are no' a lad. Lads do no' cry. You're a lass. What brought you out here alone and in a lad's clothing, besides?"

Bella did her best to squelch her tears, especially once she felt them freeze on her skin. She swiped it away with an indignant huff. "I'm looking for someone. Please be quiet."

"Who are you lookin' for? I know everyone in this town."

"What's your name?"

"Kenzie. And this is my spot you are in, so dinna think to steal aught from me."

She scowled at him. "Why would I steal something from a lad who sleeps under a tree? You cannot have much of value."

"I do so, and you'll no' take it."

"Lad, you have naught but a tin cup, an old pan, and a few dirty plaids." She rolled her eyes at Kenzie, though the wee laddie was rather cute.

"Aye, and that pan belonged to the great Loki Grant. 'Tis worth some coin, I think."

Bella sat up and stared at him. "Did you say Loki Grant? You know him? Where is he?" Pieces of the puzzle finally fit together in her hazed, partially frozen mind. A lad without a home who slept in a crate in the royal burgh...She stared at her surroundings, realizing she was in just the type of situation Loki had spent the first few years of his life in. The man she loved had lived in a location much like this one, and her heart suddenly ached for this lad.

"Nay, I dinna know Lucky Loki, but he used to live here before Alex Grant adopted him."

"Alex Grant did not adopt Loki Grant, his brother Brodie did."

Kenzie's brow furrowed. "That's what the other man said. Are you sure?"

"Aye, I'm sure. Now where is this other man?" Cute as he was, she wished to grab him by the collar and shake him.

"The lad who was here went to the tavern in Doongait."

"How long ago?" She hugged her knees tight to her chest, hoping to stop her shivering. Hell, but she hadn't guessed the cold would soak through her like this.

"Almost a sennight."

The timing could fit. Loki could have been here before he was kidnapped, before he met his sire. "What did he look like?" Bella's heartbeat sped up, excited that she might have a lead on locating Loki.

"He was tall and strong...big muscles...and he was odd looking. And he was with an older man who had darker hair. He was a bit shorter, but he was all muscle, too. I've seen him before, but I dinna know him."

"What do you mean odd looking?"

"He had one eye blue and one eye green. 'Tis rare."

"That's him!" Bella whooped and hugged the lad. "Where exactly did he go?"

"That's who?"

"That's who I'm looking for, Loki Grant and his friend, Logan Ramsay."

"'Twas no' Loki Grant or he would have told me." The boy looked so disappointed it almost broke Bella's heart.

"Mayhap he was in a hurry," she said through the chatter of her teeth.

"Aye, he was. The other man told him to hurry."

"You mean Logan Ramsay?"

"That was Logan Ramsay, the one who spied for the crown when the Norse were here?" His eyes grew wide while he leaned in toward her.

Her words came slowly between the chattering of her teeth and the shivers wracking her small frame. "Aye. Well done. You met both Loki Grant and Logan Ramsay. Now you just need to take me to them."

"But you dinna look verra good, my lady."

Bella shivered and toppled over onto her side.

CHAPTER ELEVEN

Loki spurred his horse into a gallop, hoping he could get away before his sire sent men after him. He almost made it back to the outskirts of Ayr before he heard horses. Hiding in the trees, he waited for them to pass, just noticing that it had started to rain, the kind that would freeze on the paths and turn treacherous. He didn't have his sword anymore, just his sire's dagger.

His uncle and his cousin stopped directly in front of him. "What took you so long? We thought you would have freed yourself already."

Loki smiled, but said, "Get me away from here and I'll tell you the whole story."

"Didn't like spending time with your new sire?"

Loki glowered at Logan. "He's not my sire any longer. I want naught to do with him. When did you find out something was wrong?"

"The messengers bypassed me. He sent one to my brother, one to the Grants, and one to the Camerons, but Torrian and I followed them until they split. We convinced the lad heading to Ramsay land to give us the message. Then we sent another message to the Cameron updating him."

"The man makes me ill. I waited so long to find him, and for what? He's naught but scum."

"Mayhap 'tis not for naught. You can still tell Bella's sire you are of noble blood," Torrian said, "just as you'd hoped."

"If being of his blood impresses Bella's father, then I am not interested in convincing him of my worth. Bella and I will just marry. To hell with what her sire wants. Bella and I belong together. I only have one sire—Brodie Grant."

Logan snorted, "Finally. Must be your true sire knocked some sense into that thick skull of yours."

Torrian beamed, "Aye, must have been a good swing. 'Tis one thick head, and stubborn. He finally speaks with a bit of wisdom."

Loki ignored them and flicked the reins, moving his horse along, all the time feeling quite satisfied with his decision. Logan and Torrian agreed with him, though they'd said it in their own twisted way. Didn't matter, their agreement was enough for him. Resolved with a new sense of purpose, much of his doubt fell away as he envisioned telling Bella the same.

They headed toward Ayr. Once they reached the tavern, Loki heaved out a sigh and said, "I need a bath. Do you think I'll get one in the middle of the night?"

Logan said, "Aye, I'll see to it. You're covered in blood, and you've traveled through rain without a mantle. It's a wonder the rain did not freeze you. The bath is what you need. We'll make our plans after. You are likely hungry for victuals as well. I'll have something ready for you."

The tavern owner showed Loki where he could bathe. Before he left, he turned around to face his uncle and his cousin and said, "I've got naught. Have you aught I can wear? These clothes smell and I do not wish to be reminded of my sire at all. I wish to burn them."

Logan nodded and went up to their chamber, returning with a satchel that he tossed to Loki. "Take what you need, lad, then meet us out here in the tavern room."

Half an hour later, Loki came out with wet hair and a fresh plaid over breeches. "I feel much better," he said as he joined Torrian and Logan at the table. My thanks."

"Aye, we ordered meat pies and ale. Will that suit?"

Loki sighed in satisfaction. "Aye. My sire's accommodations in the dungeon were not verra nice. The food was not much either. In fact, there was one oatcake I never could reach."

"Then eat up. You can tell us all after your belly is full."

Loki ate everything the other two didn't want.

"Judging by the colors on your face," Logan said, "I'm guessing it took you a little longer to escape because you took a beating or two. From your sire or his goons?"

"Hamish and Hector and a few others. I know their faces. I was out for a while after the first beating, but I do not know how long."

Logan grinned and waggled his eyebrows at his nephew. "You must have got a good one or two in first, aye? Your knuckles are torn up a bit. If you've learned aught from me, your answer will be a resounding aye."

Loki chuckled, then rubbed his belly and sighed. "Aye, I did. I smashed my sire's face against the iron bars a few times before they stopped me. Shite, but that felt good."

"How'd they get you in there?" Torrian asked. "You are a hell of a fighter, cousin."

"Shortly after Logan left, my father drugged me and I awoke in the dungeon."

"And how'd you get out?"

"Picked the lock on the manacles they had on me, then convinced my sire to come into the cell to talk to me. I nearly choked the rat bastard."

"Well done, nephew." Logan gave him a look that told him how proud he was. "Glad to hear you've changed your mind about Bella. The poor lass will be pleased. She's stayed loyal to you through all."

"Aye, you have a bit of time to think if you're stuck in a dungeon. I do not care what her sire wants. If Bella will still have me, I'll marry her."

"Are you choosing marriage over working for the Scottish crown?"

Loki paused for a moment before he answered. "I would like to discuss it with Bella. I'm not sure where she would prefer to live. Her sister is to marry and move away, so mayhap she would rather live here. If so, I could still work with you."

"Lad, you've only just found your way out of a bad situation. I'll give you time to think on it. No need to rush your decision. The only thing you need to do at present is fill your belly."

The door burst open and they could overhear a young lad talking to the tavern owner, upset about something. Loki perked his ears up when he heard his name.

"...and Logan Ramsay. I know they were here before, and I really need to speak to them. 'Tis someone looking for them, and she's no' good."

Loki shoved his chair away from the table and headed out into the entrance to the inn just as the tavern owner shoved the lad back out the door. "We'll have none of that here. You go back to your crates, lad."

"Hold, please. I'd like to speak to the lad."

The tavern owner turned to Loki and mumbled, "You may speak to him outside. I'll not have the likes of him inside my establishment. His odor would send my good customers away."

Loki nodded and stepped outside the door just in time to see Kenzie running away. "Lucky Kenzie!" Loki bellowed down the pathway. The lad halted and spun around, then raced toward him.

"The lass. She was asking for you and Lord Ramsay, but she's no' good now. I cannot wake her. I think she's too cold."

Loki shoved the piece of bread he held in his hand at Kenzie, then spun back to the tavern to yell inside. "Uncle Logan, I'll be back."

Logan followed him outside. "What is it?"

"He says a lass is seeking us, and she's sick with cold. My Bella is bull-headed sometimes, so it could be her. Can you find a kirk and a priest who would marry us? I'm headed to Woodgait and there's a kirk not far from there. At least I could warm her there if it proves to be my Bella."

"Aye, I know the place. We'll be there awaiting you."

Kenzie had already climbed onto the horse he'd rode to the inn, so Loki mounted his own beast and followed the boy out of Doongait toward Woodgait. Once they arrived, Kenzie dismounted, tied the horse, and ran to his area behind the tavern, waving his arm to direct Loki toward the back.

Loki didn't know what to expect, but it certainly wasn't what he found. Bella was on her side under an oak tree, her skin a grayish hue, her breathing shallow and barely visible in the cold. He knelt down beside her, peering at her in the dark before he shook her shoulder. "Bella! 'Tis me, Loki." He paused.

Kenzie stared at him, his eyes wide with admiration. "She was right. 'Tis you. You are Loki Grant, just as she said."

"Aye, lad. But I do not have time for that. We must get her to the kirk, somewhere warm." She didn't budge, so he lifted her tiny form into his arms and ran back to his horse, slipping and sliding along the way as he fought to stay upright on the ice. "Kenzie, help me get her on the horse."

Once they were ready to leave, Loki said, "My thanks, lad. I'll return with coin later. We'll be at the kirk if you want to get out of the cold."

He flicked the reins of his horse and headed back down the pathway. His uncle and his cousin already stood in front of the kirk waiting for him. He handed Bella down to Logan while Torrian held his horse.

"She does not look good, Loki," Torrian said.

"I'll warm her inside. She's just too cold. I cannot imagine how far she rode. Kenzie told me 'twas her horse he rode, and I have no idea where she found a horse." He stepped inside the church and sat on the nearest bench. "Help me get her mantle off."

Logan and Loki stripped her down to her chemise, which was miraculously still dry, then wrapped her in an extra Ramsay plaid. Loki wrapped his arms around her and whispered in her ear. The priest came out from the back room and spoke to Logan.

Loki couldn't heed them. "Bella," he whispered. "Please come back to me. I love you, and if you'll still have me, we'll get married right now. The priest is here." He rocked her in his arms, praying she would warm up. She was as cold as the highest ridge in the Highlands in January, but he wouldn't stop holding her.

The priest led him to the hearth in the back, then brought him a cup of broth. "Here, lad. Try this if she awakens."

His father had told him he had no heart, but this was proof that he did. He could feel it breaking into pieces at the thought of losing his Bella, his love. He'd never tire of telling her how much he loved her if she'd only wake up. "Bella, please, fight. Come back to me, I miss you already." He sat for a few moments in front of the fire, rocking her close to his chest.

"Loki?" A soft whisper greeted his ear and he wanted to shout to the high heavens.

"Lass? Here, I have some broth to warm your insides." He helped her sit so he could feed her the broth. He held her tight, rubbing her arms and whispering sweet words to her, anything he could do to bring her back to him. "I love you, lass. Please do not frighten me like that again."

Her hands trembled as she reached for the broth, but she was able to offer him a weak smile.

"I love you, too, Loki Grant. Do not ever leave me again…promise?"

Bella stared at the love of her life, her heart melting as his words. Was it true or was she dreaming? The last thing she could recall was arriving at Ayr on her horse and having to pay a toll in the frigid wind of a cold autumn night. She recalled naught after that except a wee lad with dark red hair covering her with a plaid. The rest was blank.

But she would swear on her life that Loki had just proposed marriage to her. Squinting at him through her still dampened lashes, she had to ask. "I'm sorry, Loki, but what was it you said to me?"

He grinned and showed her the whitest smile she'd ever seen. "You heard me, aye? You heard the word marriage?"

Squeezing his arm, she said, "Aye, and do not tell me you've changed your mind already. 'Tis quite impossible."

Loki gazed into her eyes and her heart pounded from the look he gave her. One blue eye and one green reached inside of her and grabbed her, swearing to never let go. Her heart swelled even more when he whispered, "Aye, you heard right, if you wish to marry me and make all my days happy ones, then please say aye."

"Aye, Loki. Naught would make me happier. Are you sure you do not wish to wait to marry with your family?"

"Nay, I wish to marry you right this moment if you'll have me, Bella. You've had me ever since the day you swore your love for me, but this will make our love known to everyone. 'Tis what I want."

She nodded, tears forming on her lashes. He kissed her lips, then turned to face the priest. "Father, would you do us the honor of marrying us this day? 'Tis almost morn, is it not?"

"Aye, lad, 'twould please me to marry you, as soon as the lass is warmed enough, we shall." The priest spoke to Torrian and Logan a short distance away. "Will you agree to be witnesses to this marriage?"

Torrian nodded and Logan strolled toward them with a wide smile on his face. "Aye, the two of you remind me of my sister and her husband when they married in such haste. 'Twas the best decision they ever made, and my guess is 'twill be the same for you. Whenever you are ready, lass."

Bella decided it was time, so she scooted to the edge of Loki's lap and set her feet down on the floorboards of the kirk to stand. She almost lost her footing, but hung on to Loki with a death grip until she finally managed to push herself upright. As soon as she did, she glanced at the priest and said, "I'm ready, Father, if you please."

Father nodded to her, his hands clasped in front of him. "My name is Father Brian." He held his hand out to his side. "Why do we not head to the center of the kirk so I can marry you there?"

Bella padded to the front of the church, Loki's arm wrapped around her waist for support, until they stood in front of the altar—Torrian on one side of them, Logan on the other. Father Brian began the ceremony by wrapping their hands in the blue Ramsay tartan she and Loki both wore, but Loki stopped him and reached into his sporran to pull out a thin piece of the red Grant plaid that could be used instead of the blue plaid.

Bella couldn't believe this was happening—her dreams were finally coming true. She glanced up at Loki, his tall broad shoulders, his beautiful smile, his arresting gaze. How had she managed to win his love? She was so excited she could hardly hear the words Father Brian was saying. Her wedding could not be more different than the elaborate fanfare with which Morna would be married, but she knew her marriage would be the happier one. Loki was everything to her, and she would remember this day forever. They were finally saying their vows.

When Father Brian finished and Loki leaned down to kiss her, she wished to jump for joy. Logan said, "Come, we'll have a small feast at the inn across the road, and then we'll decide what to do next. Father, would you care to join us?"

Father Brian laughed, his hands settling on his small belly. "Och, nay. I'll be staying here at my home."

Logan offered the priest a coin before moving out of the kirk and over to the tavern. There weren't many people out on the roads this morn. They sat at a table in a separate room at the inn. Logan ordered chunks of pork, eggs, mushrooms, and thick crusty bread for their breakfast. Bella's mouth watered as soon as the pork was set down on the table.

Loki's eyes danced as he watched her. "Hungry, wife? You're almost drooling."

"Aye, I'm hungry. I've had naught to eat for almost two days. I ate little traveling from the Highlands because I tried to store up food for my journey here, but then I became too ill and too cold to eat it."

Logan asked, "I'm not hungry, so eat as much as you like. How did you get to Ayr, Bella? Please, you must tell us."

"I rode with my sister to her betrothed's home, then sneaked out in the middle of the night. I did take a horse, but he has a huge stable, so I'm sure it will not be missed."

"And no one saw you?" Torrian asked.

"Nay, I waited until after midnight, so the guards were all mostly sotted. I dressed as a lad and no one stopped me." She shrugged her shoulders and piled her plate full of food. All three men stared at her. Torrian's jaw dropped open.

Logan said, "You think you can eat that much, lass?"

Bella scowled. "Aye, I can. Did I leave you enough, or do you wish for me to put some back?" Her chin lifted a notch. "I may be wee, but I'm not weak. I must keep my strength up."

Logan laughed and said, "You remind me of my Gwynie. Eat whatever your heart desires. There's plenty for all of us, and we ate not long ago. And we'll take care of returning your sister's horse."

When they finished their meal, Logan pushed back from the table and said, "I hate to bring up a subject you do not wish to hear about, but I think we must move on. I cannot believe that your sire will not attempt to retaliate after your escape. Please enlighten us a bit more on your captivity, Loki."

Bella jerked her gaze to her husband's. "You escaped?"

"Aye, Bella, and 'twas not easy. My sire had me in chains." Loki squeezed her hand and then turned to Logan and Torrian. "You have the right of it, Uncle. His last words to me were that this was not over. He also threatened to go after anyone I cared about. Much as I'd like to stay and celebrate our marriage, I think we need to move."

Bella sat forward in her chair, the color leaving her face. "But where will we go?"

CHAPTER TWELVE

Loki thought for a moment, but he knew what his decision had to be. Above all, he had to keep Bella safe. "I think we need to return to the Grants. We'll be safest there."

"Loki, my da will be so angry when he finds out we've married. I know he's frustrated both of us, but I do still love him. I want him to support us." She stared at the floor and chewed on her lip.

"Then we shall not tell him. We can pretend for a while until I earn his respect enough to approve of the marriage. I will be successful in this, wife. Our laird supported us, so we have naught to worry there, and you know my parents adore you. I think they will go along with us for a short time until I can convince your father of my worth."

Torrian interjected, "Did you forget to tell your wife that you are of noble blood? Mayhap her sire will be more accepting of you now."

"You are, Loki? Your sire is of noble blood?"

"Aye, my sire is an earl, though he was not born an earl. But it does not matter, I do not accept him as my sire, so I'll not make that claim to your father. Whose sire locks them up in a dungeon, beats him, and then chains him to a wall like an animal? I hate the bastard."

He could see tears pooling in Bella's eyes, though she tried to blink them away. "Aw, Bella. Do not cry for me. I'm fine, and we're married now." He wrapped his arm around her shoulder and pulled her close. "I have never been happier."

"But your own sire chained you in a dungeon, and look at the bruises all over you. How awful. I'm sorry your sire was not happy to see you. I did not imagine he would treat you so poorly even though he tried to use you to gain coin."

"He's a cruel man, and I have no proof he's my sire, so I'll deny him."

Logan stood up from his chair. "I'll pay the innkeeper. You get ready to leave in ten minutes. I want all of us to ride away from here as quickly as possible. There's a nice inn far north, and I think we can reach it shortly after dark. We'll stay the night, then Torrian and I will leave you to finish your journey into the Highlands. 'Tis high enough and cold enough, I do not think they'll follow you that far."

"There is no need for you to go with us." Loki settled his hands on his hips and looked from Logan to Torrian. "I'll protect my wife."

"Aye, we do need to go, and I've a few guards to travel with us, besides. We'll spend the night in a warm place, and I think 'tis a deserving spot for a pair that's newly wed. I'll not have my nephew sleeping with his wife on icy ground for the first night of their marriage. Plus, these auld bones of mine prefer to be inside this time of year."

"We can sleep under the stars. We shall be fine. Avelina did." But Bella shivered a little in his arms, as if chilled by the mere thought.

"Avelina married in the summer and slept on a warm ground with the fae and her husband to guard her." Logan gave Bella pointed look. "And in view of last night…"

"He's right, wife. You were dangerously cold. I would have you sleep inside a building tonight. We cannot risk your well-being." He leaned down and kissed her soundly on her cheek. "And I look forward to it. Now let's get ready to move. I'll see what I can find for food to carry with us on our journey."

When they were preparing to mount their horses several minutes later, Loki said, "Uncle Logan, I'd like to leave by Woodgait if you do not mind. There is one more thing I must do."

Logan nodded his agreement. "I see no problem with that since it's not far, we just need to get moving."

Loki lifted Bella onto his horse, then mounted behind her, his long hair flowing in the wind. As soon as they made it to Woodgait, Loki slowed his horse to search for Kenzie. Mayhap someday he would be back for the laddie. He hoped it would happen, but he at least needed to pay him for saving Bella. "Kenzie?"

No one answered. Logan prompted him, "Be quick about it, lad. We should not tarry long."

Loki jumped down from his horse and ran behind the inn, but Kenzie was nowhere to be seen. He searched the area, but though the lad's things were still there, there was no sign of him. Loki grabbed two coins from his pocket and left them inside the pan. Where was he?

"Let's move, nephew."

Loki knew they needed to hurry, so he rushed back to Bella—his sweet Bella, looking absolutely beautiful on his horse.

They rode for hours, but fortunately, their trip was uneventful. Bella fell asleep in the middle of the day, and her sweet bum sat directly against Loki. He'd had an erection off and on during the day depending on whether he was speaking to his wife or his cousin. But now that she was sleeping, she was totally relaxed and her soft globes were pressed against him. It made him want to stop and toss her skirts up on the next pile of leaves they passed. Or perhaps he could hold her while her back was against the tree. At this point, he'd even be willing to try making love to her on horseback. Anything at all to give him release.

"Loki!"

"What?" he scowled at his uncle, who just grinned at him.

"Good thing we're not far from that inn, do you not agree?"

Loki groaned and stared straight ahead while his uncle laughed.

"I know where you're at, lad. Been there before. Still happens to me every time Gwynie rides in front of me. Unavoidable."

Torrian smirked. "I'm so enjoying this, cousin. Many thanks, Uncle Logan, for inviting me along on this wee venture. I've never had this much fun at home."

"You'd pay for those words if I did not have a sweet wife in front of me," Loki snarled.

Just after dark, the path widened and they noticed a couple of torches ahead. They'd actually made it to the inn ahead of schedule. Loki kissed Bella's shoulder until she awakened.

She wiped the sleep from her eyes and dismounted. Her knees

buckled as soon as they hit the ground, but Loki caught her. "Loki, 'tis a beautiful inn."

Logan said, "Aye, there are not many this far north, but 'tis well known. The couple who runs it takes good care of their guests, and she's a great cook. Hopefully, there are no other travelers already staying here this night. I'll go check and see what I can arrange."

"You're right, 'tis beautiful," Torrian added.

Logan returned quickly with a smile on his face. "Perfect. They have one private room for the newly wedded couple, and Torrian and I can sleep on pallets in the main room with a few guards. The others can sleep in the stables around back. 'Tis a large enough building for all the horses to warm up and bed down for the night. They've a full pot of stew just made today, plenty of bread, and good ale." He turned to the guards. "Lead the horses out back, then join us for supper before you settle down.

Bella moved inside the door and curtsied to the couple. The tavern was quite large, equipped with two long trestle tables, a hearth to cook in on one end, and a table and utensils in front of it. There were a couple of pallets off to the side as well as a small room in back with a few pallets and a garderobe. A staircase at the other end led upstairs.

The couple, Gus and Fiona, busied themselves at the hearth, getting trenchers and goblets of ale ready for the travelers. After a moment, Fiona hurried over to Bella and said, "If you please, follow me." She led the way upstairs, so the young couple followed her. She could look over the railing and see everyone warming near the fire, sharing an ale and laughter. There were two chambers off the balcony, and they were in the far room. Fiona opened the door to their chamber and bowed her head.

Bella stepped inside and gasped. "Loki, this is beautiful." She turned to Fiona and nodded to her. "My thanks. 'Tis lovely."

"There's a basin of fresh water for you, my lady. The bed is clean. Do you wish to join us for sup or would you like your food here?"

Bella glanced at Loki and said, "We'll join you for sup. You do not need to wait on us. We'll be down in just a bit. My thanks, Fiona, for your fine care."

The moment Fiona ducked out the doorway, Bella threw herself into Loki's arms. "Loki, this is the nicest bed I've ever slept in. I've always had a pallet. Look at the pillows and the furs! Did you hear her call me my lady? And look at the dried flowers on the table. They are lovely."

"You are happy, wee one?" Loki sat on the bed and tucked her into his lap.

She slipped her arms around his neck and whispered, "Aye. I'm nervous about tonight, but I'm so happy to be your wife. And this is the most wonderful inn I could have asked for."

Loki whispered, "Good. I want my wife happy." His mouth descended on hers.

His lips were soft and warm at first, but then he became more possessive, ravishing her lips, teasing her with his tongue. She returned every last bit of his passion, loving the taste of this man, her husband. He angled his mouth over hers and deepened the kiss, sucking on her tongue, but then released her and kissed a line down her neck. The brute knew exactly how to make her breathless, and she moaned as soon as his tongue touched a sensitive spot in the front beneath her collarbone before moving even lower.

The door flew open and Logan stood there with Torrian and a few guards behind him, laughing and teasing. Bella blushed the deepest shade of red imaginable, but then started laughing along with the rest of them because Loki's breathing had become as ragged as her own.

"Do not start too soon or there'll be naught to eat. You must come down and join us first. You cannot have the whole night to yourselves. We have to drink a toast or two to the newly married couple." They headed back down the balcony and the staircase, but left the door ajar, teasing them as they left.

Loki kissed her cheek. "I'm sorry, Bella," he whispered in her ear.

"'Tis all right. There would have been more teasing if we'd married at the Grant keep. Shall we join them, do you mind, Loki? Mayhap they'll all get sotted and forget about us."

"Nay, I do not mind. We need to eat, but I'll not stay there long. You are way too tempting, lass. I've waited a long time for this night."

When she was sure the others were too far to hear, she whispered, "You'll be considerate of me tonight?" Her shoulders hunched up next to her ears in a shrug as she waited for his answer.

Loki lifted her off her feet and into his arms, his hands caressing her bum as he kissed her hard on the mouth. Hellfire, he'd never make it through the toast without embarrassing himself, would he? He'd wanted this lass for too long, and now she was his forever. What more could he ask for? Aye, he'd take good care of her. When he was finally able to pull away from her, he gulped to catch his breath, holding her tight against his hardness. He whispered in her ear, "Are you feeling what you do to me, lass? You'll see that I promise to take verra good care of you, and I'll do it all—" he kissed her neck, "—night—" he kissed her throat as she leaned her head back, "—long…"

He slid her down his length and said, "And that's a promise."

Logan bellowed loud enough to shake the rafters, so Loki set Bella down and ushered her out the door and down the staircase. The others stood and Logan and Torrian handed each a goblet of ale as soon as they descended the staircase. "Loki and Bella, a toast to many years of happiness and bairns."

Torrian laughed and threw his ale down. "You're the first."

Loki gave him a puzzled look. "The first what?"

"You're the first of the Grants and the Ramsay bairns to marry."

Loki smiled and wrapped his arm around Bella's shoulders. "I am, 'tis true." He held his glass up and said, "Here's to you being the next one, Torrian."

Torrian paled and said, "Ummm, nay."

"Why not?" Logan asked. "I like the sounds of that, though I have not thought of the perfect match for you. I'll have to consider it…or mayhap my Gwynie already has an idea." The man's face lit up with the glee of taunting his young nephew. "Time for food, my belly is rumbling."

Once they were seated, Fiona and Gus brought out mutton and boar meat pies along with two loaves of fresh baked bread. "You're a bread lover, are you not, wee one?" he whispered to his wife.

Bella leaned into her husband, murmuring, "Aye."

Loki whispered as quietly as he could so as not to embarrass her, but he could not resist the urge. "I hope I please you enough tonight for you to look at me that way when we're alone."

A fast elbow to his ribs prompted an, "Oof," from him. Perhaps he should have kept his thoughts to himself, for the woman he loved was turning a deep shade of red.

"Loki!" was all she managed to get out before she buried her face in his shoulder.

He could tell from the mischief in his uncle's eyes that the older man was about to latch on to Bella's discomfort, but Loki gave him a pointed look that stopped him just as he opened his mouth. He snapped his jaw closed.

Torrian said, loud enough for all to hear, "Probably makes you a wee bit uncomfortable being the only lass, does it not, Bella?"

Her gaze swung to Torrian and she nodded. The others looked chagrined, though that might also have something to do with the dark glare Loki was giving them.

"Bella, have I ever told you how shy Gwynie was the day we married? Best day of my life. She preferred to sleep under the stars, as I did, so that's where we spent the first sennight of our marriage. 'Twas a wee bit warmer then than 'tis now, just as it was for Avelina and Drew."

"Aye, my thanks for finding the inn for us. 'Tis lovely and makes it special," Bella said.

Gus brought out more food—a feast of rabbit stew, pear tarts, and apple pastries. Loki noticed Bella didn't eat her usual amount, which he took to be a sign that she was nervous about the coming night.

Before they dug into the sweets, Loki stepped back from the table and held his hand out to his wife. "Bella and I will leave you to the ale, but we'll take a pear tart with us if you do not mind, Fiona."

Loki accepted the wrapped pastry from Fiona and then guided his wife ahead of him so he could protect her from the rush of well wishes and shouts of vulgarities that oft accompanied a newly wed couple. Once they started up the staircase, he gave her a wee shove and said, "Go inside and close the door. I'll handle them."

CHAPTER THIRTEEN

Bella raced to the end of the balcony and then entered the chamber and closed the door behind her, her heart racing from all the comments. She'd thought about their wedding night many times, especially after listening to all the tales of skirt tossings from some of the looser kitchen maids, but now that it was here, her nerves were on edge.

She had paid close attention to what those women had said each time the topic came up. They'd told her the first time stung—like having a bee caught inside your female parts fighting to get out—and any time after that felt more wonderful, like warm honey spreading through your insides. She wasn't quite sure what that meant, but she wanted to get past the bee stinging part.

She remembered the wash basin and thought to freshen herself for her husband before he came into the room. Hurrying so she wouldn't be caught in the middle of it, she dropped the sliver of soap on the floor. Her husband came in just as she was bending over to retrieve it.

"Och, my Bella, what you do to me."

She jerked back to a standing position, horrified to have been seen in such a position, but when she straightened her skirts and turned around, the look on his face was that of a famished lad who was about to go hunting.

"Loki?"

His gaze traveled from her head to her toes. He barred the door and said, "Do not give them another thought. Uncle Logan is sleeping at the bottom of the stairs, so they'll not bother us again."

His voice—husky, deep, and hungry— called to her, "Come here, my beauty."

He always looked at her with desire, but the expression on his face now was so much deeper. Aye, he wanted her, and the knowledge of that made her feel proud and beautiful. Her mouth went dry as she crossed the room to him.

"Turn around, lass."

She did as he commanded, and he worked his way through her laces, untying the gown. The more he untied, the more he fumbled. The thicker his thumbs became, the deeper his growl grew. Glancing at him from over her shoulder, she had just a glimpse of what a man wanted from a woman, and a new understanding of true love blossomed inside her. Becoming bolder, she settled her hands on the bodice to keep it high enough to cover her breasts, and when he finally finished, she turned around and dipped the bodice down slowly, revealing her tender globes, and rubbed her thumbs across her nipples as Loki had done many times.

He sucked in a breath, as if in pain, and said, "Bella, my Bella, what a beauty you are." He reached for her and lifted her in the air so that her gown fell from her hands. He raised her up more so he could suckle her nipple, but her head hit the rafters and she squeaked. "Bella, I'm so sorry."

"Loki, you are too tall to do that." She rubbed her head as he lowered her to the floor, sliding her down the front of him so she could feel his hardness through his plaid. "Oh my."

"Och, indeed." Once her feet hit the floor, he quickly tossed off his boots, plaid, and breeches. His tunic followed, and before she knew it, he stood in front of her unclothed. "Enough, sweet one. We're moving to the furs and pillows before I hurt your head again."

Her quick intake of breath stopped him. Only then did he seem to notice how she was looking at him.

"What is it?"

"Loki, you are all bruises. They beat you terribly. Does it not hurt?" Her eyes misted as she stared at the evidence of what his short captivity had been like.

"Nay, they no longer hurt. Do not think about them, please." He picked her up and tossed her onto the piles of furs, then lowered himself over her. It was impossible to stop her body from writhing.

"What is it?" he asked, perplexed.

"Loki, these furs are so soft and teasing against my skin."

With a groan, his lips fell on hers, searing her with his desire. His tongue mated with hers, teasing her, tantalizing her until she wanted to scream. All her nerves left her, and she embraced everything he wished to do to her, with her, giving her trust to him completely. She knew he would do everything in his power to make this experience wonderful for her.

She knew this because he would love her forever—the same way she had promised to love him.

His lips traveled across her jaw, then moved to her breast, teasing her with just a flick of his tongue over her hardened nipple. She arched into him, wanting him to take her nipple full into his mouth.

"Tell me, Bella. What is it you want?" He flicked his tongue over her other nipple and received the same response.

"I want...I want..."

"Say it. Tell me." He teased her again, licking a path around the areola of each breast.

"I want you to..."

"To what? Tell me what will make you happy." His hand pinched her nipple and she moaned.

"Your mouth, suck me, please..."

He grinned and obliged her, suckling her until she wanted to cry out, unsure of what was happening to her. Threading her fingers through his long locks, she tugged him closer. His mouth moved to her other nipple and his hands caressed her belly, her hips, and then crossed over to her private place.

Some unknown force inside her spread her thighs apart as soon as he touched her curls and even the softest of touches sent needles of pleasure shooting through her. Though shocked at her own boldness, she didn't want him to stop. Once his finger entered her, she moaned and caught his gaze. "I don't..."

"What is it?" His tongued moved to her belly, flicking in various spots before finding her nub and teasing her there.

She clamped her legs together, shocked at what he had just done.

"Nay, Bella, allow me to taste your sweetness. You are so slick for me."

As she clutched his taut biceps, her legs flew open on their own. She moaned and closed her eyes, digging her fingernails into him. "I want…"

"What do you want, Bella?"

"You, please, you, Loki." She was desperate for something, though she knew not what.

"Lass, you've tortured me enough. Your passion threatens to unman me. I need you, too. I need to be inside you."

She took one look at his hardness and panted, "You'll never fit, Loki, it won't work…"

"Aye, lass, we'll fit perfect. I'm sorry I must hurt you, but 'twill be better after."

He brought both hands around her hips, then traced them across her sensitive bottom, teasing her back and forth until she spread her legs again. He dipped his fingers inside her, making her moan for him. "Bella, you are so beautiful and passionate."

He teased her with the tip of his cock, moving it back and forth against her entrance until it was slick with her juices. "Now, Loki, please."

He growled and gripped her hips, plunging through her barrier until she screeched, "Stop, please stop. It hurts, you're too big for me, Loki. Please."

"Nay, love, I'm not," he said, catching her gaze with his. "We were made for each other. Just be patient and you'll see. 'Twas the worst just now."

She whimpered as she gripped his shoulders.

"Do you not recall the day you said you would love me forever?"

"Aye, I will always love you."

"Then trust your husband." He hadn't moved once since she'd asked him to stop.

The pain did start to ease as she stared into his eyes, her heart ready to burst with the love she had for him. She could see from the sweat on his brow and the clench of his jaw how hard this was for him, stopping for her, holding his weight on his elbows. A moment later, the pain had mostly disappeared. She shifted against him to test it.

"Bella, if you do that again, I will not be able to stop," he murmured, his voice pained. "I've waited a long time for you."

She moved to bring him out and back in again. "'Tis all right, Loki. It does not hurt anymore. What do we do now?"

Loki groaned and grasped her hips as he buried himself deep inside her, then pulled out again only to peek at her again. "All right?"

"Aye, more, please."

Loki drove into her and a wave of sensation sent tendrils of pleasure shooting through her. Shocked at the wonder of this feeling, she moved with him, the pleasure building inside her until she wanted to explode, her body tingling in places she'd never noticed, building to a crescendo she didn't know what to do with.

As Loki thrust into her again and again, an unknown sound issued from the back of her own throat. Then he reached down between them to caress her nub, and after two more thrusts, she careened over the edge into a vortex of pleasure. When she was able to open her eyes, she watched as her husband did the same, a fierce growl erupting from him that would have frightened her if she weren't in his embrace.

But she was, safe and happy and protected from the rest of the world.

Loki rolled onto his back and tugged Bella close, resting until their breathing returned to normal. "Did I please you, my Bella?"

"Aye, that was ... I never..." She breathed in deep and sighed. "That was wonderful, husband."

"You are not angry that I went too fast? My apologies if I rushed, but those mewling sounds of yours put me over the edge. I've wanted you for so long."

"Nay, I'm quite pleased. You were right."

"About?"

"We do fit perfectly." She kissed him soundly. "Just as you said."

He sighed, pleased that he'd satisfied her and he hadn't been too rough with her. She was his, and he was proud of it. He'd take good care of her, just as his adopted sire had always cared for his wife. They'd see he'd be a good husband. Bella was his world, a world he wished to stay in forever.

As Bella rested her head on his shoulder, she whispered, "Where will we go, Loki?"

"What do you mean?"

"Where will we live? My sire will be furious we've married without his permission. I do not know if we should live on Grant land." Her fingers caressed the flat plane of his abdomen.

"Wife, you know our laird can say he forced the marriage."

"Nay, I know my sire. He'll hold his anger forever. I know you do not want to acknowledge the earl as your father, but it might convince my father to approve of the marriage."

"Nay, the Earl of Cliffnock has no honor, and I want naught to do with him."

"But you do not have to ever see him again, Loki. Just use this to calm my sire's rage. My sister is gone, and he's the only family I have left. He does love me, and I love him."

Loki rolled Bella onto her back and settled himself above her so he could gaze into her eyes. "I want your father to respect me for my character, not for some foolish title. I meant what I said before. We can hold off on revealing our marriage until I earn his respect. I'll do it somehow, Bella." He kissed her nose. "I'll do it for you, for us. I want us to be a happy family. We'll have bairns someday, and they'll want to know their grandsire. Just give me some time."

"I wish for the same, but I will not be able to be apart from you for long. I'll agree, but only if you promise me no more than three moons." She gripped the hard muscles in his forearms as if hanging on for life.

Loki thought for a moment, then conceded. "I'll agree to that. As long as you understand something else."

"What?" Her gaze searched his with uncertainty.

"That your sire is no longer your only family. In three moons, you'll have a hall full of aunts, uncles, and cousins, along with my mama and papa, and a new brother and two sisters."

Her face broke into a huge smile. "Aye, 'tis true. How wonderful it will be when I am a true member of your family. Do you think they'll be happy, Loki?" She held her breath as she awaited his answer.

"Bella, my mama already wanted us to marry. You'll see how much they love you already, just as I do." He kissed her and suckled her tongue until she pulled away, her eyes bright.

"I cannot wait to be part of your family. Do not make me wait too long, husband." She clutched his face in her hands and whispered, "I do love you so."

"The only problem we'll have is explaining why you are riding home with me." Loki sighed, his lips pursed in thought.

Bella's eyes widened. "I had not thought of that. What will we say? Aye, we'll have to come up with a good story or my sire will whip me himself."

"Well, you were with your sister. Where did you tell her you were going?"

She rolled her eyes. "Uhhh…"

"Bella? You left without telling your sister you were leaving?"

"I had your sister pen a note for me."

"And what did it say?"

"I told her you had been kidnapped and I was going after you. 'Twas the truth."

"My wee Bella." Loki clucked his tongue at her as he rolled onto his back again, pulling her with him. "We'll tell her you were lost in Ayr and we found you. 'Tis the truth. We do not need to mention our marriage just yet. 'Twas Kenzie who came to find us because you were so cold. Your sire will be glad we found you, and Logan and Torrian were with me, so there is no reason for him to think it improper. Even though they leave us, we still have the guards as chaperones. We'll talk to them about our plan."

"I hope you are right, Loki. My sire's belt is not verra nice."

"He'll not whip my wife. You are to come to me if he threatens any such foolishness."

She didn't answer him.

Loki rubbed his thumb across her cheek. "Bella…you are my wife now. He has no rights. You promise to come and get me if aught happens?"

She nodded her head, but the movement was so slight it was almost imperceptible.

"Wife?"

"Aye, I promise."

Why did Loki not quite believe her?

"There's one other thing I need to ask you, wife." He paused, taking a moment to put the fear into words. "Do you think I'm cold-hearted?"

"You, cold-hearted? Och, nay, Loki. How could you ask such a thing? You love all your cousins. I saw you dance with Ashley because she's afraid of lads. Besides, you have protected your family again and again. You're a soft-hearted lad, if you want my opinion."

"My father's men say he is hard-hearted, and they think I am the same because I don't show pain."

"Not showing pain does not mean you have a hard heart. Look at Lady Madeline. She has the biggest heart of all. That's a daft notion. Do not listen to them. I'm surprised you can even think such a thing of yourself."

"Well..."

"Well, what?" she prodded.

"Well, there's one thing I think I do have in common with the earl."

"Tell me more."

He paused, hating to admit this one truth about himself, but he had to tell her. "I have always wanted to tell my parents how much they mean to me, how much the adoption changed my life, but each time I try, my tongue becomes muddled and doesn't seem to work. I get so addled that I cannot think of what to say. Probably because I still carry the fear of being abandoned again."

"Have you told them you love them? I know you would do aught for them."

"Nay," he replied, "The words just do not come."

"Loki, you've told me you love me. Why not them, especially your father? Even I love my father, though he does often try my patience. I have many fond memories of him when I was younger."

"I've had great difficulty, but after seeing what my true sire is like, I'm hoping I'll be able to thank them. Blackett made my parents seem even more special."

"When the time is right, you'll say the right things. They know you love them, but 'twould be nice for you to express your feelings in words, especially to Lady Celestina."

"You are correct. Now I just need to decide how to do it." And in his mind, he thought it would be the final testament to him being different from his sire. He would demonstrate that he was not hard-hearted by telling his parents what they meant to him. He'd told his wife, now he would tell the rest of his family.

"And Loki? You do not have to ever fear being alone again. Now you have me."

He hadn't thought of that, but she was right, wasn't she?

CHAPTER FOURTEEN

The next morning it was time to say goodbye to the other half of their party. Loki promised his uncle he would consider working for the crown in the spring. First, though, they needed to get things settled with Clan Grant.

"Aye, and if I do not get the laird's heir back to his clan soon, my brother will hang me by my ballocks." Logan said, giving his nephew a sly look.

Torrian, already seated on his horse, had a huge grin on his face. "Aye, but this was such a great trip, Uncle Logan. We'll have to do it again some time."

Logan rolled his eyes as he turned to face the married couple. "Travel safely, and send a message with any news about your sire." He gave Bella a kiss on the cheek and then slapped the flank of their horse. "On home with you both. Good luck with your sire, Bella. He'd be a fool not to accept Loki as your husband."

Logan had left three guards to travel with them. Even though the next part of the journey was a rough climb over steep inclines, Loki liked it best of all. The majestic peaks of the Highlands around them were topped with snow, and they cast a white glow on everything. The leaves had mostly fallen, but some reds and golds lingered on the trees, while the green of the pines remained.

Later in the day, Loki tugged Bella tight against him to protect her from the cold wind whipping around them as they moved through a narrow pass in the forest. He had the sense they were no longer alone, or soon would not be, so he ordered a man to ride ahead of them—something he'd never done before. Usually he preferred to be in the lead, but now his priorities had changed. Wee Bella was his main concern. "Ride ahead. I sense someone is headed this way."

The guard nodded and galloped out of sight.

"What is it, Loki?" Bella tipped her head back and stared into his eyes.

"I'm not sure, but we are close to Grant land. If someone is coming, it should be someone we know." He stopped his horse and turned so he could listen to the wind. "We're so far north, it must be someone from our clan. Not many would venture this far into the Highlands at this time of year."

A few minutes later, their guard returned with a grin on his face. "Just a few Grant warriors ahead. They're awaiting us."

Loki flicked his reins and moved ahead, a smile breaking across his face as soon as he came upon the Grant contingency. His sire was in the lead, and as soon as Brodie saw Loki, he rode forward, moving away from all the guards. Loki led his horse directly up to Brodie's. "Where are you headed? Do you need me along?"

Brodie chuckled. "Nay, we're coming for you. We received a message you were being held for ransom. We were confident Logan Ramsay would handle everything, but I wished to see you with my own eyes. I've brought the coin to pay if necessary. What happened?"

Loki shrugged one shoulder.

A feminine voice interjected. "He escaped. He was held in a dungeon and chained to the wall, but my husband outsmarted his captors." Bella crossed her arms and nodded her head for emphasis.

Brodie quirked his brow at his eldest son. "You escaped chains? And did I hear you correctly, Bella? Did you call him your husband?"

Loki nodded, wrapping his arms around her and tugging her close. "Aye, we married in Ayr, but we'd like to keep it a secret until I can win the approval of Bella's sire." Loki was happy to see their marriage pleased his sire, he could tell by the expression on his face and the way he looked at Bella. More important, Bella could tell he was pleased they had married. How blessed he'd been the day he met Brodie Grant.

"Congratulations and welcome to the family, Bella! Loki, you've chosen well and your mother will be verra happy. I will respect your wishes and not mention it until we meet with your laird to discuss it. Bella, do not mention your marriage around any of the guards or word will travel. I might add that 'tis good to see you are safe, lass. We worried when you disappeared, though my wife and I had a good idea of where you'd gone."

Bella blushed a shade of pink. "My apologies, but 'twas the only way I knew to learn more about Loki."

"'Tis all right, lass. You are both here and happy." Brodie chuckled and turned his horse around.

Loki was relieved that his adopted father still referred to himself as his father and Celestina as his mother. Thank the stars above they hadn't given up on him now that they knew about the earl.

They headed for the Grant castle, and Loki was surprised to see the number of guardsmen who came out to escort him to the keep. Brodie moved to his side as the guards cheered him on. Naught was mentioned about why he'd been captured, but everyone seemed impressed that he'd escaped from his captors. There was also naught said about the fact that Bella and Loki were arriving together.

He was happy to be home. Once they dismounted from their horses, they crossed the cobblestone courtyard to applause and greetings from his clanmates. He wanted to hold his bride tucked against him, but she stepped away from him. If they were to perpetuate the ruse that they were not married, they would need to act like it.

As he neared the door leading in to the great hall, Alison and Catriona raced toward him. Each hugged one of his legs once they reached him. "Loki, we're glad you are home. We were so worried. Do not ever leave us again."

He returned their hugs and then moved on to the woman standing on the steps, tears flooding her cheeks and her arms outstretched in greeting. Celestina hugged him and said, "Saints above, I'm glad you are home safe, Loki." She stepped back from him and cupped his face. "I was so afraid we'd lost our first son."

"Nay, Mama," he kissed her cheek. "Your son is hearty, do not worry about me." Love swelled in his heart, and he hoped he'd soon get the opportunity and the courage to tell his parents how much their loyalty and support meant to him.

"You will never know how worried I was that you would not return to us. I was afraid you would find a mother or father to love more."

"Nay. You need not worry about that ever happening. Come inside and I'll explain everything to you." He wrapped his arm around her shoulder and led her toward the door.

But the door flew open as soon as he reached for the handle, and before he knew it, Alex Grant stood in front of him. Loki was surprised to see that he was almost eye to eye with his laird. Naught would make him happier than to be able to look him in the eye.

"Loki, 'twas a short trip on Brodie's part. They met up with you on the way?" Alex grasped his shoulder, and after Bella and Celestina had entered the great hall, he led him through the door. "My guess is you have a story to tell. I'd like to hear it as soon as you've had something to eat."

"If my laird approves," Loki said, "I'd ask to speak to you now in private, with Arabella and my mother and father also in attendance."

"Agreed." He waved to Maddie, who hurried over to their side.

Maddie gave Loki a fierce hug, her eyes damp with tears. "Welcome home, Loki."

"Maddie," Alex said, "would you have them bring food into the solar? You are welcome to join us if you would like."

Uncle Robbie came up behind Loki and clasped his shoulder. "Welcome home. Mighty proud of you for making it out on your own."

Loki thanked all of his well-wishers, but his eyes were fixed on Bella. She seemed a bit nervous, but not enough to give anything away. A little while later, Alex ushered them inside his solar, getting everyone situated while they waited for the food and ale to arrive.

Once the food had been brought in, Brodie closed the door and Alex asked, "Who wishes to start?"

Loki said, "I will. As soon as we arrived in Ayr, Logan checked in with Hamilton, who gave us his instructions to find out anything we could about missing royal jewels. Torrian and I attended an event at the royal castle, and managed to get some information from a couple of goons."

"And what was that?"

"That the Earl of Cliffnock claimed I was his son." Loki cleared his throat before glancing at his mother, wishing he could avoid causing her any pain. "Edward Blackett, the Earl of Cliffnock, declares himself to be my sire. Logan and I traveled to his keep the following day, and he requested that I stay for two moons to get to know him better."

Loki heard a slight intake of breath from his mother, but he forced himself to continue. "I refused that request, but agreed to stay a couple of nights, so Logan left. As soon as they left, I was drugged, and when I awakened, I was locked inside a cell in the dungeon."

Celestina whispered, "Is it true? Is the earl is your true sire? And what of your mother?"

Though it was only the laird's place to speak in such a situation, Alex allowed the question. It was a true testament to the respect he had for Loki's mother. Loki wanted to look away from her, but he did not. He stared into her eyes as he answered her question. "Mama, he claims to be my sire, but whether or not 'tis true, I don't accept him as my sire. I only have one, and 'tis Brodie Grant. The earl claims my true mother died in childbirth giving birth to my sister, who also passed."

Celestina choked on her sigh of relief, trying to hide it but failing. Loki wished he could take away all of her pain and discomfort, and he hoped this information would help.

Brodie wrapped his arms around his wife and asked, "And the reason you were living in a crate in the royal burgh?" A flash of anger burst in his eyes.

"He says I ran away when my mother died. At first, he was too distraught to notice, and by the time they searched for me, it was too late. They couldn't find me." Loki allowed that to settle for a moment. His mother and Maddie were both tearing up and dotting their faces with linen squares. "They did not live in Ayr, but in Perthshire at the time. 'Tis anyone's guess how I arrived in Ayr." He ran his hand down his face. There was something else he recalled—something about how he'd been naught but an extra mouth to feed—but there was no need to tell them that. Nay, he would not spend any more time on the lout.

After a short pause, Alex said, "Please continue about the events at the earl's castle."

"When I awakened, the earl came to speak to me. He claimed he deserved coin after all he did for the crown during the battle with the Norse. So he wished to extract coin from you, from Quade Ramsay, and from the Camerons and Lochluin Abbey. Apparently, he knew about all of our family's connections. Messengers were sent to all three places. Torrian and Logan intercepted the messenger headed to the Ramsays and Logan sent his own messenger to the Cameron to advise him to ignore Blackett's messenger. They were unable to catch the man headed to you."

Alex nodded back to Loki, pausing for thought before he stretched out his hand in a signal to continue.

"I was able to grab Blackett's head through the bars of my cell and slam it against the iron a few times before his guards could stop me. I took a beating that knocked me out for an unknown period, and when I awoke, I was chained to the wall."

"Did you learn aught about the earl that we should know?" Alex asked.

"Only that he has no honor. He claims my mother had the same eye coloring I have. 'Tis how he knew I was his son. Though I admit 'tis possible he fathered me, I refuse to accept him. You should know that he plans to continue his quest for the coin he feels he deserves."

Alex asked, "Why do you question his story? I could believe that a wee lad would run away after his mother's death."

"Because I don't remember it. If I ran away, I think I would recall running through the forests or arriving in Ayr. But I have no knowledge of my arrival in the burgh at all. He said I was five or six summers, and I think I would recall something about it. He has a guard named Hamish who claims to remember me, but I have the strangest feeling around him. Someday, I'll recall something about the man."

"And how did you get away?"

"Uncle Logan taught me how to use a tool to open a lock. There was one hidden in my clothing, so I managed to free myself from the manacles. I had to convince my sire to come into the cell, and then I stole his dagger and used it against him."

Alex quirked a brow at him as his hand came up to rub his chin. "Well done, lad."

"Torrian and Uncle Logan were already on their way to break me out, so I met them just outside the Cliffnock castle."

"And Bella? How does she fit into the story?" Alex tipped his head in her direction.

Bella started to speak, but when Loki noticed she was trembling, he tugged her onto his lap—much to the surprise of most of the people in the room. The poor lass was not used to being in the laird's solar or being questioned by Alexander Grant. "Bella had heard I was being held captive, so she sneaked away from her sister's keep and came after me. We found her in Ayr and I asked her to marry me."

Celestina and Maddie gasped, then both of them broke into smiles. Brodie embraced his wife, and Maddie squeezed Alex's hand, which prompted him to tug her onto his lap before signaling for Loki to continue.

"Bella and I married at a kirk in Ayr with Logan and Torrian as our witnesses, but we would like our marriage to remain a secret until I can earn her sire's approval."

Celestina and Maddie's faces went from smiles to scowls in but a moment.

Alex asked, "And is this what you would like also, Bella?"

Bella nodded. "I want my father to want Loki to be part of our family. He said he would find a way to convince him to support our marriage, and I believe in my husband."

Alex pondered all he had heard for a moment as everyone waited, but then he lifted Maddie off his lap and came around his desk. "Welcome to the family, Bella," he said. "Congratulations to the two of you."

Celestina jumped out of her chair to hug first Bella first and then Loki, crying with happiness. A loud banging sounded at the door. They all froze, and then Alex moved over to the door.

He swung the door open and said, "Who dares to rudely interrupt the laird in his solar?"

Bella's father stood on the other side of the door. "Is Bella here? She's here and she did not come to me?"

CHAPTER FIFTEEN

Bella jumped and hid behind Loki, but then thought better of it and moved behind Brodie.

"Nevin," Alex said, "mind your manners in my keep. Your daughter is here and safe, but I can clearly see she is shaken by her experience."

Nevin moved over to his daughter, grabbing her by the hand. "Bella, you frightened me so. I thought I'd never see you again. I know I'm an ornery auld man, but you are my daughter, and I've just lost one to her husband. I cannot lose you, too. When I arrived for Morna's wedding and you disappeared, you gave me a horrible fright."

Taking her completely by surprise, he hugged her, then let her go brusquely before turning to Alex. "Forgive my harsh tone, my laird. The lass is a wee bit stubborn and will be the death of me yet."

"Understood, Nevin. She is a bit headstrong, I will agree with you."

Bella's eyes widened at her laird's statement, but kept quiet. How she wished Loki was by her side this very moment to comfort her.

Her sire coughed into a linen square and continued. "Where did they find you? And please tell me that the one who doesn't belong had naught to do with this."

Alex barked, "You'll not speak of my nephew as such, Nevin. He belongs as much or more than anyone."

"My laird, forgive me, but you know my wife requested that

Bella marry one of Grant blood."

"He's as close to our blood as you'll ever find, and one you should be proud to have as a son-in-law," Brodie said in a level voice, controlling his temper.

"Where were you, Bella?" Nevin repeated.

"They found me in Ayr. When I heard Loki had been taken captive, I traveled to Ayr to find him, but I passed out from the cold and Logan Ramsay, Torrian, and Loki found me and took care of me until I was better. I'm sorry, Papa, but I had to go. Please do not be angry."

"You missed your sister's wedding to chase after him?" Not waiting for Bella's response, he spun on his heel and walked away.

"What do I do?" She glanced to the group, her shoulders drooping.

Alex said, "Loki will sleep with the men in the guard's building, and you may sleep here in the keep."

"Aye," Celestina said, "you may have Loki's chamber. I'll just say I invited you to stay with us. Your father does love you. Perhaps he just needs time to absorb everything."

"That's an excellent idea," Maddie said, "and I will talk to Nevin after he has had some time to calm down."

Alex's gaze narrowed as he stared at his wife. "I do not know if I agree with that."

Bella watched Alex and Maddie. The entire clan enjoyed witnessing the affection and strong love between their laird and his wife, especially the way Maddie had learned how to twist Alex into agreeing with her wishes. Though she was a little rounder in the hips from all her babes, Maddie was still beautiful and Alex had great difficulty standing in the same room as her without touching her.

Maddie smiled at him as she reached up to rub her fingers on his forearm. "If Nevin is anything but polite, I shall come find you, husband." Maddie's mother had been English, so she and Celestina sounded alike in many ways.

Alex grinned, as if admitting to her power over him, and wrapped his arm around her waist. "Promise, love?" He leaned down to kiss her cheek.

Bella asked, "Would you like me to go with you, my lady?"

"Nay, I'll go alone, Bella. But if I find him agreeable, I'll come and get you. It appears you had a difficult time in Ayr as well. You should rest now that you're here safe. And we will all help Loki achieve his goal, I promise you both that. Do you not agree, Alex?" She tipped her head up to gaze into her husband's eyes.

"Of course, sweeting. Now I must move on with my duties. Bella, welcome." He kissed her cheek, and when he left the room, Loki and Brodie followed behind him.

Loki glanced over his shoulder at her and winked, which was enough to cause that sweet ache in her heart.

⧉

The Earl of Cliffnock sat at his dais, drumming his fingers on the table, scowling at the front door.

"Why do you frown so?" Hamish asked from the spot next to him. "You cannot blame your own flesh and blood for being clever."

"I frown because I finally had my son here, and he got away from me." He continued to stare at the door as if mesmerized by something.

"Are you surprised? I'm for certes not surprised. He's your son. Now he's not only clever, he's also a braw, strapping man. He was a challenge for us, and there were three of us against him."

"I remember. The lad could outsmart me at the tender age of four summers."

Hamish chuckled. "He was a cunning boy."

"How much do you think he remembers?"

"I do not think he recalls a thing about his life in the cottage. He denied remembering his mother, so I doubt he'll ever recall the rest. I think the blow took care of his memory. Why? Does the thought of his memory returning make you nervous?"

"Aye, I'd prefer for him not to know too much about me."

Hamish gave him a puzzled look. "Why would it matter if he remembers you tried to get rid of him?"

The earl glared at him. "He could still come in handy for us. He's got a clever mind, and with the right training, he could help us improve our status. But he has to trust me, and remembering that his father let him go willingly will do naught to create that trust."

The front door burst open and Egan came flying in with Gus

trailing behind him. "My lord, we have good news."

"I hope what you're about to tell me is better than the news you brought me about Loki having left the burgh." He chewed on the inside of his cheek as he awaited their response.

Gus's face lit up. "Aye, I think 'tis verra good news for you. You'll be quite pleased."

"All right. What is it?" His gaze narrowed at his men as he tipped his head back to stare at them.

"Loki has taken a wife." Gus smiled as he revealed the big secret he had uncovered.

"He what?" The Earl of Cliffnock bounded out of his chair in shock.

"He married in Ayr. Father Brian married the two of them just before they left the burgh."

Edward Blackett chuckled, louder and louder until he started laughing uncontrollably. "What a fool. Now I have a way to get to him. Did you see what she looks like?"

"Aye. Her sister is married and lives in Perthshire."

"And where are they now?"

"They took quite a few guards with them, and are headed back to Grant land. We just followed until we knew what their plans were."

The earl shook his head. "I tried to warn him about lasses, but he chose not to listen to me. Once I have her, he'll do aught I ask. He's newly married, he'll be beside himself when she turns up missing." Blackett rubbed the stubble on his chin, his mind churning with all the possibilities. The wee bastard would not out think him this time.

"Did we do good, my lord?"

"Aye, you did this time, Egan. We shall wait a fortnight or so before we make our plans, but then we'll finish this matter. I want the coin the king promised me, and I will get it whether it comes from the Grants, the Camerons, or the Ramsays." He smiled and stroked his chin again. "We'll have more wealth that we can use. I never thought I'd see the day, but finally, I'll get what I deserve." He clasped Hamish on his shoulder. "Our day is here, and I have my son Loki to thank."

⬿⬾

A few hours later, Bella returned to the great hall rested, just in time to find Maddie adjusting the hood on her mantle. "Your pardon, my lady, but do you go to visit my sire?"

"Aye, I'd hoped to catch him now."

Bella implored Maddie, "My lady, may I please go along with you?"

Maddie pressed her lips together. "Hmmm, Bella, I'll allow it. Mayhap it would be best for us to go together. Mayhap we should go see him right away rather than allow him time to simmer. What do you think, my dear?"

She nodded eagerly. "I would like to see him and explain what happened without mentioning my marriage to Loki. If you agree, my lady." She couldn't help but twist her skirts just at the thought of seeing her sire. "He has not found one to marry yet, has he?"

"Not that I am aware of, Bella. Come, let us go now and see to his comfort. I do not wish for him to mull over this situation overmuch."

Bella and Maddie set out of the great hall for the cottages in the outer bailey, the usual guard trailing behind Maddie. Bella's cottage was not far from the lists, so she hoped to catch a glimpse of her husband bare-chested. The men had gone straight to the lists after leaving the meeting. Regardless of the weather, Loki always seemed to strip down as soon as he started sparring.

"Bella, I'm sure this will all work out. Loki has always been such a strong, helpful lad. I'm sorry that his true sire was such a disappointment to him, but I believe all worked out for the best. It appears he is much better off with Brodie and Celestina as his parents. Do you not agree?"

"Aye, my lady. Loki feels the same way." Bella turned her head again for another glance at the lists. This time she saw her braw husband swinging his sword overhead, and she smiled to herself, still amazed that he was finally hers.

The laird's wife was watching her with a smile on her face. "Bella, you remind me of when I first met Alex. I would watch him in the lists and my heart would burst with pride, though sometimes he would act as if he wished to murder someone. I never could guess what he was thinking. Can you guess Loki's thoughts?"

Bella swung her head back so she could look at her companion. "Nay, only occasionally." Then she blushed at where her thoughts had taken her, for she could always guess at her husband's thoughts when he wanted her. He would get a distinct glint in his eyes.

A moment later, they found themselves in front of her father's cottage. Maddie knocked on the door. Nevin answered quickly, bowing to Maddie and inviting her inside. "Please come in, Mistress. But you'll see my cottage could use some cleaning." He cast a quick glance at Bella when he mentioned the disarray.

"Aye, 'tis lovely to see you again, Nevin." Maddie strode into the cottage with such grace that Bella just hid behind her.

Her sire apparently wasn't pleased to see her. "Is that the daughter who ran away from her own sister's wedding?"

Once the door closed, Maddie made her way to the middle of the room before she began, "Nevin, I'm sure you are glad to see your daughter again." She paused to see his reaction.

"I would have been more pleased if she'd had the respect to come here first," he mumbled, his eyes narrowing at his daughter.

"Papa, I was with Brodie Grant, and we had to see our laird first. Surely you understand." She stood to the side of Maddie with her head bowed, hoping the presence of the laird's wife would continue to soften him.

"I want to know why you rode in on Loki's horse. 'Tis unacceptable to ride with him when you are unmarried."

"Papa, he and Logan Ramsay saved me from the cold. I could have died. It was better for me to ride with someone or I would have grown too cold again."

His voice became a bellow. "What were you doing leaving your sister's to travel all the way to Ayr on your own? And to follow a lad I have forbidden you to see? Why must you disobey me in this matter?"

Maddie gasped just as the door flew open, almost flying off its hinges. Alex Grant ducked to get inside the doorway, but as soon as he did, he stood in front of it, his bulky frame blocking anyone from leaving. "Did you dare to raise your voice to my wife?" he bellowed. "If you did, you can leave this cottage and find another off my land."

Rushing to his side, Maddie grabbed his forearm, "Nevin is upset. Do not worry."

Bella backed into the corner, watching her laird's anger and her sire's response. Why was everything turning upside-down on her? She'd been so happy to be married, accepted by her husband's family—every one of them. But her own sire still refused to accept the man she loved. They were doomed for failure. She'd have to accept her sire's rejection, as cold as it seemed.

Alex dropped his voice to whisper to his wife, "Maddie, stay out of this, please." He kissed her cheek and then placed his fists on his hips and glowered at Bella's father.

"I'll ask you again. Did you raise your voice to my wife?" The laird's voice bounced off the walls of the small hut, making Bella wish to cover her ears.

"Nay, my laird." Nevin shifted his feet a few steps backwards. "Nay, I was speaking to my daughter who defied me. I would never speak to your wife in such a way."

Alex leaned down so his face was even with Nevin's. "I'd prefer it if you don't speak to any lass in such a tone. Do you understand me? Treat your daughter kindly."

"Aye, my laird," Nevin whispered. He glanced at Bella. "Forgive me, Bella. If you wouldn't mind assisting me with cleaning up the cottage, I'd much appreciate it."

Bella nodded, moving over to the table to collect the dirty dishes and place them in the basin.

Alex gave his wife a kiss and left, nodding to Bella on his way out.

"My lady," he said as he cleaned the crumbs off his chair for her, "please have a seat." He collected other items and put them away, busying himself while Maddie sat down.

"Nevin, surely you do not still hold Loki's parentage against him, do you?"

He turned to face Lady Madeline, his gaze on the rushes on the floor. "My lady, I have naught against young Loki, he appears to be a nice lad. But my wife made me promise to marry the girls to either noblemen or to members of Clan Grant, that is, lads born into the clan. I only try to do as my dear wife requested."

"I think you should get past that. If your dear Bessie stood in front of me today, you know she would agree with me and allow the marriage."

Bella tried to keep her tears inside, not wanting anyone to see how much her sire's rejection hurt.

"Nay, my lady. I must disagree with you. On this, my Bessie was adamant."

"Surely, you cannot hold Bella's feelings against her. She's a young lass."

He refused to lift his gaze to either of them, but continued. "I do not mean to be cruel to Bella, but she works in your kitchens now. She can sleep there. I'm sure I can take care of myself, so I am no longer in need of her. I'm sure she'll be of benefit to your Cook."

Bella hung her head and left, not wanting to hear the rest of the conversation. She'd never be with her husband. Never.

⤳

After hearing how poorly Bella's meeting had gone with her sire, Loki decided there was no sense in waiting. Now that Bella was no longer living with the man, mayhap he would agree to bless the marriage. After all, the man had practically disowned her, though he hadn't used those words. Loki had discussed the mattered with his father and they had agreed to pay a visit to Nevin.

Once they had been admitted, Nevin scowled at both of them. "I assume this is about the same issue? Must we continue to talk about my daughter? Please do not belabor this. She made her decision to not abide by my rules, so now she is living in the kitchens."

Brodie didn't bother to explain that Bella was sleeping in Loki's old chamber while he slept with the guards. They had discussed this on their way down the hill, and they'd decided it would be best not to anger Nevin by revealing the details of their arrangement.

Loki cleared his throat. "If I may, I'd like to once again request that you allow Arabella to be my wife. I promise to protect her and treat her kindly."

Nevin glared at Loki for a moment, clearly wanting to make an impression before he spoke. "Nay, you'll not be marrying my daughter."

Brodie replied, "And what is it about my son that you find objectionable, Nevin? We've known each other a long time. I stand in front of you asking you to honor my son's request.

Arabella and Loki care for each other, and they will make a good pair."

Loki stood to the side, not having seen a temper in his sire often.

"You know why, Brodie. He's not a Grant. If he were your true son, I'd be honored to have Bella marry him." Nevin's lips set in a grim line over clenched teeth. "I've told all of your family about Bessie's request. I must honor her."

Brodie opened and closed his fists three times before he spoke again. "He's my son and his name is Loki Grant."

"You adopted him. I understand that, and I have no trouble with the lad living with our clan, but he's not a blood Grant. If my Arabella is to marry, it will be to a man of noble blood. I've explained it before. Now why must you continue to question me?"

"Nevin, you are fully aware our laird can order the marriage if he pleases."

"Aye, but if he was planning to do that, he would have done it by now. My laird honors the relationship between my sire and yours. They were the best of friends, and I do no' think he will act against my wishes." Nevin returned to his chair and turned his head away. "Leave me be."

"And your daughter's happiness means naught to you? Because she prefers my son."

Nevin's expression did not change.

Brodie's face reddened and he looked as if he were about to punch someone, but he controlled himself. "Nevin, this will never be forgotten." He turned to Loki. "Son, let's take our leave. We're talking to a fool, an auld fool."

Loki stared at the rafters and sighed. It was not to be just yet.

CHAPTER SIXTEEN

Loki jerked up in his pallet, panting. His gaze searched the room, but there was nothing amiss. The rest of the guards were sleeping. Finally, the memories settled in. He had been dreaming...again...another horrific dream of his childhood. He rubbed his face to try to erase the awful sensations coursing through his body, but they did not fade so easily.

After grabbing his plaid, his sword, and his boots, he headed outside. He paced in circles under the starless night and then made his way over to the loch. Standing there, he stared down at the glassy surface as if something could rise out of the cold water and tell him he had imagined every bit of it.

But it didn't happen. This was the third night in a row that memories of his life as a wee one had kept him awake. One night he had dreamed of his mother, another night about his father. But this night's dream had been the worst...

Hamish. He'd dreamed of Hamish. He sat down on a cold rock and relived all that he'd just experienced. There was no choice but to suffer through it again, for he believed it was all true.

This dream had been different from the others. While the dreams of his mother had been fleeting images and thoughts, sometimes just a smell, the nightmare of Hamish had been as detailed as if he had lived it.

He was quite sure he had. He'd just discovered why he could not recall how he had made it to Ayr.

The nightmare began in a small hut. The cottage had two rooms in it, and he was alone in one with Hamish. He could hear his father yelling at his fair-haired mother, but the only thing he recalled about his mother was that she was sobbing and saying "Please, Edward" over and over again.

He had no idea what she wanted, and he could not recall anything his father said, but what he did remember was that he ran through the door and told his father to stay away from his mother.

His father punched him in the face, his mother cried out, "Nay, Edward!", and the next memory he had was riding in a cart. He woke up under a large blanket, the wheels of the cart hitting rocks and stones, bouncing him up and down. He peeked out from beneath the blanket to see where he was going. Hamish was riding the horse that pulled the cart, and he could see the moon overhead, the stars twinkling in the dead of night. When the cart finally stopped, he sat up and uncovered himself, only realizing his eye was swollen after he tried to brush the sleep from them. Poking his face in other spots, he realized his father's fist had bruised him this time.

This time. Loki put his face in his hands trying to grapple with his thoughts. Had his father beaten him frequently at a young age? Never had Brodie Grant once raised a hand to him, and his uncles had never beaten their bairns either.

Loki forced himself to recall the details from the rest of the dream.

Hamish had pulled the horse into a clearing in the woods. After dismounting, he stalked to the back of the cart, grabbed Loki by the neck, and hoisted him out of the cart.

"Finally, I'll do what I've always wanted to do with you, you wee wise arse."

Loki didn't say a word, but just stared at this man he hated.

"Your sire has finally had enough of your wise remarks and told me to do as I please with you." He grinned at him. "You opened your mouth a few too many times, and you think you're smarter that everyone else, do you not?"

Loki couldn't help himself. He knew he shouldn't say aught, but for some reason, he wanted the last word with this cruel man.

"'Tis not hard being smarter than you, you piece of shite."

It felt good to curse this man—so good that he smiled. He saw a familiar look in Hamish's eyes—the blind fury that usually preceded his fist. The big man lifted Loki out of the cart and pummeled him, throwing him a good distance through the air. When he landed, Hamish stalked to his side, leaned over him, and whispered, "Your sire never wants to see you again, so I thought I'd enjoy taking your last breath, lad, but instead I'd rather have the animals feed on you."

Then he strode away and left him there to die.

Aye, this dream was real—he knew it without a doubt. Tears streamed down his face. The memories were brutal, but it explained why Hamish and the earl had treated him so horribly. They'd always hated him, apparently threatened by the acuity of his mind. His own father had sent him off with a brute, and the brute had left him to die. For some unknown reason, his mind had protected itself from the painful memory for years.

After he brushed the tears from his face, he did the only thing he could do. He raced to the keep and made his way to his parents' chamber. He sneaked inside, not wanting to wake his brother and sisters, for he had to see his Bella.

She was in his chamber, asleep, but as soon as entered the room, she rolled over and held her arms out to him. Loki climbed under the covers, and she gave him a questioning look, as if she suspected he'd been crying.

He placed his hand over her mouth and said, "Please, Bella. Can we not talk? I just need you desperately. Will you have me, my beautiful Bella?"

Bella nodded and he closed his eyes, sighing with pleasure as he helped her remove her gown. He kissed her deeply, stroking her tongue with his, trying to let her know how much she meant to him. Trailing his lips down her neck and across her chest, he took her nipple in his mouth and suckled her. She moaned and spread her legs for him as he reached down to the vee between her curls, only to find she was slick with need for him. He sighed as he sank into her sweet flesh.

"Bella, I love you. Promise me you'll never leave me?"

"I promise, Loki. I love you, too. I was just dreaming about you."

He moved inside her, a slow rhythmic tease that he wished would last forever. He slid all the way out before driving into her as far as he could, earning a guttural moan of delight from his wife—a sound that sparked him like no other. He so loved her passion. This time he watched her as he slipped out of her sweet passage and plunged deep inside her again. Her legs spread wide as she tried to take him in deeper, building a yearning inside him that threatened to explode.

"Faster," she whispered, her breathing ragged as he reached underneath to clutch her sweet bottom and pull her closer. He caressed the softness of her cheeks until she groaned, then pulled out again and plundered her again, this time finally crossing the point of no return. He drove into her again and again, stroking her to a frenzy he'd never seen in her before. He gripped her hips and thrust into her until he felt her insides squeeze him, the sign she was about to go over the edge. He reached down and caressed her nub and she screamed, but he covered her lips with his, keeping her sounds from echoing into the night. As she tumbled into bliss, he followed her, just barely managing to keep from shouting for all to hear as he buried his seed inside her.

He loved Bella like no other.

Loki leaned his head against her cheek as he fought to level his breathing, feeling her hands as they rubbed his back.

"Loki?" she panted.

"Aye?"

"Are you all right?"

He paused to inhale the scent of her hair, her skin, his Bella. "Never better, love, never better."

Bella wiped the sweat from her brow as she worked the bread dough in the kitchens. They'd been back a sennight, and she was still forced to live apart from her husband. She tired of the separation. The night he had crept into her bed had been one of their most special moments. He'd slipped out before dawn to make sure his sisters didn't hear him, and the bed had seemed so huge and cold without him.

Once finished, she set the dough on the table, then made her way to the sink to wash some of the dishes. Nola, a lass much taller than Bella, started her usual taunting.

"Where's your lad now, Miss Bella? I have not seen Loki sniffing your skirts in a while."

"'Tis none of your concern, Nola. Find someone else to tease."

Nola grinned and her face lit up. "A wee bit sensitive about

Loki Grant, are you?"

Bella set her hands on her hips, but reminded herself how often Nola played this same game. She loved to get someone's goat about anything, and today Bella was her target. Determined to ignore the fool, she continued with her work, humming a tune that had been played by the last minstrel to visit the keep, refusing to make eye contact with the witch.

"I see he's sleeping with the guards. I've heard he's been dallying with lots of lassies."

Bella did her best to ignore Nola. She could hear a couple of other kitchen maids snickering behind her. "Nola, I'm not interested in hearing about anyone's whoring ways."

"Nay, but we all know you're in love with the lad. I heard you years ago when you promised to love him forever." She chuckled and leaned against the broom she had, placing one hand on a generous hip. "Did you really believe that the laird's nephew would lower himself so much as to marry a lass who works in the kitchens? You are a bit addled if you did."

Bella closed her eyes, summoning the strength to ignore the lass. The other maids had started to gather around to watch the scene. Unfortunately, she had few friends in the kitchens, and the other maids tended to follow Nola around. Cook had gone to visit someone, so they were without supervision for the moment. Bella vowed to continue her work in silence.

"I heard he's got one that hangs like a horse. What say you about that, whore? You've had it in your mouth, have you not? We all want to know." Nola moved in so close that she stood within an arm's reach of her.

There was a chorus of laughter and gasps from the other gathered maids, but Bella ignored them.

"Since you are no longer interested in the laird's nephew," Nola leaned down to whisper in Bella's ear. "Mayhap I'll swive him myself and show him what a real lass is like."

That was the comment that toppled Bella over the edge. She moved so fast that Nola could not possibly have guessed what she had in mind. Bella leaned over as if to pick something up off the floor, but instead grabbed Nola's left leg and swung it up in the air, forcing her to lose her balance and land flat on her arse. Suddenly, quiet descended on the kitchens as the other maids waited to see what would happen next.

Once Nola toppled to the ground, Bella fell on her and twisted her arm to hold her in place.

"You'll mind your own business, do your work, and leave everyone else alone, especially my Loki."

Nola whimpered as she stared up at Bella, moving nary a muscle. "Aye, I'll stop, just as soon as you let me go."

"I'm not ready to do that yet."

"You're hurting me, Bella. I'm going to tell Cook when she returns."

"You sound like a wee lassie of five summers all of a sudden, Nola. Why the change?"

"You have my arm twisted and I cannot move. Leave me be." Nola's hands tried to release Bella's grip, but she wasn't able to budge her.

Nola had gone too far this time. Bella looked at the others, all of them staring at her as if she'd grown a pair of wings on her back. "You must promise to stop taunting others. We're all here to work; we do not need your bossy ways."

Nola nodded, gasping, "I promise."

Cook came into the room and stopped short. "Bella? What in hellfire has happened here?"

Bella released Nola's arm. "Naught, Cook. We just needed to settle something, and I believe we did."

"Is that right, Nola?" Cook asked.

"Aye. All is settled," she ground out. She took her time returning to a standing position and then she stomped away, rubbing her neck.

"Bella, why do you not go home for a couple of hours?"

Bella opened her mouth to argue, but then decided against it. Cook knew how the other lasses all taunted her because of her small size, and she'd been dealing with their torment for a while. Mayhap it would be best if she got away for a wee bit. Nola had upset her terribly.

The thought of loose women slipping into the guards' sleeping chamber made her quite ill. She'd heard of others going after lads that way, but she trusted Loki, didn't she?

CHAPTER SEVENTEEN

Loki jerked his head when a small form caught his eye. His wee Bella tore through the outer bailey in a hurry, heading into a grove of trees. Anxious to see her, he walked over to speak to Robbie and his sire, who were in charge of training in the lists today.

His uncle just nodded and pushed him toward the trees. "I saw her. Go see to her, but be discreet about it."

Loki nodded to both his uncle and his father, then took off toward the small forest. He did not stop until he reached the path that meandered through the trees. There was no sound of footsteps, but then he heard his love sobbing, down the path a ways yet. He followed the sound of her voice until he found her huddled under a pine tree sobbing. Sitting down beside her, he lifted her onto his lap and whispered in her ear, "Bella, sweet Bella, what has you so upset? You are my strong lass."

Bella wrapped her arms around his neck and sobbed into his shoulder, gut wrenching sobs that pierced his soul.

"Bella, what is it? Are you hurt?"

She shook her head.

"All right then, did someone say something to you?"

She nodded, pulling back to gaze at him with red swollen eyes.

"Bella, it cannot be that bad, can it?"

"That depends."

"On what?" He waited while her breath hitched thrice more.

"On whether you have allowed another lass into your bed. Nola says the lasses are lining up to visit you in the guards' chamber."

He smirked, glad to see the problem was not something life-shattering.

"'Tis no' funny, husband." She shoved against his shoulder. "You would not be smiling if they spoke of me with another."

He lost his smirk in an instant. "Nay, I would not. My apologies. But lass, I love only you—and you are the only one I want in my bed. Have I not told you this before? Stop your tears. The wench told her lies to irritate you."

She fell back against his shoulder, her arms wrapping around his waist. "Aye, but she said the Grants would never allow you to marry a kitchen maid."

Loki caressed her back as she leaned into him. "It would appear they are wrong."

She moved back again and stared at her lap. "Aye, I know 'tis not true, but can we not live together? I do not want to be around Nola any longer. At least she will stop her teasing if she knows we are married."

"We agreed to give it three moons, did we not? I tried talking to your sire once, but he did not wish to listen."

"He will never accept you. The way he spoke to me in front of my lady...I will never matter to my sire, Loki. 'Tis not worth the wait."

Loki didn't like to see her so defeated. It hurt to be away from her, but he still felt he needed to do this for her. Whether or not her sire was a reasonable man, he knew she wanted him in her life. "Bella, it will be better for us in the long run if I manage to earn his respect. How about if we cut it to two moons?"

Bella pouted, gazing at Loki with her big blue eyes, tears still sneaking onto her cheeks occasionally. "One moon."

Loki chuckled. "Aye, we need to bargain? Is that what you wish?"

Her chin jutted forward as she squeezed his forearms. "Loki, what does it matter? If he does not give in after one moon, he will never give in. And what if I am carrying our bairn right now? Then everyone will say you were forced to marry me when the truth comes out."

Loki thought for a moment. "Aye, 'tis true. I do not wish to cause you any embarrassment, wife. And I do know how ruthless some of our clanmates can be. My aunts and uncles do not understand that, but I know how it feels." He took a deep breath and sighed. "All right, my Bella, I'll agree to one moon from today."

She grinned and kissed him full on his lips with a smack. "My thanks, husband."

Loki turned his head quickly, becoming aware of yelling back near the keep. "What is that? Can you hear what is happening?" He helped Bella to standing, then took her by the hand and led her closer to the opening in the trees. "Bella? Whose cottage is it that everyone gathers around? Can you tell?"

"Loki, 'tis my sire's. Come, we must see what is happening."

The two ran down the hill toward the cottage, only to find a crowd had gathered outside. Bella's sire stood at the front of the group, his eyes blazing with fury.

"There they are! And there's the monster who followed my daughter into the woods. Who knows what he's done to her? He's asked for her hand in marriage and I've turned him down several times. Now look at what he's done. He's ruined her…ruined her for sure."

Loki was stunned. He didn't know what to say, so he turned to his wife and whispered, "Bella, Bella, I'm so sorry."

Bella just stared at the crowd. He could tell from her expression that her spirit was crushed. She turned pink first, but when the entire crowd turned to face them, her cheeks turned to a deep shade of red. Her eyes grew wider the longer the others stared, but Loki didn't know what to do.

Her father rushed toward them, his finger outstretched toward Loki, spouting vile accusations. "He needs to be sent away. Get him off Grant land! Look what he's done to my poor Bella. Look at her!"

Loki could take no more. "Stop accusing my wife. She's done naught wrong and she deserves only respect from you and everyone else."

A gasp spread through the crowd as others members of the clan continued to gather around them.

"Your wife? You cannot just expect us to believe that. You're a liar!" Nevin pointed his finger at Loki.

"Nay, Bella and I were married in front of a priest named Father Brian in Ayr. And we had two witnesses, Logan Ramsay and Torrian Ramsay. She's my wife, and you'll stop insulting her." Loki reached for her hand and tugged her over to his side, wrapping his arm around her protectively.

Nevin's face turned beet red and he spewed curses to the sky, but then he spun around and ran toward his house. "I shall fix this. You'll not lay false claims…" His foot tangled in a tree root and he sprawled forward. As he made a hard tumble to the ground, his leg hit a rock. Bouncing off it, he rolled onto his back screaming.

"Papa! Saints above, are you all right?" Bella ran to his side, only to be waved away.

"Leave me be, daughter. You've caused all of this. You and that lad of a different clan." His finger pointed at Loki, but then he screamed in pain as he attempted to move his leg.

Someone in the crowd shouted, "Look, his leg is bleeding." A bump showed through his breeches, about midway between his ankle and his knee, and the cloth was soaked with blood.

"My leg…I think 'tis broken. I cannot move. Help me, someone, please." Nevin writhed in pain, moving back and forth in the grass.

"Someone get Lady Caralyn."

Loki didn't know what else to do, but he could not just stand by. He moved forward and scooped Nevin up into his arms as if he weighed no more than a feather. "Bella, lead me to his bed."

Bella ran ahead of him, leading him to the cottage door.

"Put me down, Loki," the man bellowed. "Tis all your fault. Look at me, just look at me."

Bella threw the door open and led Loki to her father's pallet so he could settle him down on it.

The older man squirmed and bellowed, but Bella leaned over and cried, "Shush!"

Her sire stopped instantly and stared at her in surprise.

Bella continued. "I'm sorry you're hurt, Da, but the only one to blame is you. You spun around and ran too fast. I'm sorry to tell you this way, but 'tis the truth. Loki and I married near a moon ago. We are husband and wife, and we will live as such, and I'm sorry if you want me out of your life."

Moments later, the door opened and Caralyn entered with her husband, Robbie, carrying her tools as one of the clan's healers.

Bella turned around and ran out the door, Loki following.

Bella and Loki had moved in together in his parents' chambers in the tower. They slept in Loki's room on the upper level. Bella had returned to speak to her sire the day after his injury, and she had helped clean the cottage, but then he asked her to leave. Not having any other recourse, she had asked him to send her a message if he ever desired to see her again.

It was late at night, Celestina had gone over to the great hall to sew by the fire with Maddie, and Loki and Braden were on the floor playing horse with Alison and Catriona. Bella and Brodie watched them, each of them smiling at the antics.

Braden and Loki were down on all fours, and Catriona rode on Braden's back while Alison rode on Loki's. The object was for them to race from one end of the chamber to the other. Brodie was in charge of declaring the winner each time.

Loki loved to tease wee Alison, so as they headed back across the chamber, he made the sound of a horse and tossed Alison up in the air a wee bit, as he'd already done many, many times.

Only this time, she grappled for Loki's tunic and missed, falling off of him with a thud. As soon as she landed, she started to scream and cry.

Bella and Brodie ran over to her, and Loki rested back on his knees in shock. "Alison, are you all right? I did not mean to hurt you."

Bella took one look at her husband's face and her heart broke. She could see how upset he was that he'd caused the accident— his goal had been to make Alison laugh, and now she was crying.

Brodie picked the wee lassie up in his arms and settled her on his lap in the chair. She continued to whimper, and from the way she held her body, it was obvious she was in pain.

"Braden, fetch Aunt Caralyn."

Braden took off at about the same time Celestina flew in through the door. "Heaven above! Alison, what is wrong? I heard you crying from the stairs."

Alison was crying too hard to answer.

Celestina asked her husband, "What happened? My wee lassie. Oh! Oh!" Celestina kissed her cheek, clearly wishing to grab her and hug her, but afraid to jostle her.

Alison's finger pointed at Loki.

Brodie said, "Alison, 'twas an accident. You'd been quite happy playing with Loki. He did naught wrong."

Concerned for Loki, she turned to look at him in time to see him turn a strange shade of green and race out the door. Bella thought she should go after him, but decided to give him a minute. She wished to see how wee Allison was doing first, hoping she would be able to tell Loki there was naught wrong with her.

Caralyn came in and checked Alison thoroughly, then turned to address Celestina. "I think she may have broken the bone that is at the base of her neck. I thought it was her arm, but it's not. There really isn't anything I can do for it either. She'll just have to be careful for a moon or so."

Alison whimpered and said, "No more horsie?"

Caralyn smiled and kissed her cheek. "No more horsie for a while. Here, Celestina, why not put this in some broth. 'Twill help her to sleep."

"I can move my arm, Aunt Caralyn?" She gingerly wiggled each finger before moving her hand, her wrist, and eventually her arm.

Caralyn showed her where her injury was. "See, I think 'tis broken right here, and if you touch it there, 'twill hurt badly."

"Then what do I do?"

Celestina took her wee daughter from Brodie's arms and settled her onto her lap.

"Don't touch it and I think you'll be fine. Just be careful lifting and pushing things because it might hurt."

Now that she knew the extent of the injury, Bella hurried off to find Loki. There was no sign of him in the great hall, but she eventually located him on the bench in the garden, his shoulders slumped.

"Loki, she'll be all right. Aunt Caralyn thinks 'tis the bone under her neck that is broken. She can move her arm; she just can't lift much."

Loki tugged Bella on his lap and set his chin on her shoulder. "I cannot believe I did that. How could I hurt a young lass like that? My parents will never forgive me. Never. They'll probably want us to move to our own cottage, Bella. Be prepared. Remember you promised never to leave me."

"You're being silly," she said, reaching up to stroke his face.

"They'll not send us away. Your sire said 'twas an accident. Why are you so undone about it? We all know 'twas not apurpose."

"You do not understand how much my mother loves Alison. She's the babe of the family, and she adores her. She'll never forgive me." He stared into space, acting as if he'd lost his best friend.

They sat there together like that for a few moments, Bella stroking Loki's back, Loki staring off into the distance, and then Brodie came down the walkway and sat on the bench next to his son. "Loki, she'll be fine. We know 'twas an accident. Alison can be a wee bit dramatic when she's hurt, and it earns her Celestina's undivided attention for a short time, which is her mission in life. Do not let her sobbing concern you. She is not crying at all now."

"Da, I felt so bad when you picked her up and she screamed. You know I'd never do aught to hurt any of you, aye?"

"Aye, Loki. You were playing with the lassies and they were loving it until she fell. There'll be no horsie for a while, but other than that, she'll carry on just fine. Though you can expect to see her on Mama's lap for most of tomorrow. I know my youngest, and she'll stay there if she can."

Brodie stood and grasped Loki's shoulder. "Do not be too upset about it. She'll be fine by morning. I'll leave you now. Come home when you are ready."

Bella's heart lifted, but as soon as Brodie moved away from them, she noticed her husband still looked defeated. "You do not look like you believe your da." Lately, she'd seen this look more and more on her beloved's face. Was it her fault? Had it to do with their wedding?

Loki stared over her head. "I do not feel better. I hurt a wee lassie."

"You'll see sense on the morrow when she's fine."

Somehow, Bella didn't believe her own words. Something was wrong with her husband, and he would not share his feelings with her. What would happen next?

CHAPTER EIGHTEEN

Loki shot up from his bed, rubbing his eyes. Bella awoke beside him.

"What is it, Loki?"

"Naught, Bella. Go back to sleep." He kissed her cheek and covered her with furs. "I'll return shortly."

Loki grabbed his plaid and stole down the staircase and out the front door of the tower. Things had been better all day. Alison had recovered for the most part, and no one seemed to hold the accident against him.

Bella had gone to see her father and asked if Loki could visit as well, but he had emphatically denied that part of her request. Still, he had allowed her to help him since his leg was broken, and he needed assistance, though the clan had been wonderful bringing him food according to Maddie. Though Bella no longer worked in the kitchen, she spent her spare time helping Celestina and Maddie whenever she could. Life was better than it had been.

But strange bits of memory had returned to Loki over the past sennight, and tonight, they'd finally materialized into something recognizable. He sat down on the bench in the garden and blew on his cold hands. He had dreamed of his mother. She was pleasing to the eye, but not beautiful like Celestina. Fair-haired and plump, she always had a smile for him. He tried to see the color of her eyes, but couldn't.

In his dream, his mother had sat on the side of his bed, staring at him and brushing her fingers through his long locks. "Loki, you are naught like your sire. I know he told you that you were, but you are not. 'Tis the reason he does not always favor you. You're quick-thinking and warm hearted, which bothers him. He thinks lads should be cold-hearted, but you are not. Do not believe the things he says."

At first, he had assumed he was experiencing the memory of some long ago day when his mother had tucked him in, but the next section of his dream proved him wrong.

"Loki, you were blessed the day the Grants took you in as their kin. Do not be so afraid to tell them how you feel. They will not think any less of you, and I know what you're thinking. They have no desire to send you away from the clan. You are an important part of their family, and they all love you. Stay and tell them the truth. Do not believe the lie your sire has planted in your mind."

That bothered him more than anything else she could have said. It was as if she knew every little thing he had been thinking—fearing.

He worried the Grants might decide to send him and Bella away. There had been too much happening for the clan to keep him around—too many accidents, too many threats.

First, he'd hurt his wee sister. Aye, he hadn't done it intentionally, but it had happened.

Second, Bella's sire was furious that Loki had wedded his daughter without his permission. He had heard the gossip. Alex had gone to visit Nevin to see how his leg fared, and Bella's sire had spent his whole visit discussing Loki Grant and why he didn't belong.

Third, his true sire was a threat to everyone. They'd left him in Perthshire, but what would he scheme to do next? Would he risk delving deep into the Highlands to carry out his threat?

Fourth, his sire had promised that if Loki ever married, he'd come for his wife. He shouldn't have married. He shouldn't have returned to the Grants and put them in jeopardy.

But the question that troubled him the most, bringing with it a fear so strong that it settled deep in his gut, was whether he truly was like his sire. Was his soul as rotten to the core as the earl's? Did Bella's father see something in him he'd been trying to hide from by being helpful and honorable?

He was lost, totally lost, and he knew not where to turn.

The next morn, Loki had kissed Bella goodbye and was headed out to the lists. He passed the solar and heard male voices. The situation was not at all uncommon, as his sire often sat in the solar with his two brothers discussing the clan and its issues. But something caught his ear when he passed by the door. His name.

He did not want to eavesdrop, but he felt frozen in place, unable to move. Had he heard what he thought he'd heard?

Alex said, "I think 'tis a wise move. He would be good over there, and I think it would be better for their marriage."

Brodie replied, "I know you think he should go, but I do not think the time is right yet."

"Why not? He's mature enough. He can take care of Bella. They'll be fine there."

Robbie added, "You do not want him to move, Brodie, but Alex's solution seems to be the best for all concerned."

Loki forced himself to place one foot in front of the other. This was it. They were going to get rid of him. They were planning to send him away. His greatest fear was coming true. He was about to be abandoned by his parents, and Bella would probably leave him, too, as soon as she learned they were being forced to move away.

He had just reached the front door when two of the guards came forward, escorting a messenger. "Loki, bring the lad to the solar for us."

Loki nodded and the guards left. The messenger appeared confused, but then the man pointed at him. "You're Loki Grant?"

Loki, though wary, nodded. "Why?"

"My message is for you. Your aunt didn't know you were still alive. She wishes to meet you."

Loki didn't know what to say. "My aunt?"

"Aye, she said to tell you that she's your mother's sister. She wants you to visit her in North Perthshire." The messenger handed him a piece of parchment. "Here are the instructions for where she lives."

Loki thanked the lad and took him to the kitchens for refreshments after his trip. He returned to his chambers immediately afterward. Perhaps this was just what he needed. A trip could give him the time he needed to come up with another plan. Who knew how soon before his laird decided to send him away, wherever it was? If he searched out his aunt, mayhap he'd learn if his dreams of his mother were true.

Bella came in behind him. "I thought you'd already left for the lists. Why are you back so soon?"

"Bella, come sit for a moment." He pulled her over to the bed and set her down next to him. "Listen to me. I know this will not make sense for you, but I'm going to leave on a short trip. I just discovered that I have an aunt—the sister to my mother—and she wishes to meet me. She lives in North Perthshire, and I have to go see her."

"Fine. I understand completely, Loki. Give me a few moments and I'll pack. You deserve to learn about your true mother, so this could be a wonderful trip for you." She jumped up from her spot and tugged a satchel out to fill it with clothes.

"Nay, Bella. I'll not take you with me."

Bella froze in her spot and turned back to look at him. "What are you saying? You should travel with your wife. We have naught to hide. I'd like to meet your family, too." Her hand settled on her hip as she watched him.

"Bella, my sire threatened to hurt anyone I cared about. That would be you. I cannot take the risk of having you with me in Perthshire again. This sounds like a true request, but it could also be a trap. I'll not put you at risk. Plus, your father still needs you, and so does Celestina since I hurt Alison."

"Loki," she swatted her hand at him, tears misting her eyes. "Stop being like that. You did not hurt her, and you'll protect me against your sire. I want to go with you. Please. We are finally able to live together. Do not leave me alone again."

Loki tugged her close and cupped her face in his big hands. Hellfire, but he hadn't expected her to fall apart like this. How could he make her understand he needed to do this on his own, needed to see some things for himself. He hated to see her cry. "Bella, I love you, but I cannot risk having aught happen to you. You are too important to me. I'll return as soon as I'm able, but for now, I must go." He dropped his hands and packed his satchel in a matter of minutes, then kissed her cheek. "I love you. I'll see you soon."

"Wait, Loki," she chased him around the chamber as he filled his bag, "I know why you're doing this and 'tis time you admitted it to yourself."

"Why I'm doing what?" He answered her, but continued with his task.

"You think you are not worthy of the Grant name. You think you do not belong here because your true sire is a bad man."

Loki froze in shock, wondering how his wee wife could have guessed the truth so quickly. "What?"

"You think just because my sire doesn't think you belong and some of the guards do not think you belong that mayhap you do not, but naught could be further from the truth."

Loki turned away from her, hiding the anguish he was sure showed on his face, fussing with his things. How in hell had she figured that out?

"Can you not see the truth?"

He stopped what he was doing to stare at Bella. "And what is the truth?"

She gazed into his eyes and reached for his hands. "The truth is that you belong here more than anyone else, because you have earned the right to be a Grant warrior. The others are here because they were born into the Grant clan. You have acted as the highest of all warriors, more honorable and steadfast than any of the others, always protecting those who cannot protect themselves. What more could the chief of any clan want of his men? You have proven your worth time and time again. Everyone knows it but you."

He drew in a deep breath and released it before speaking. Pinching the bridge of his nose with his fingers, he said, "Mayhap that was true of me a decade ago, but what have I done since then to deserve the honor of being a member of Clan Grant? At this point, I've only caused pain and risked the Grants' safety due to threats from my own sire."

Bella didn't answer, but then he had not expected her to answer. It was the truth, plain and simple. He returned to his task.

She yanked on his arm to get his attention again. "None of that is your fault. You helped save Jennie Grant, you've been a member of the guard for years, and you devote your time to training others. You have had the honor of protecting the laird's family, and you've started training with Logan Ramsay to do work for the Scottish crown. You helped save Gracie and Aunt

Caralyn and your mother. What more could you expect from yourself?"

Loki spanned the distance between them and kissed her cheek. "Good to know that my wife believes in me, Bella. I do love you for it, but I think you cannot deny my reasoning." He finished his packing and headed to the door.

Bella flounced back onto the bed. "Drat, Loki. I thought you loved me."

He grinned at her as he walked out the door. "You know I do more than aught in the world. Now be safe until I return."

She leaned out the door as he descended the staircase. "Did you tell your sire where you're going?"

"Nay, I'll be back before they miss me. Trust me."

Bella stomped around the room, cursing as she paced for the better part of an hour. She'd already tried talking to a couple of Loki's cousins into traveling with her, but they refused. How she wished Torrian were here. They were all afraid of the laird's temper, though she hadn't seen it much. Jake and Jamie swore they'd never go against their father again, though they would not tell her why, but they did promise not to inform anyone and warned her about asking any guard to go with her. They would all tell rather than risk the wrath of their laird. Drat that stubborn husband of hers. She'd just have to follow him on her own like she had done before, though she had one serious problem she needed to fix first.

She had no idea how to get to Perthshire. Chasing down the staircase, she headed to the kitchens. A messenger must have just told her husband about his aunt, and if so, the man would still be somewhere in the keep.

She found the messenger at a table near the kitchens, and he explained exactly how to get to Perthshire.

"You do not mean to go yourself, do you, lass? I already gave the message to Loki Grant."

"Nay, I just wanted to be able to repeat it to his sire." She took a seat next to the lad.

"Which one is Loki's sire? I should find him and repeat the message to him before I go."

"I'll take you to him." Bella jumped out of her chair.

"Do you mind if I finish my meat pie first?"

Bella frowned, but she sat down again, drumming her fingers on the table as she waited.

A short time later, the messenger said, "All right, take me to the Grants so I can deliver the message again."

Bella shot out of her chair and led him to the laird's solar, then knocked on the door. As soon as she did, she slipped away, not wanting them to stop her from leaving on her own.

She'd find Loki Grant if it killed her. And then he'd never leave her again.

⟳

Loki sat on a log in the clearing, wondering what he would say to his aunt. His father was a rat bastard, but mayhap his mother was as sweet as his dream had indicated. If that were true, perhaps he would have a little more confidence that he could be a good man.

Everything in his life was now a mess. He had doubts about everything, most of all about himself and his lineage. Before he would feel settled, he needed to face his past.

Finally, he stood up and headed to the row of four cottages, hoping what he found inside was better than what he'd found in Cliffnock. He scraped a hand through his long locks to try and untangle them, checked his plaid to make sure he was presentable, then moved up to the door of the first hut. After knocking three times, he shook out his tingling fingers and stood back, hoping someone would answer.

A man opened the door, so Loki said, "Good eve to you. I'm looking for Flora." The man pointed to the third cottage over. After thanking him, Loki headed over to knock on the correct door, but it flew open with a bang as soon as he reached it.

A slight woman stood in front of him, and her hand flew to her chest as she gaped at him. Her voice came out as the lowest of whispers. "Loki? Loki Grant?"

"Aye," he replied. "Are you Flora?"

"Och, saints above, aye." A pair of sturdy arms appeared behind her, pulling her back into the hut.

"Come, Flora, sit down before you pass out and hurt yourself. Lad, come on inside. Please."

Loki ducked under the doorway and moved inside the hut,

uncertain of what his next move should be. Their hut was clean, but they had little more than what was necessary. Flora had gray hair held back in a plait and kind, blue eyes. She couldn't stop smiling at Loki, a wistful look in her sharp gaze.

"Here, lad, sit at the table with your aunt," the man said. "If she acts as if she's seen a ghost, 'tis because she has. She was told by your sire that you died alongside your mother." His uncle was just a wee bit taller than his aunt, mostly bald with a long gray beard.

"When we heard Blackett claimed to have found his son and you were now Loki Grant, I had to see you for myself. Thank you for coming."

Loki perched on the stool across from where his aunt had seated herself. Tears formed in her lashes, threatening to spill onto her cheeks. "The Lord above has blessed us this day, Gordon. I thought I'd never see my sister again, yet a part of her sits in front of us."

"Aye, 'tis true, Flora. Loki, we were told you ran away after your mother died. Your father said he found your body dead in the forest and buried your body with your baby sister. Flora, here, prepared your mother's body for a proper burial, and it devastated her not to be able to place her two dead children with her. It would seem Edward was full of lies, though I'm not surprised to learn that."

Gordon took a seat on the stool next to his wife. Flora, meanwhile, continued to stare at Loki. "Forgive me for staring," she finally said, "but you look so much like your mother that it warms my heart, and I wish to never forget you."

"Do you mind if I ask what my mother looked like?" he asked, excited to finally have the chance to learn more about her.

"Oh, not at all. Your mother was my younger sister, and she was a beauty. Her hair was a bit lighter than yours, more golden. She was a thin woman when she was young, but her hips widened after giving birth. I swear on God's land that she had the biggest heart of any woman I knew, and there was naught that she loved more than you, her only son."

Loki settled upon hearing that the woman in his dream matched the one his aunt was describing to him, making it much easier for him to believe his mother's comforting message. His aunt and uncle seemed good natured, and as genuine as any two people he'd ever met.

"What did you think of my sire?" he asked.

Flora scowled and turned her fierce expression toward her husband. Gordon chuckled. "Your aunt has difficulty speaking ill of any Scot, so I'll say it for her. We never liked Edward Blackett. He was as crooked as a winding stream—the type of lad who would sell the shoes from his own mother for a cheap coin. We never had much use for him. In fact, 'twas a sad day for both of us when they married, but circumstances forced their hand."

His aunt continued for him. "Your mother, Ciara, made the best of a poor situation. She was a good-natured lass who would do aught she could to help anyone. Your father was a cruel man."

Gordon cleared his throat. "Here now, Flora, 'tis best for the lad to make up his own mind about his sire."

Loki said, "I have already made up my own mind about the Earl of Cliffnock, and I do not acknowledge him as my sire. The earl chained me to the wall of his dungeon the day after he met me in the hopes of garnering coin in exchange for my freedom."

Flora's hand came up to her mouth in shock. "My poor sister! It hurts to think of what he must have done to her. Mayhap 'twas a blessing for her to move on. Oh dear." She shook her head repeatedly as she worked over this new information. Then she lifted her gaze back to Loki and a sad smile lit up her features. "But now I am blessed with a nephew. I am truly grateful you have come to visit us. You must have questions for me. Go ahead and ask whatever you wish."

She sat back and Gordon tugged her hand into his large paw. That act of genuine affection tugged at Loki, making him miss his wee wife.

Many questions popped into his mind, so he started with the one he needed to know most. "Was I pleasing to my mother? She did not hate me like my sire does?"

"Nay, lad. You were the light in your mother's eyes, she loved you so. She named you Lucas. I'm not sure when your name changed to Loki, but I knew you had to be her boy when I heard you were the lost son of Blackett. Och, the tales she used to tell me about you. To hear her tell it, you were more cunning than your own father. You were a quick-thinking lad, and one who would always help another in need. I saw the good in you every time we visited. Do not doubt your mother's love for you. She adored you." She choked on that last sentence, so overwrought with emotion she brought out a linen square to dot at the corner of each eye.

He liked the sound of that, he was the light in his mother's eyes. That brought up another question. "Do I get my eye color from my mother? My sire told me so. 'Tis unusual, as I'm sure you know."

Her eyes widened as she stared at him, as if she had not noticed that he had one eye blue and the other green. She glanced at her husband, and he gave her a slight nod of encouragement.

She stuttered at first, but then said, "Your mother's eyes were blue." She hesitated before she continued, kneading her hands in her lap. "Both of them."

Loki pondered this information before he questioned her again. "My sire's eyes are brown. How could that be?"

Flora paused again, glancing at her husband once again before she answered. His aunt mumbled a type of prayer, or so he thought, then gave the sign of the cross on her chest before she spoke.

"Edward Blackett is not your true sire, but I know not who your true sire is. Your mother would not tell me."

CHAPTER NINETEEN

Loki rode back to the Grant keep, his mind more muddled than ever. He still did not know who had sired him. In view of where his family had lived, he doubted anyone noble had ever visited his mother, so he conjectured that his true sire was not one of great wealth. He only hoped the man had more heart than the earl did. It gave him a wee bit of peace to think that the cruel Edward Blackett had not been the only man in his mother's life.

He did have some good news to take to Bella—at least in his view. His mother had been much like the sweet woman from his dreams. The knowledge that his mother had possessed a kind and loving heart helped center him. Perhaps more important, he now knew that his mother had adored him. That short statement had meant everything to him. He would cling to it for a long time.

He arrived at the Grant stables just about the time his gut started churning. The stable lad grabbed the reins of his horse and took off toward the building without speaking. An eerie sense of quiet greeted him that he did not like.

Something had happened—he could feel it in his bones. He strode toward the great hall, his pace increasing as he traveled, for he did not like the looks he received in the bailey. What in hellfire had happened in his short absence?

As soon as he stepped into the great hall, his sire, Robbie, and Alex all turned to greet him. Celestina sat by the hearth with Maddie and Caralyn. None of them spoke, yet they all stared at him as if they awaited news. Somehow, he knew they weren't after information about his aunt.

And then it hit him. "Where's Bella?"

"We were hoping she was with you," Brodie replied.

"What? Bella did not go with me, why would she be with me?"

Alex motioned for Loki to come closer. "Sit down, lad. It won't do you any good to run right back out the door. Bella disappeared not long after you left. She was seen here shortly after you rode to see your aunt, questioning the messenger who brought news of your aunt, but no one has seen her since. She was not noticed leaving either."

Loki let out a short bellow. "Bellaaaa...." Hellfire, but he should have known. She had sneaked away to find him before, and now she'd done it again.

He fell onto the bench in distress and looked up at his family. "Bella was angry that I was leaving without her, but I could not return to Perthshire with her. My sire—" he stopped himself, almost smiling at the realization that the earl was nothing to him, "—nay, the earl threatened to hurt any lass I cared for, so I didn't wish to risk her safety. The message could have been a hoax."

Celestina whispered, "Was it a hoax, Loki?"

He shook his head, "Nay, I met my mother's sister, who is a sweet, wonderful woman. I suspect my mother was the same way. My aunt told me that Edward Blackett was not my true sire—my mother confided the truth to her, and besides, my mother's eyes were both blue. I count it as a blessing, but I doubt I'm of noble blood."

Brodie strode over and hugged his son. "It never mattered to us, but I think you know that, son."

Celestina hugged him and said, "I knew we would discover your mother was as soft-hearted as you are. She must have been a wonderful woman."

"My aunt confirmed that my mother died when my sister was born. She was told by Blackett that I died after running away and was buried with my dead sister. She and her husband Gordon buried my mother."

"I'm so sorry, Loki," Celestina said. She reached for his hand and squeezed it.

"So you did not see any sign of Bella along the way?" Robbie asked.

"Nay, but there are more ways than one to get from here to

Perthshire. Daft lass! I'll leave right away and go find her."

Brodie held his hand up, "Give me an hour to arrange for a group of guards to go along with us. 'Twill be much better to have a group to check out the different paths. Get yourself some food and ale, pack up more provisions, and we'll leave right away."

Loki hated to admit it, but his father was right. Planning could make the difference between finding Bella and losing her forever.

⬱

Bella twirled in a circle, trying to make her mind up which way to go, but she had a strong suspicion that she'd been through this area before.

She moved away from her horse and perched on a nearby rock for some rest. She picked up a pile of rubble so she could fling a few stones to help settle her temper and her fear. After several days, she was finally willing to admit the truth to herself. She was lost, and she had no idea where to go. The very rock she sat upon was familiar, so her latest attempt to find her way by following the rising and falling of the sun had failed.

Fortunately, she hadn't run into many fellow travelers along the way. The one traveling minstrel she'd come across had thought her a lad. But as she stood up to stretch, a group of horses suddenly came into view. Tearing off in the other direction, she found a clump of trees to hide behind, hoping they would pass on by without bothering her, but two of the horses headed directly at her. She screamed and ran as fast as she could, only to find herself scooped up and thrown across the back of one of the horses.

"Got her!" a male voice yelled.

"Good. We'll get her back to Blackett by nightfall."

"She's a wee thing. We could stop and play with her for a bit."

"Nay, you won't unless you want the earl to slice off your ballocks. He said we were not to hurt her."

Bella's heart pounded out of control. The name told her she hadn't been kidnapped by just anyone—Loki's father, the Earl of Cliffnock, had her in his clutches. How could she be so daft? Poor Loki. One of his worst fears had come true and it was all her fault. What in hellfire would they do to her? Though she was relieved to hear they weren't planning to stop and rape her, it didn't calm her one bit. The earl had chained his own son to a wall. What would he do to her?

By the time they arrived at a castle several hours later, Bella's entire body was bruised from bouncing across the horse. As soon as the man riding behind her dismounted, he grabbed her and yanked her off the horse, causing her to fall to her knees. "Get up, you lousy wench."

"Hector, leave her be. Just take her to Blackett so you can do his bidding."

Bella stumbled to standing as the two men discussed her as if she weren't there.

"Hamish, did anyone ever tell you that you are a bore?"

"Close your mouth and bring her along."

Bella did her best to kick out of Hector's grip, but he was much too strong for her. Her best efforts were a mere irritation for him.

When she kicked him in the shin the second time, Hector raised his hand to strike her, but his companion yelled, "Do not do it unless you wish to spend a fortnight cleaning garderobe trenches." Hector glowered at Hamish, but he lowered his hand nonetheless.

The rest of the trip into the keep was uneventful. Once they were inside, Bella was tossed onto a bench at one of the trestle tables while Hamish left to find Blackett.

A little while later, a man with a perpetual sneer on his face came down the stairs, his face lit with excitement. "So you're my son's wife. How happy I am to see you. We'll bring your husband to his knees, and then we'll have all the coin in the Highlands. You'll see." Turning to face Hamish, he said, "Take her upstairs and lock her in the chamber room at the end of the hall. Have the maids bring water and pottage, and she can just sit there and wait for her husband to come after her. If they're recently wed, he'll be here in less than a sennight. I'll send my messengers out now." His face lit up with glee. "Finally, I'll get my just rewards." He pointed his finger at Bella. "I warned your husband of what would happen if he married, but he's not as bright as he believes himself to be. 'Tis only fair that I get my due."

Hamish dragged Bella upstairs, only stopping when they reached the door at the end of the passageway. He opened it with a key and tossed her inside. After barking orders to one of the maids, he came back inside with a basin of water, which he set on the side table. "Make it last," he said. "Who knows when I'll remember to come in here again?" And with that, he disappeared.

Bella paced the room until a kitchen maid came in carrying her food. She had a trencher of pottage and a small hunk of cheese. The maid kept her eyes down and left as quickly as she had entered. The very next moment Bella tumbled onto the bed, curled into a ball, and sobbed her eyes out. Loki would be so angry with her foolishness that he would probably leave her here to suffer. That thought only made her wail louder.

Loki paced the great hall, spewing curses to all who dared stand near him. The memory of how cold Bella's slight body had been in Ayr tormented him. What if she was dead? What if they never found her?

Brodie clapped a hand on his shoulder. "Son, I'm sure she's with Blackett. The tracks told us there were two horses, and her horse was found wandering nearby. The earl would not waste the opportunity to kidnap her."

"I know that's probably true. I just wish there was more we could do. After what he did to me, I cannot fathom what he would do to a lass the size of Bella. How will she be able to hold up?"

"He will not hurt your wife. They need her unhurt and able to speak. Ransoming her is his only chance for the fortune he desires. He'll take good care of her."

Alex had agreed. "Do not worry overmuch. I highly doubt she'll be mistreated."

He hoped they were right, because he'd kill the rat bastard for touching his wife.

They huddled over the dais during the meal for quite a while, planning for their departure the next day. Loki was shocked to discover the number of guards Alex planned to send with him. He'd thought to beg for ten guards, but Alex planned to send five score.

Loki stared at his uncle. "One hundred guards? I appreciate all you're trying to do, my laird, but do you think we need that many?"

"Loki, if the earl has managed to find Bella, he will use her to get to you—and to me. Men like that do not change their ultimate goal, only their strategy. The only things that could stop him are success or death."

"My apologies for bringing this situation into our clan."

"You did not bring it upon us, the Earl of Cliffnock did. He probably also intends to go after the Cameron and Ramsay coffers. Five score guards will put an end to all of this. I cannot afford to allow that kind of evil to grow in the Highlands. We must stop him now."

Loki mulled over Alex's response, but he knew the Grant way was to always be over prepared. It was probably why they so rarely lost.

"Tell us again where his castle is located, Loki," Brodie said.

"He's northeast of Ayr and Glasgow. Not far from Drummond land or the Ramsays. I'd like permission to ride ahead of the group to see what I can find. If I come up empty, I will continue on to Ayr. Bella found her way there before, perhaps she will do so again."

"There's quite a bit of proof that Blackett already has her," Alex said. "I understand your need to make sure she is not lost and injured, but I'm confident that she is with Blackett." Alex leaned back in his chair, his hands folded in front of him, a common thinking position for him. "If you feel the need to ride ahead, then take ten guards with you and go. If his castle is not far from Ramsays, then we'll meet you there and plan accordingly. Let's hope Logan has been rustling up information. Mayhap he's received a message instead of us. 'Tis another reason for us to spend a night or two there, plus I can get provisions for our men before we move out."

Alex glanced at Brodie and then Robbie. "Robbie, you'll stay back and protect the clan, aye?"

"'Twill be my honor."

Brodie stood from his seat. "Loki, I'll travel with you. We'll head out within the hour. Alex, we'll meet you as soon as we can."

Loki headed out the door, but paused when he saw his sire was headed to the tower rooms. He changed course and joined him. Once inside, they found Celestina pacing the room while the lassies sat playing with their dolls. Celestina whirled around to face them when they entered. "You must leave soon?"

Brodie strode to his wife and wrapped his arms around her. "Aye, sweet one. We must end this as quickly as possible. I know 'twill be difficult for you, but 'tis best for Bella if we go now." He kissed her forehead, then picked up each of his daughters and kissed their cheeks. "Be good for your mama and help her. Tell Braden he's to help Uncle Robbie."

"Aye, Papa." A chorus of voices greeted him. "Bye, Loki."

Loki fussed with his sisters while his father gave his mother another kiss, then turned to head out the door. He raised his hand to his mother and said, "Bye, Mama." His first thought was to rush away after his wife, but he stopped and strode over to his mother to give her a warm hug. "We'll find her, I promise."

Celestina said, "Please find her soon, Loki. She's such a wee thing and I do love her. She's young and foolish yet, but she loves you."

Unfortunately, Loki recalled just how small Bella had seemed when Kenzie had brought them to her. "We will, Mama." He left the room with one thought on his mind, and he couldn't figure out why he hadn't thought of it before.

Kenzie. Kenzie had found Bella before, and Kenzie was also in Ayr. He recalled exactly what it was like to be alone in Ayr. He had always made it his business to make sure he knew every bit of gossip in town.

Lucky Kenzie could be the key to everything.

CHAPTER TWENTY

Loki and Brodie paid the toll outside of Woodgait and led the ten guards into Ayr. They headed to the castle first to see if Brodie could uncover any information about Bella there, but the trip was fruitless.

Loki sat outside the castle with the guards, still on horseback, while Brodie entered the castle. When he returned, Brodie told Loki, "The only thing the king is presently worried about is the theft of a few jewels from his royal coffers, but that has naught to do with the earl. King Alexander had very little to say about the Earl of Cliffnock. Seems he's been quiet lately, which is not his norm."

Moving back through Doongait and on to Woodgait, Loki slowed his horse. Brodie gave him a look of curiosity, which was not a surprise—Loki had not told him aught about Kenzie. As soon as he neared the inn, he shouted, "Kenzie!"

The young lad shot out from behind the building, his eyes alight with excitement. "You came back for me?"

A surprised look filled Brodie's face, followed by a small grin as he took in the young lad in front of him. Loki wondered if his sire remembered this spot.

Loki replied, "I did come back for you. Kenzie, this is my sire, Brodie Grant."

Brodie gave each of them a weighing look. "Seems I've seen someone like this before," he finally said.

Kenzie jumped up and down. "Aye, I live where Lucky Loki lived, so someday I'll be lucky, too."

Brodie returned his gaze to his son, curious to see what would happen next.

"Kenzie, have you seen the wee lass you found before?"

"Bella? Aye, Blackett's men have her at the castle," he said with a scowl. "I tried to tell the sheriff, but he would not listen to me. She could be hurt. I don't like the earl. He and his men are mean. And I can help you find her. I sneaked behind them one day, so I saw where the secret tunnel to the castle is hidden."

Loki's mouth curved, for this was just the discovery he'd been hoping to make. "How do you know she's there?"

"Because Blackett's second came through to hire a bunch of men to guard his castle. He also hired the best archer in England to kill someone. Never said who, but they say he's the best." His nose scrunched up. "I heard Ramsay's wife is the best of the Scots."

"You heard right, now continue. What else did you hear about Blackett?"

"The second said Blackett would be attacked soon and he needed help. He promised a lot of coin, so some Lowlanders went with him. But some that left came back. I overheard them talking. They said Blackett was holding someone's wife at his keep, and he would bring all the Highlands down on them. 'Tis why they left. They did not wish to fight the savage Highlanders from way up north. Are you a savage? You do not look like a savage." He peered at them such a serious expression it almost made Loki choke.

Holding a hand down to the laddie, Loki said, "Do you wish to travel with me? I'm not riding in to an easy situation, but I could use your help. We are always looking for someone who can uncover information for us without raising suspicion." He wouldn't discuss it with his sire now, but Kenzie was going home with him to Grant land. He could live with him and Bella, or wherever he wished to live. They'd make it work somehow. He couldn't desert the lad again, not when the cold winter was about to bear down on him.

Brodie cocked his brow at Loki. "Like you did with me," Loki glanced at his sire, speaking only loud enough for him to hear.

Brodie nodded. "Suits me if it suits you. He seems like a resourceful lad."

"I'm coming," Kenzie yelled out, "but let me hide some things first so no one steals from me." He tore back behind the building, and Loki saw him dash into the trees.

Loki waited until the laddie was out of hearing distance, then explained to his sire. "He found Bella when she was about to fall from her horse from cold and exhaustion. He wrapped her in plaids, then moved her in the back before he came to find me."

Brodie nodded. "That explains everything."

Loki hung his head as he whispered, "He also found a pan with the initials 'LL' inscribed with a knife in the middle of the bottom."

Kenzie raced toward them, only a plaid in his hand.

"Do you have anything else of importance, lad?" Brodie asked, an unreadable expression on his face.

The laddie gazed up at Brodie Grant, hesitant to answer for some reason. "Aye, my lord."

"What is it?" Brodie asked, in a quiet yet stern voice with which Loki was quite familiar.

"Uhhh…"

"Speak up, lad."

Kenzie swallowed and said, "My mama sewed me a fabric puppy before she died."

"Then you better get something that important. We won't be coming back."

"Aye, my lord." Kenzie hurried through the walkway and returned with his well-worn puppy. "Where am I going, my lord?"

"Home," Brodie replied. "'Tis time for you to go home with us after we're done with this wee skirmish."

Kenzie's face lit up as he stared at Loki in delight.

Loki gave his father an appreciative look and then held his hand down to the laddie. "Aye, you're moving in with the Grants. Welcome to the clan."

By the time they arrived at Clan Ramsay, Kenzie had just about talked their ears off. Loki and his sire left the guards in the outer bailey, then made their way to the stables. As soon as they stepped inside the great hall, a special woman made her way over to Loki, and he couldn't keep the smile off his face. Alex's sister Jennie Grant, now married to the Cameron chieftain, strode over to them.

After she greeted Brodie, she wrapped her arms around Loki and said, "I'm so glad to see you, Loki. I'm sorry to hear about your wife, but I look forward to meeting her once she is home safe. Is she not the same lass who told you she would love you forever? Arabella, is it not?"

"Aye, she is the same lass."

"I'm so happy for you. Come and see Aedan and our children, though they are no longer wee." Jennie led him over to the table and introduced him to her daughters, Riley and Tara, and their son, Brin. He'd met them when they were young, but years had passed since their last meeting.

Loki pulled Kenzie out from behind him and said, "This is a new member of the clan, Kenzie. We brought him with us from Ayr. I think he'll be able to help us. He's very astute."

Her eyes lit up with surprise, but she simply said, "Well, if he's anything like you, he will be a clever lad." She ruffled the laddie's hair and found him a spot at the table. "Are you hungry, Kenzie?"

The laddie's face lit up as he nodded. Loki thought his head might roll off his neck, he nodded so hard. He recalled what it felt like to have an empty belly. "We haven't eaten in a while, Jennie."

Brenna Ramsay greeted them and sent the kitchen maids for food. "These lads look mighty hungry, Fiona. Stew, lots of brown bread, and some baked apples for them."

Kenzie tipped his head back to look at Brenna, excited at what he'd just heard. "I've never had baked apples before. Will they still be warm?"

"Aye, they'll be warm, and you'll have the chance to try plenty," Brenna said with a chuckle. "I hear you have much work ahead of you. We'll fill your bellies first." Kenzie sat down at the table, anxiously awaiting his food while he took in all the people in the Ramsay hall.

Alex emerged from Quade's solar and beckoned for Loki and Brodie to join them. When Kenzie gave Loki a questioning look, Loki waved at him. "Eat, lad, we'll catch you up when we've decided what to do."

And then he and Brodie joined Alex, Quade—the Ramsay chieftain, Aedan Cameron, and Logan in the solar. Torrian came in from outside to join them at the last minute.

Once seated, Logan quickly filled them in on the situation.

"We've received our note asking for coin in return for Bella's life. We are pleased to see he's handling it this way since it is now in Blackett's best interest to keep her alive."

Loki ran his hand down his face and rested his elbows on his knees, staring at the ground. "Hellfire, I did not want it to come to this."

"I'm pleased," Alex said. "The bastard sent a note to the Cameron, also. He needs to be stopped."

Aedan folded his arms across his chest. "This is the second time I've received notes from him ordering me to empty the coffers of Lochluin Abbey. I agree with Alex, we must put a stop to this. The monks and the nuns are verra upset and frightened."

Loki raised his head quickly to give his uncle a perplexed look. "Explain why this pleases you, if you'd be so kind, my laird?"

"The alternative was that your wee wife was lost in the woods in the Highlands in the winter. At least we know she is alive, warm, and being fed."

Loki shot out of his chair. "You do not know that. The man is a bastard. Who knows what he'll do to my wife. He could be..."

Brodie pulled on his hand, encouraging him to sit again. "We do not know aught for sure, and there's no point in conjecturing. Actually, that is incorrect. There is one thing we do know for certain. Bella is a strong lass. Need I remind you the strength in your mama? You need to believe in your wife."

Loki sat, realizing he spoke the truth. An image of the gentle Celestina Grant running down a pathway as she swung a large branch at a Norseman popped into his head. Bella was strong, too. He'd have to believe in her, or he wouldn't be able to continue. "All right. I believe in my Bella. So what is our plan?"

Logan said, "Simple. We collect a bag of coins, then we take eight score of guards and surround their curtain wall until they release Bella. There is no other option."

"Aye, there is," Loki said, "or at least there is something else we can try while we wait."

"And what is that?" Logan asked.

"The lad we brought with us says he followed Blackett's men. He knows the location of the secret tunnel they use to get inside the castle walls. He also told me they hired the best archer in all of England."

"Then this should prove to be a great contest," Logan said with a grin. "We have Gwynie on our side."

"And you," Brodie added. "You're one of Scotland's best archers as well. We'll put you in the trees alongside Gwyneth."

"Not sure about that, but I will have a talk with the lad. He's the one from Ayr, is he not? What's his name?" asked Alex.

"Kenzie," Loki replied. "His parents died of the fever, leaving him to fend for himself on the roads in the royal burgh."

"Then he is definitely wily enough to help us," Alex said, giving Brodie a pointed look.

"When do we leave?" Loki kneaded his hands, so worried about his Bella he could barely think of aught else.

"First light. You agree to stand back and let me handle things, Loki?" Alex said. "You're a fine warrior and a clever guard, but you are too close to the situation to think clearly. You need to let me handle this scum and deal with him. Find out what the boy knows, and we'll see if 'tis of use tomorrow. Personally, I hope we come to full battle with the earl. He's not going to stop until he gets riches from one of us."

❧

Bella paced the floor again, unable to settle no matter how she tried. She knew what Loki would tell her about saving her strength, being ready to run, being observant—all the qualities of a fine spy.

But she couldn't stop herself. Fortunately, the louts hadn't bothered her much. She'd been allowed out to use the garderobe, and only the maids came into her room. She'd vomit for sure if any of Blackett's men dared to touch her.

She'd said a thousand prayers for forgiveness, hoping the laird and Loki would both forgive her for her foolishness. Would they come for her as a clan or would Loki be forced to carry this battle out on his own? How she hoped her laird was behind him, that he had willingly sent extra guards with him. Every once in a while, she could hear conversations in the chamber next to hers, so she put her ear to the stone wall and tried to eavesdrop. Still, she hadn't learned much of use.

She heard more sounds from the adjoining room, so she sat back down on the pallet and put her ear to the stone again. This time, she could make out everything.

Voice #1: "How long before they arrive?"

Voice #2: "I expect them any day now."

She was surprised she could hear them so clearly, but she suspected they'd imbibed quite a bit of ale, making all of their voices louder. She thought the first man was Hamish, and the second was Blackett.

Voice #3: "Tell me exactly what you want me to do."

Whose voice was that? She did not recognize the lad.

Voice #2: "We'll know more once they're here, but I plan to bring her out to get Loki to come forward with the bag of coin. We need to get him alone. If he has any warriors there to assist him, he'll be too dangerous."

Voice #1: "I'll beg you to allow me to go hand to hand with the lad. He's a smart arse, and I'd like to whip his arse."

Voice #2, now sharp and louder: "Nay, you'll not jeopardize our wealth for your sick need to beat him to a pulp. The archer will take care of them both."

Bella almost shouted, but she managed to hold her shock inside. Take care of them? Did he mean…

Voice #3: "So the only two you want me to kill are the lass and the lad?"

Voice #2: "Unless this erupts into a full battle, in which case you'd be expected to take out as many as you can, though I only want you firing on my instruction. The plan is that when he walks forward alone with the bag of coin in his hand, you'll kill them both. I'll grab the coin and immediately send guards outside the gate. We need to be conscious of the fact that Ramsay has an expert marksman who's a woman. Make sure you know where she's located."

Voice #3: "I've heard of her skills. I'll keep an eye out for her."

Voice #1: "So what do we do now?"

Voice #2: "We wait."

Bella's hand shook because she knew all too well that she and Loki were the lass and the lad they meant to kill…and there was no way of getting a message to her beloved.

CHAPTER TWENTY-ONE

Loki would just as soon vomit as think about all that could go wrong on their mission. This is the first time he'd had these feelings roiling through his gut, and he knew why. This time his wife was in danger.

Kenzie tipped his head back to stare up at Loki. "I promise I'll do a good job."

"Do you recall everything you need to do?"

"Aye. I need to lead people to the secret passage leading into the Cliffnock castle. Then I'm to find Bella's room to tell her not to worry."

"Aye, and what else, lad?"

"I'm to lead her out if I get the chance, but if not, I can hide, then find my way back to Logan. He'll tell me what to do next."

"Good job. You're sure you recall the way to the secret entrance?"

"Aye, I memorized it in case I ever needed to use it."

Loki and Kenzie rode toward the front of the group, alongside Brodie, Alex, and the Cameron. The laddie peeked around Loki's waist a few times, hoping to see all the warriors behind them, but it was an impossible task given the rocky terrain.

Seeming to intuit what the laddie was thinking, Brodie said, "Kenzie, we're going down a hill ahead. You'll be able to see the warriors soon."

"I will?" The top of his head banged into Loki's as he shot straight up to speak to Brodie.

"In a few minutes, you'll get to see how many are behind us."

Brodie smiled at him, clearly remembering when Loki was no bigger than the wee lad who now rode before him.

When they were nearing the bottom of the hill, Loki allowed Kenzie to grab onto him, turn around, and peer over his shoulder at the massive number of warriors following them. "Saints above, I've never seen so many men on horseback. Look, Loki, can you not see them yourself? They go on forever."

Loki glanced over his shoulder for a second, just so he could try to see them as Kenzie did. He remembered what it felt like to be under ten summers and spying the Grant warriors for the very first time. It was the kind of view that made a man wish to be a warrior. "Aye, the Grant warriors are an impressive sight, are they not? 'Tis one of the reasons the Norseman ran away with their tails between their legs."

"Are there any savages? Do you think they'll have to fight the earl? Will I get to watch?"

Loki thought about all the danger they were about to face. "I hope not. Death is not pretty, and I want my clan and my Bella to survive this day."

"We'll get those fly-bitten whoresons." Kenzie lifted his hand and scrunched it into a tight fist, his face burning with the same fury Loki had felt as a young boy after seeing a Norseman in action.

Loki thought about life on the road and how different it was from life at the Grant keep. "I do not mind it here, but you'll not speak such language around my wife or my mother. But you'll learn."

Kenzie's shoulders slumped. "I'm sorry, Loki. You'll still take me, will you not? You will not dump me back in Ayr?"

"Aye, you'll still go with us."

Brodie had to shout to be heard above the din caused by the group behind them. "Do not feel embarrassed, Kenzie. Loki used to call everyone he did not like a "surly pig-nut," and it took a while before he learned to mind his tongue around his mother. You will."

Kenzie giggled, his eyes casting a quick glance at Loki to verify that it was true. A moment later, as if possessed by an unseen force, his entire countenance changed in reaction to the sight in front of them. "There it is. We're there."

The line of warriors trailed down the hill and lined up under Alexander Grant's instructions, forming a sea of Highlanders in front of Blackett's curtain wall.

"You'll need to keep silent now, lad, and when I drop you off my horse and tell you to run, you'll head to the secret entrance without question. Understood? You know who is to go with you."

"Aye, my lord."

Once his men, the Ramsays, and the Camerons were all in place, Alex moved his horse forward. Brodie, Loki, and two other guards rode in tandem with him. They made their way to the gate and waited for the guards to appear. One of the men stuck his head out without opening the gate and Alex said, "I need to see the earl."

"Aye, the Earl of Cliffnock is on his way. Shall I give him a message when he arrives?"

"Nay." Alex paused, then continued. "I'll talk to him myself."

"Hope you brought the coin."

The guard headed back into the tower room.

A few moments later, the gate raised and Edward Blackett came toward them on horseback, Hamish on one side, Hector on the other. There was also a third man Loki didn't recognize. Hamish and Hector flashed evil grins at Loki.

"How nice of you to bring your full contingency, Grant, but it will not be necessary."

Laird Alex Grant, the mightiest warrior in all the Highlands, replied, "This is far from my full contingency, about a quarter, but I did not think I needed more than this. Add a few Cameron and Ramsay warriors, and we still have a nice group. Do you wish to be a fool enough to take us on? Shall I send for more men just so you can realize what you are up against?"

Blackett chuckled. "That will not be necessary. You can use all the show you wish, but I have Bella, and if you use even one of your warriors against me, I'll slit her throat. The man with her has his instructions. Any battle and she's a dead woman. You do not even know where she is."

"State your demands."

It was amazing to Loki that there was not even a rustle of clothing from the enormous force behind them while the Grant spoke. He never tired of watching the laird in action. His men knew what was expected of them. Logan had drawn his horse up next to Loki, and Gwyneth could just barely be seen within the trees—seated and ready to move when instructed. Kenzie was quiet in the saddle in front of him, though Loki could feel the pounding of his wee heart. The lad's mouth was slack as he stared and listened to all that was taking place around him, his usually constantly moving body frozen in awe.

The earl shouted for all to hear. "You know what I want. There was no need to bring this force against me. But since you ask, I'll be quite specific. I want Loki to approach me alone carrying the bag of coin, and I want your soldiers to back away from him. When I see Loki headed this way, alone, I'll have my guards bring Bella forward. Once all of this takes place, I'll consider making the switch."

Alex nodded, but not before he glanced at Brodie, then Logan, then Aedan, and finally at Loki—his expression telling each of them that they would move ahead with the plan they'd agreed upon in advance. This dumb maneuver reeked of inexperience and greed. It was exactly what Alex, a brilliant strategist, had predicted the earl would do, and they had planned accordingly.

"Good," Blackett replied, tugging on the reins of his horse to turn back toward his keep. "I'll be waiting for young Loki and the coin. When he makes his approach, I shall return. But not before."

Alex Grant moved his right hand, curling his fingers around the reins of his horse in the signal they had agreed upon. As soon as he did, Brodie and Alex's horses reared back, startling the earl's guards. Loki turned his horse just enough to hide Kenzie, then dropped him to the ground while twenty guards moved into position behind Alex and Brodie, a synchronized dance to draw the eyes away from the important movement on the opposite side of the field. Loki moved his horse in front of Kenzie, giving him the chance to dodge into the trees unseen with the other two, while Gwyneth climbed into the trees. They moved their horses deeper into the forest so they could circle around to the secret entrance of the keep. All of Blackett's men still eyed Alex Grant, whose sword arm had swung out in a wide arc, the sun glinting off the fine blade.

Alex's horse landed on his front hooves with a snort and Alex chuckled, winking at Blackett's men as he moved away. Then he galloped in the opposite direction, a power play that left some men quaking in their boots. Alex Grant was not to be toyed with, he had the finest sword arm in the land of the Scots. When Alex retreated again, Loki followed him. Then he climbed off his horse and grabbed the bag of coin from a warrior in the middle of the group.

The battle had begun. Unfortunately for Blackett, he would have no idea what had taken place until it was too late. Thus far, everything had gone as expected.

Bella couldn't see outside, but her hackles had risen a long time ago, so she knew something was afoot. She couldn't stop thinking about the conversation she had overheard the day before. The earl intended to kill both her and her husband, no matter what the Grants did.

She followed the same circle she'd already worn in the floor as she reviewed all the possible scenarios, but the light sound of scratching near the door stopped her in her tracks. She jumped to the chair in case it was another mouse—or worse yet, a rat—but the door flew open and a young lad hurried into the room. It was the very same lad who had caught her when she'd fallen off her horse in Ayr.

"You, again? Why are you here?" Grabbing the material around his neck, she pulled him close enough so he could hear her whispers. "Who are you?"

Kenzie's hands went to his hips and his back went as straight as a sapling. "Kenzie, how could you not remember me? Loki sent me. He…"

Too anxious for his news to wait, Bella practically tugged him off his feet. "Loki? Tell me, tell me before I lose my mind!"

He squeezed her hands until she let go of him. "He said to tell you not to worry. They will get you out." He grinned, a grin that told her he knew how wonderful those words would make her feel. "I cannot tell you what is to happen, but they are coming for you and you need to trust him."

Boots pounding on the staircase down the passageway greeted them.

"I have to leave now. He will save you." He wriggled his nose with a look of surety that slowed her beating heart, then left.

Loki, please come and get me, and do not let him kill you.

Loki rode his horse toward the portcullis, the sweat on his palms seeping into the cloth bag holding the coins. Mayhap the fabric would weaken enough to lose coins. The thought of the earl watching his ill-gotten wealth fall into the grass almost made him smile.

Of course, it would never reach that point. He had faith in Alex Grant, in his adopted sire, and all of his clan.

Aye, his clan—the clan he belonged with no matter what travesty could possibly befall him. And even if his laird wished to send him off somewhere, he'd do whatever was asked of him without question.

Why?

Because he trusted them. His laird, his adopted parents, and his clanmates had always offered him their support. He was truly blessed to be part of the Clan Grant, the type of clan that had allies as valuable as the Ramsays, the Camerons, the Menzies, and the Drummonds. He hoped he could earn their respect this day.

Knowing they stood behind him, he rode toward the keep with confidence. Once he reached the portcullis, he slid off his horse, his gaze watching every corner and angle for something unusual.

The guard screeched at him, "Move off to the side. Leave your horse behind."

He walked toward the gate, his gaze searching for any sign of Bella. He noticed the area around the keep was quite empty—the clan members he'd seen here on his first visit had apparently deserted the earl. He was told to wait outside the gate for the earl to come to him.

That's when his world collapsed. The Earl of Cliffnock lumbered toward him, his hand holding a dagger to the delicate throat of his wife. Loki had no moves. Alex had told him not to worry, that the situation would be handled from inside. When activity exploded in the keep, Alex and his men would be ready to attack. But there was no sign of Kenzie or the others.

What if Kenzie had failed?

"Set the bag down, but don't come any closer. I want it on that tree stump over there. I'll not play the fool again, Loki." The earl's eyes danced with a look of superiority.

Hamish came out from behind him. "No wise arse remarks today, Loki? Are you sure you do not wish to take me on? One wee fight. Whoever brings the first to the ground wins. What do you say? The earl gave me permission to fight you, just once."

Loki stood, his gaze not moving from the earl's. "Here's your coin. Release my wife—we have an agreement." He placed the sack on the tree stump Blackett had indicated, his gaze locked on the dagger at Bella's throat.

Hamish continued to throw his best taunts his way, but he would not allow the brutish man to distract him from his focus.

His father said, "I do have an agreement with Hamish. He wants a fight with you. I'm of a mind to allow it. What say you, son?"

"I'm not your son, and I am naught like you. Free Bella as you promised. I am not interested in battling with Hamish. I only want my wife."

The grin that exploded on Edward Blackett's face told Loki the man had known all along that he was not his sire.

"Nay, 'tis true, you're not really mine. You are too much of a lass like your mother."

Loki ignored the laughter from the opposing guards, his gaze still fixed on Bella.

Then the only thing that could sway his mind happened.

Hamish reached over and rubbed Bella's bottom, and she chirped, a sound that traveled straight to his soul in an instant.

CHAPTER TWENTY-TWO

Loki would kill the rat bastard for touching his Bella. A loud growl erupted from him and he dove at Hamish, throwing three punches at the man's face before he could react. Hamish swung his leg out, catching the back of Loki's knees and dropping him to the ground with a roar. He punched Loki in the belly twice before he was able to roll away.

Blood ran down Hamish's face, and to Loki's disgust, the animal actually licked it and smirked as he hopped back onto his feet. The two circled one another, Hamish taunting Loki, Loki refusing to respond. Taking the older man totally by surprise, Loki flipped onto his hands and hit him hard in the chest with both feet before he landed upright again. He then pounced on him and pummeled his face. After throwing two punches to the man's belly, Loki grabbed him by the throat, swearing to choke the life out of him. Just then, Hamish kicked him square in the ballocks, bringing him to his knees. Hamish had to fight to get back to his feet, gagging to regain his wind, while Loki fought the sheer pain of the blow. Just as he made it to his feet again, Hector tossed his sword at Hamish.

"A sword against an unarmed man? Fair contest, aye?" Loki blew the hair out of his eyes and fought to level his breathing, reminding himself that being in control was more important than having the most powerful weapon. His sire and his uncle had taught him well, and he would be victorious. Uncle Alex had often told him that all his training could ultimately be for only one fight, but that fight would mean life or death for him or a loved one.

How true his words were.

Hamish swung the sword over his head and heaved it toward Loki's middle, but he easily spun away, causing the older man to stumble. Taking several steps away, Loki tried to come up with a plan to best the sword. But there was no need. Logan appeared behind him on his horse and tossed him a sword.

Satisfaction crossed his face as the cold hard hilt of the sword rubbed against the calluses of his hands. This was his sword—the sword crafted by Brodie Grant for his son. He swung the weapon a couple of times away from Hamish to get the feel of it again, then he waited for the lout to move toward him. Patience, Uncle Alex had often told him—patience, skill, and brute strength would always win the day.

Hamish moved his one hand, a move Loki had been trained to watch for, something that meant a warrior was about to switch his grip. At the exact moment when Hamish changed hands, Loki swung his sword in a wide arc, a move he'd practiced many times. But this time was different, for this time his swing was fueled with hatred for the man who'd mistreated his mother and with fury for the man who'd dared touch his wife.

Throwing his entire body behind the force of the arc, he caught Hamish in the arm first, causing blood to shoot up from his body, then buried the sword deep into his belly.

Hamish's eyes turned dull as he crumpled to the ground, clutching for something—anything—to avoid the fate he'd sought. Instead, the life force drained from every part of him. "Wise-arse bastard."

Loki grabbed the hilt of the sword and twisted it, forcing an eerie sound from Hamish's throat. "Rat bastard. This is from the wee lad you left in the forest alone to die."

He turned to the earl and whispered, "Let. Her. Go."

The earl shoved Bella toward Loki, grabbed the coin, and raced back toward the portcullis.

He ran toward the gate screaming, "Close the gate once I'm in and the archer is out!"

It had been torture enough for that awful man to hold a knife to her throat while her husband was in a fight-to-the-death with that brute. But Loki had prevailed. For a moment, she had allowed herself to hope they'd survive. Then the earl shoved her away and ran toward the keep—and Loki took off after him. "Nay, Loki! The archer has instructions to kill us both. Let him go!"

Loki continued to run until he caught up to Blackett and grabbed him from behind. He tossed the sack of coins over his shoulder as if they were oatcakes full of air, then leaped toward the earl, his fist wrenched back over his shoulder, ready to deliver the blow.

"Nay, Loki," Bella screamed. "He'll kill us both! He's coming our way." There he was, riding from inside the bailey, now in a full gallop.

Bella turned to face the Grant force behind her, unable to comprehend why they were not moving. They simply sat their horses in place and watched. She wanted to slap each one until they listened to her. Her throat had almost closed in fear, but she managed to holler to Brodie Grant. "Please, I overheard them. The archer has instructions to kill us both."

Blackett's guards began to slowly close the gate as Blackett approached the opening, but Loki yanked him back and punched his face with enough force to throw him to the ground. The guards rushed down the staircase to assist him, leaving the gate open, but a wee lad popped out of nowhere and pelted their heads with rocks from behind, making them tumble head over arse to the ground.

Blackett scrambled to get up, but the archer bore down on them, riding his horse toward the gate with a mask on, his bow out and his arrow almost nocked. "Kill them now! What are you waiting for? You have your instructions!"

Bella gave one last heart-wrenching scream as the archer came closer, almost upon them. "Help us! He'll kill us both! Please stop him."

Loki took out his knife and stabbed the earl in the chest just as the archer turned his arrow toward them. Bella threw herself at her husband, screaming, "Naaay!" when the archer suddenly changed his direction and shot the arrow toward the curtain wall, taking out the last guard left by the portcullis.

Bella ran at the archer and tugged on his leg, trying to unhorse him, scrapping and swinging with all her strength, tears flooding her cheeks and yelling, "Leave him be, leave him be."

A warm pair of strong arms picked her up by the waist and

tugged her back. "Bella, Bella, 'tis all right." It was her husband, alive and well. "That archer is my cousin, Torrian."

"What?" Bella's entire body locked up, unsure what to think or say. "He's your cousin?" She glanced up, suddenly realizing Torrian Ramsay was indeed on the horse.

"Aye, Bella. He was part of the plan all along. Torrian was to get on the inside to replace their archer. Kenzie helped him get inside with Uncle Logan. They took the archer out and Torrian stood in his place after the earl and his men left for the gate with you."

Bella's head exploded in a fireball of emotion, taking her breath from her, but she regained enough of it to turn around and shove at Loki's chest. "You knew 'twas him, and you did not tell me? Why did you not tell me?" She pushed him again, using enough pent-up power to cause him to stumble.

He never let go of her. "Bella, how could I tell you when you were imprisoned on the inside? Kenzie told you to trust me, did he not? He did not have time to leave a detailed message."

She moved to shove him again, but at the last minute she threw her hands around her husband's neck instead and started to sob.

Loki whispered in her ear, "Sweet Bella. I'll never let you go. You know that, do you not? You know I love you."

She pulled back without releasing her death grip on his shoulders, "You planned this all along? This was the way it was supposed to happen?"

Torrian ripped his mask off. "Sorry, Bella. I did not mean to frighten you."

Brodie Grant pulled his horse up beside him, cleared his throat, then answered, "No' exactly that way it was meant to go, was it, lad?"

Logan and Gwyneth joined them next. "Nay, but I did enjoy the show you put on," Logan said. "I was almost ready to signal to Gwyneth to kill the fool when he kicked you in the ballocks, but you held up well. I did not wish to take away your glory moment, and you seemed to be handling yourself."

Bella pulled back to glare at Loki again. "Did you have to fight the man, husband? I thought he would spear your innards several times. You could have ignored him."

"Bella, he touched you. I vowed to protect you and I did." He forced her gaze up to his. "I said I'd protect you, did I not?"

Her face erupted in tears again and she collapsed against him, her arms around his waist and her face buried in his chest.

Alex, still on horseback, waved his hand to two score of his guards and sent them inside the curtain wall to manage the rest of the earl's guards, then rode up to Loki's side without saying a word.

Loki glanced first at his father, then at Alex. "My apologies, my laird. Seems I lost my temper when the rat bastard touched my wife."

Alex gave a rare smirk. "Aye, you do not like anyone touching Bella." Midnight snorted and pranced a bit around the two. "I must admit 'twas a fine show you put on for all of us."

"Seems we've taught the lad a thing or two over the years, Alex," Brodie said with a smirk.

Bella peered up at her husband, just realizing what he'd done for her. He'd fought for her honor, like any knight would do. She leaned her head on his shoulder and whispered, "Many thanks for rescuing me, husband."

Loki locked gazes with her and said, "If you promise never to run off alone, I'll promise never to fight in front of you like that."

She scowled, but nodded. "My apologies, but you left me again."

Wee Kenzie barreled over toward them. "Did I do good? Did I do what I was supposed to do, my laird?"

Torrian reached a hand down to pat Kenzie on his shoulder. "Aye, you did a fine job with the guards on the wall, lad, and getting us inside."

The laddie's shoulders straightened as he glanced at Brodie and Alex. "My laird, will you keep me in your clan? May I still go to the Highlands with you?"

Bella said, "Loki, we're bringing him home with us?"

"Aye. You know he reminds me of someone." He ran his fingers through the curls in her hair. "Does this please you?"

"Aye, I want him to come home with us. He can live with us if he prefers."

"Aye, Kenzie," Alex said. "We'd be most pleased to have you along. You did a fine job. As did Loki."

"I did, did I not? Och, and guess what I found? They tried to hide it in the hall, so as soon as they left, I took it." Kenzie pulled out a small velvet bag from inside his tunic. "I wonder what's inside."

Loki held his hand out and said, "Dump it out."

Kenzie pulled on the ties and opened the bag. Peering inside, he shouted, "Saints above. Look!" He tipped the bag sideways and a line of jewels fell into the palm of Loki's hand. Rubies, sapphires, and emeralds.

"Look, Gwynie," Logan said. "Kenzie found the king's missing jewels."

Bella stopped crying long enough to stare at the gemstones. "Oh my."

Kenzie shook the bag and said, "Wait, there's one more item in here." Out tumbled a ring with a square ruby in the center and a small diamond on each side.

Logan said, "A wedding ring, just as I've always promised you, Gwynie."

Gwyneth snorted. "What would I do with a gem like that? It would get in the way of my archery, though it is quite handsome. I think the king should present it as a gift to Bella for all she's been through."

Bella gasped as she stared at the stones in Loki's hand.

Loki kissed her cheek. "Would this make up for all you've been through, lass?"

Clinging to him, she shook her head. "Nay, I do not like to watch you fight like that. I was so frightened." It was all over, but she had difficulty accepting that fact.

Loki returned the stones to Kenzie's velvet sack. "Well done, lad. We'll send it with Logan to return to King Alexander. It would seem Blackett did not only try to steal from us." He caressed Bella's neck as the men continued their conversation.

"Loki, 'twas some fine swordplay you demonstrated," Alex said. "You made me mighty proud to have you in our clan. Mayhap you'll be the best swordsman of your generation, and you can take the title from me."

"Nay!" Bella wailed without thinking, then collected herself enough to say, "My apologies, my laird, but please do not make him fight like that. I cannot handle it."

Loki tugged her closer, kissing her forehead. "I doubt you'll ever be put in such a position again, wife. 'Tis over."

"Brodie, settle the guards inside, make sure all is calm here, then head home. I'll take a group to the Ramsays, then we'll battle the weather behind you. Is there aught else you need to do, Loki?"

"Actually, I'd like to take my wife to the tavern. We'll spend the night, fill our bellies, then head back in a day or two, if you agree."

"Aye, I'd like a warm bath, and I have not slept at all. 'Twas terribly cold, and I've had verra little to eat."

Logan added, "And we know the lass loves to eat, do we not, Torrian?"

Bella hid her face again as her face turned pink, but then she announced, "I think I deserve it this time."

"Aye, you do, lass," Torrian said.

Alex glanced at Brodie. "Do you agree, brother?" One of the guards retrieved the bag of coins and handed it to Alex, who gave some coins to Loki. "If so, I'll leave three guards to travel with them."

Brodie gave Bella a sympathetic look. "Aye, Loki, take her to the inn so she can enjoy a warm bath. The two of you could use a good night's sleep before you travel. 'Twill not be an easy trek through the mountains this time of year. Do you want us to take Kenzie with us?"

Loki glanced at Bella, and the two of them shook their heads at the same time. Bella whispered, "He needs a bath, too, but please do not tell him. He should stay with us."

"Gwynie and I will travel with you to Ayr, but we'll take the jewels to King Alexander and spend the night in the royal castle," Logan added. "Torrian, let Kenzie ride with you to Ayr. You can spend the eve at the tavern with the three of them. In the morn, Gwynie and I will gather our guards, stop at the inn to collect you and return to our keep. You can have our horse then and follow along with us. Loki will need two and Gwynie can ride with me."

Loki found his horse, helped Bella up, and climbed up behind her. "Aye, 'tis time to relax and enjoy each other's company."

⁂

Once they arrived in Ayr, Loki and Torrian headed to the tavern with a few guards while Logan and Gwyneth continued on to the royal castle.

Kenzie asked, "Torrian, are you going to the Highlands with us?"

"Nay, I'll head back to Ramsay land. You'll go with your family. I'll see you in the spring, I'm sure. But for now, some warmth, some food, and some family."

Bella announced, "And a bath."

"Nay," Kenzie hopped down from the horse and stared at her. "Not a bath. I hate baths."

Loki took one look at him and said, "You need a bath, Kenzie. You'll bathe before we eat. All of us will."

His chin dropped to his wee chest. "Must I?"

"Aye, you must. And if you do it without whining further, I'll buy you a fruit tart."

"Suits me fine." The bribe was enough to restore brightness to his expression and he dashed inside, only to be stopped by the man at the desk.

The man tried to order him back out of the tavern, but Loki said, "He's with us. We'd all like to bathe—downstairs for the men, upstairs in the best chamber for my wife. We'll take a full meal for all, including the five guards we have with us."

"Aye, my lord. We'll take care of everything." Once the arrangements had been made, Loki led Bella toward the stairs.

"Kenzie, go with Torrian," he said, calling down to the lad. His wife continued on her way, clearly eager for her bath. "You'll bathe with the men while I situate Bella."

Kenzie stopped and spun around to check where Loki was headed, then followed him to the staircase. He whispered, "But if you go up there, you'll see a girl naked."

Loki would have choked for sure if he'd been drinking anything. He turned back to the lad and said, "Well, that would suit me just fine since she's my wife."

The lad stared at the floor, his face contorted. "But do you really like girls, Loki? Because I do no' like them."

"Well, someday, I promise that you will like lasses, but for now, 'tis acceptable if you do not."

He jumped closer to Loki. "But I do like Bella. She's the only lass I like."

"Good, because I love Bella. You go run and take that bath now so you can get your fruit tart. I'll return in a bit."

Kenzie yelped, "Aye, I have to hurry!"

Loki chuckled all the way up the staircase, wondering if he'd ever felt the same way. He must have at some point. He gave the door a light rap before he opened it, peeking around the side in time to see Bella preparing to climb into the tub.

"Hurry and close the door," she squealed, covering herself the best she could. "I'm so cold I did not wish to waste this hot water the lads just brought up." She stuck her foot into the water and moaned.

Loki froze and stared at her, that sweet moan going straight to his cock, now begging to be set free. "Bella, you should know by now what that sweet sound does to me." He unclasped his brooch and dropped his plaid to the floor, tossing his boots to the side and removing the rest of his clothes in a flash.

Bella stared at his hardness. "That happened just from my moan?"

"Aye, and the sight of you, too." His words came out in a husky tone even he did not recognize, but he moved quickly and lowered himself into the tub before she submerged herself.

"Loki, you're taking up the entire tub." Her hands went to her hips.

He said, "Do not move, lass." He leaned over and flicked his tongue over her nub, causing another moan to erupt from deep inside her.

She leaned toward him, her hands grasping his shoulders, but then she fell into the tub and he flipped her around to tuck her bottom against him, water sloshing everywhere.

"Hand me the soap, lass."

She did as instructed, leaning back against him, and Loki lathered every inch of her body that he could reach, while she did her best to quiet her moans.

Once he finished, he helped her into a sitting position and managed to turn her around without slopping too much more water out of the bath. He repositioned her legs and said, "Ride me, sweet Bella."

She kissed him hard on the mouth, sucking on his lower lip and then plunging her tongue inside his mouth. Loki leaned his head back as she continued her assault, and when she ended the kiss, she gripped his shoulders and reached down to slide him inside her.

After a couple more thrusts, she took him full inside of her, then pulled off him. He groaned and reached for her hips, tugging her back, but she resisted. Understanding dawned at him as he peered up at his wife. She wished to be in control this time. He guessed it was only fair after what she'd just been through.

He lathered his hands again and caressed her breasts, paying particular attention to each nipple as she moved over him again, taking him inside and picking up her rhythm. Her gaze locked on his as she continued. She rode him hard, and when he could take no more, he reached under the water and touched her sensitive bud, forcing her over the edge. He stared into her eyes as passion consumed her, holding out for as long as he could until her contractions pulled him along with her.

Loki knew what heaven would be like.

CHAPTER TWENTY-THREE

Loki and Bella slept soundly in a huge bed, and Kenzie and Torrian took their repose on pallets downstairs. When Logan and Gwyneth arrived the next morning, they packed their satchels and met as a group in front of the inn. The sun shone bright in the bluest of Scottish skies—a mild, beautiful day for the time of the year. "King Alexander wishes to thank you for your loyalty to the Scottish crown," Logan said, nodding to their group. "He also wishes to thank Kenzie for retrieving his gemstones. By the way, what clan are you from, Kenzie?"

His shoulders slumped. "I do not like to use my clan name. We lived alone because my sire did not get along with his clan, and I do not know where they are. It makes me sad to mention it. Must I tell you?"

Logan patted his back. "Nay. 'Tis not necessary. The king wished to offer this token to you, Kenzie, in appreciation of your hard work." Logan held up the ruby ring. "Though you cannot wear it, he thought you might like to present it to a special person."

His face lit up as he took the ring in his fingers, moving it back and forth to catch the sunlight reflecting off its surface. "Many thanks. 'Tis my choice? I've ne'er touched aught this special before."

"Aye, 'tis your choice."

"Then I choose Loki." He turned to Loki and said, "You saved me from the cold, and you had to fight hard yesterday."

Loki took the ring into his fingers, rotating it for all to see its beauty. "Many thanks, Kenzie. I'm happy to bring you home with me. But I wish to ask a question, and I want an honest answer."

"I'll tell you, honest and all." Kenzie's expression told Loki how much the wee lad already looked up to him.

Would he ever have believed that someone would look up to him? A few at Clan Grant would find this fact hard to believe, and a moon ago, he would have never believed it either. But so much had happened to him in that short time, and one person had stayed loyal and faithful to him through it all, no matter what he'd done. Bella. She deserved it more than anyone.

"May I give it to someone I love? 'Tis not a ring I would wear, but I have no ring to give to my wife. May I present her with this ring?"

"Aye, I would like Bella to wear it." He turned to Bella, a hopeful expression on his face.

"I do not know," Bella said shyly. "'Tis so beautiful. Mayhap you should hide it."

Kenzie hopped up and down several times. "Nay, do not hide it. I want to watch the sunlight on it. I'll never see it if you hide it. If you wear it, every time I see the ruby 'twill remind me that our king is proud of me."

Bella hugged him and held her finger out for Loki to place it on her finger. Loki kissed her quickly and Kenzie giggled. "You kissed a girl, Loki."

Logan said, "Well done, Kenzie. Your choices would make your king proud. We'll take our guards and head to our castle. We wish you a safe journey. Let the guards do as they should, Loki. No more playing hero with these two along."

"Torrian, you can ride Gwynie's horse." After climbing up behind Gwyneth, he turned and said, "And Kenzie? I kiss girls, too." He twirled Gwynie around, threw her head back, and gave her a loud smack on her lips.

Kenzie giggled again and turned away.

They all waved goodbye, then headed for their own horses.

Kenzie skipped along behind Loki and Bella, firing questions too fast for Loki to answer. "So is the Grant castle as big as they say? Do you think they'll allow me to stay? Mayhap I could find a job to do...I know! I could be a stable lad, and I promise to work verra hard."

Loki grinned and continued over to their horses, casting a sly grin at Bella, who was clearly as amused as he was by Kenzie's exuberance.

"Oh, wait! Loki. Did you say during supper that you wish to marry your wife again? There's a nice priest here who would love to marry you proper. He's a Blackfriar at the kirk on the other side of town, but I like him."

"Bella and I are married proper, lad. I just mentioned that mayhap we would have a celebration back in the Grant hall someday. We do not need to be married again." He leaned over and kissed Bella's cheek before he helped her to mount her horse.

"But you really would like Father Prestwick."

He scurried over next to Loki, peering up at him with such hope in his face, it took him back a few decades. He remembered feeling the exact same way about Brodie Grant. "Kenzie," he said as gently as he could, "we really do not have much extra time. Winter is coming to the Highlands soon, and 'twill be a harsh enough trip as it is. If we delay any longer, it could be disastrous." Loki lifted Kenzie up in front of Bella. That was a mistake, because now Kenzie could look at him eye-to-eye.

"Please, Loki. Father is the only one I need to say goodbye to. He's the only one who would wonder what became of me. He gave me food many times and let me sleep in his kirk when the coldest nights fell in winter."

He couldn't deny the look in the lad's eyes, so he peeked at Bella, who gave him a slight nod.

"I promise 'twill be quick."

Loki spun around and mounted his horse. "All right, lad, but only for a few moments." He motioned to their guards to follow.

Kenzie's face lit up and he clapped his hands. "You'll no' regret it."

"Lead the way." Loki tipped his head in the direction of the kirk, wondering when he'd turned into such a soft-hearted fool.

Once they reached the kirk, Kenzie jumped down and ran over to Loki's horse, tugging on his hand. "Come along, I promise you'll love Father Prestwick."

"Bella and I will wait outside. You run in and give Father a hug."

"Nay—" Kenzie's face fell, "—I want you to meet him. 'Twill only take a moment. Please?"

Loki sighed and slid off his horse, then wrapped his hands around his wife's waist and helped her dismount. "Bella, let's go inside and warm up for a bit." He turned to the guards, "We'll return shortly."

Kenzie pushed the door open and ran down the aisle, calling for the priest all the while. Loki and Bella followed him inside. The kirk was remarkable, and the tapestries and woodworking were some of the most beautiful Loki had ever seen. The altar had red cloths trimmed in gold threads, covered kneelers, and thick pillows with carefully tended needlework on each one. The lad disappeared through a door to fetch the priest, presumably in the Blackfriar living quarters behind the altar.

A few moments later, Kenzie came through the door tugging on the hand of the priest, a tall man with brown hair peppered with streaks of silver. He had a kind smile, and when he finally managed to pull away from the wee lad, he bowed to them, his hands clasped together at his waist. He stood in front of the altar, a distance away from them yet.

"Greetings and welcome to the House of Our Lord. I am Father Francis Prestwick, and I'm pleased to hear you will be taking Kenzie to your home. He is a good, hard-working soul, whom I will miss dearly. He reminds me of my own son."

Loki and Bella stayed at the back of the building, Bella seated and Loki standing next to her, his hand on her shoulder. "We promise to take good care of him, Father."

"The lad tells me you are Loki Grant of the legend of the Norse battle?"

"Legend? I'm not sure about that, Father, but aye, I am Loki Grant and this is my wife Bella." Loki took a few steps in the direction of the friar.

Kenzie bolted down the aisle and yanked on Loki's hand. "Come closer, you must see Father Prestwick closer."

His mischievous grin made Loki pause—the lad was clearly up to something—but he decided to venture closer to the priest anyway. Loki had to admit the man had a certain pull to him. He moved down the center of the aisle, Bella following directly behind him.

As he approached the priest, Loki dipped his head, then lifted his eyes to meet the other man's gaze. Bella gasped behind him and wee Kenzie was practically dancing on his feet behind the priest, a wide grin on his face. "Do you see what I see, Loki?"

Aye, he did. The priest's eyes widened as he stared at Loki. "Are you the son of Ciara Blackett?" he choked out.

Loki nodded, unable to speak for a moment. The priest had one blue eye and one green eye, just as he did. Loki glanced at Kenzie and whispered, "You knew."

Kenzie nodded, a grin still on his face. "You are the only two I ever met with eyes of different colors, and yet they are exactly the same. Do you no' think 'tis odd? You would no' have believed me if I told you. You had to see for yourself."

A fine tremor shook the priest's hands as he whispered, "Excuse me, I think I need to sit down for a moment."

Loki helped him to a nearby bench, then sat down beside him. "Are you all right, Father?"

"Aye. If you'll give me a moment to collect myself, I'd be happy to explain." He reached inside his robe and pulled out a linen square, wiping his forehead and his cheeks before he set it back inside his robe. "Kenzie, would you do me the favor of taking Bella into my chambers? You can find a piece of fruit for each of you."

"Aye, Father." Kenzie held his hand out to Bella, who leaned down to kiss Loki's cheek before she left.

Father cleared his throat and folded his hands in his lap, looking at them for a moment before he raised his eyes to Loki. "Edward Blackett is not your true sire. I am, as you may have guessed. Our eye color is quite unique." He twisted his hands together in his lap. "Before I was a priest, your mother and I met at a kirk not far from where she lived. She was the sweetest woman I've ever had the good fortune of knowing. I noticed bruises on her frequently, so I asked her one day if it was her husband who gave her the bruises." He paused to stare into space, as if seeking strength to continue. "Our relationship grew from there. Even though she was married to another, I loved your mother. I committed a sin against our God, but I loved her with all my heart."

Tears misted in his eyes, and before he continued, he ran a shaky hand through his hair. "One day, when I could no longer tolerate her living with that beast, I confronted Blackett. I confessed to our transgression and declared my love for your mother, hoping your sire would allow Ciara to leave her marriage. I was hoping to reason with the man, but he would not consider allowing her to leave. As soon as he saw me, he knew I was your father, and I believe he guessed that the babe to be born was also mine. I lived alone in a cottage not far away."

Father Prestwick gave the sign of the cross on his chest before he continued. "I left that day more determined than ever to convince Blackett that your mother and I belonged together. She carried our bairn and I wished to be the father I should be to both of you. But I decided to give him time to absorb the truth. It never occurred to me that he would react the way he did. Word reached me two days later that your mother had died in childbirth along with your sister, but I'm not sure I believe it to be true. I often wondered if he killed all three of you out of anger." He broke into a quiet sob. "He told me you ran away and they found you dead in the forest. I had no idea you still lived, or I would have searched all the earth for you." Crying openly, he reached for Loki's hand. "I'm so sorry. How can you ever forgive me? I had no idea."

"Did you not wonder when I was here living on my own? Had you not heard of Loki then?" Loki wanted to believe that this was his father, but why had he not come to him sooner? They had been so close to each other here in Ayr.

"Your mother named you Lucas. I never knew you as Loki, so I never suspected the stories could be about you. I was also out of the country for many years. Once I recovered from the shock of losing you all, I decided to become a priest in the hopes of becoming a better man. I traveled to London and did not return for quite a while. Every day I beg for forgiveness, but I never expected to find you at my doorstep."

"Father, I was adopted a few years later by a wonderful clan in the Highlands. It was my great fortune to have been brought into their family, though I wish I'd had the chance to get to know you and my mother."

Loki gazed at his father, his true father. He was a kind-hearted, loving man—one who had made mistakes and paid for them dearly. This was neither a man of noble blood nor a man of the greatest clan in the Highlands. But he was Loki's father, and he wished to accept him.

His sire continued, "I beg your forgiveness for my failures. It would be an honor for me if you would allow me to be a part of your life, in any small way, but I also understand if you choose to deny me. Whatever you decide, I hope you continue to honor the parents who raised you, wherever they are, and I will say many prayers for them this night."

Loki stood and helped Father Prestwick to his feet. "I am pleased to meet you, Da, and I welcome you into my life. The three of us are headed deep in the Highlands. You are free to join us—my clan is the most welcoming clan you will ever find—but I wish to return to them. They are my first family, and I treasure them." There, he'd actually said it, and it felt good because he knew it to be true.

"You are happy then?"

"Aye, I have never been happier. I was adopted by the most wonderful couple in the land of the Scots, and I married the love of my life." He didn't need to explain anymore. Somehow, he knew his sire had already been through enough hell. The man didn't need to know more about the time he'd spent living in a crate behind the inn.

Francis Prestwick smiled. "This pleases me. My thanks for the invitation, but my place is here for now. Mayhap you would be inclined to visit again next summer when the winds blow warm again."

"Aye, I would like that. You are welcome to visit the Grants at any time."

"And please promise to send me a message if you ever need aught."

Kenzie and Bella returned with an apple for Loki. "Father, would you like one? Do you mind if I give Loki an apple to take along on our trip?"

"Nay, take as many as you like, lad." He stared at his son for a long moment, as if memorizing his features.

Loki reached over and pulled the man into his embrace. "It was a pleasure meeting you, Father Prestwick. Take care."

⤜⤛

It was a long trip through the Highlands, but Loki found himself grateful for the extra time to think. Kenzie chattered with excitement most of the way, though there were a couple of frigid windy days that had forced them to huddle in a cave together at night just to survive.

When they drew close to the Grant land, Kenzie's face lit up. "Are we there yet? Are those the Grant towers I see up ahead?"

Loki nodded. "Aye, they are. If you look closely, you can see the men in the Grant lists off to the side of the curtain wall."

Kenzie's fingers jerked into the air to point so many times, Bella reached over and stopped him. "Lad, you'll knock us both off the horse if you continue to be this excited by aught you see," she teased.

"My apologies. I'll try not to swing my arm." He clasped both arms around his waist, squeezing tight.

"If you squeeze any harder, you'll knock yourself off the horse and take her with you," Loki said, trying and failing to hide his smile. "Just relax, lad. I know 'tis hard." He recalled riding to Grant land with Celestina on a cold winter day much like today. Celestina had been wrapped tight in furs and Loki had thrown the restrictive coverings off his body as soon as the Grant lists came into his view, practically tossing her off the horse as well.

It was a good memory, but some of his memories from the past were as fresh as a deep cut from the sharpest sword. He hoped to rectify that today.

As soon as they arrived, the stable lads greeted them and helped them with the horses. Kenzie babbled at the lads, who looked at him with naught but confusion. "Someday, I'll be working with you out here. I'm good with horses, I am. I've had to calm some of the wildest before, so I'll be a big help. And I can also…"

"Kenzie, my parents await us inside. You can chat with the lads on the morrow."

"I'm coming. I could eat something, too. Do you think they will feed us? I could eat a lamb pie and a whole loaf of bread, maybe some oat cakes, some pottage. I wonder if Cook knows how to bake apples here. What do you think?"

Bella swung his hand into hers and tugged him along behind her. "I think we need to get inside where it's warm. Come!"

Everyone in the great hall greeted them warmly, but Loki noticed his parents were nowhere to be seen. "Kenzie, sit down and eat. I need to take Bella to see my parents."

"If you insist, I will." He scampered over to the table, hopping randomly as he traveled.

"Bella, do you mind?" He placed his hand at the small of her back. "I'd like to speak to my mother. If you'd like to eat first, you may. I'll be right back."

"Nay, I'd like to go with you." One glance at her beautiful face told Loki she knew what he was about, and she wished to support him.

The two made their way to the tower rooms, a comfortable silence between them, though Loki's mind was anything but silent. He wasn't quite sure how, but he was finally going to say what he needed to say.

His parents sat by the hearth in their tower rooms. Catriona and Alison reached him first, and it heartened him to see that the wee lassie seemed to have made a full recovery. Once he'd hugged both of them and clapped Braden on the back, he said, "We brought a young lad with us, do you mind going to the great hall and making him feel comfortable while I chat with Mama and Papa?"

His brother clasped his shoulder and answered, "Sure, Loki, we'll go. I'd like to meet this Kenzie everyone has been telling me about."

Brodie made his way over to Bella, and Loki could see his mother's gaze on him, her happiness and unconditional love washing over him like the softest of furs. He stood by the door like a statue.

He didn't know how. Hellfire, he had been so certain he would finally be able to tell her how he felt. He'd rehearsed it over and over in his mind on their trek.

Bella, Celestina, and Brodie chatted as he leaned against the door, attempting to organize his thoughts, failing miserably as comment after comment brewed in his mind only to be tossed aside as insufficient.

How did one do it?

How did one person thank another for taking him from squalor? For renewing his hope and faith? At the age of seven or eight summers, he had feared he would be forever cold, forever hungry, forever lonely....nay...forever alone. Instead, Brodie and Celestina Grant had made him forever loved, forever grateful, and forever happy and full of life.

"Loki?" It was his mother's voice, the sweet cadence that was a comfort to his soul. "Are you all right?"

"Mama, I just wanted...I would like..." The words just wouldn't come.

His sire wrapped his arm around his mother's waist. "Son?"

He tried again, forcing the words beyond the lump in his throat, "I met my true sire. He's a Blackfriar, a nice man. I'll tell you about him sometime. But I just wanted to tell you..."

He saw the quick twinge of disappointment in their eyes before they masked it. Och, how he hated to cause them pain. Then he knew. No more. It was in his power to comfort his mother, and he would do it.

Bella stood off to the corner, his beautiful Bella, and as if she could read the words in his heart, she gave him a slight nod of encouragement.

"I just wanted to tell you that I appreciate all you've done for me, loving me the way you have—" he paused for long enough to see the delight emerge in his mother's eyes, "—and that you will always be my true parents. You took me in when I needed it most, and you've been wonderful every day since then, and I will be forever grateful...forever."

His mother ambled toward him, her steps shaky and graceless, which was completely out of character for her. She'd always waited for him to come to her. "Oh, Loki. You know we love you, and I'd be overjoyed to hear about your true sire." She reached up to wrap her arms around him at the same time that his father grasped his shoulder.

His mouth opened, and the words he uttered were weak, but audible nonetheless. "I love you both."

"Loki, did something happen we are not aware of?" Brodie asked.

"Nay, I just...it took me a long time to believe I deserved to come here, but now I do. And I understand what was in your hearts when you took me in."

"Do you?" His mother cupped his cheeks to bring his gaze down to hers. "Do you understand what it was like for me to be locked in a chamber for most of my life, with no friends or family who loved me?"

His head ached terribly from the truth of her words. "Aye, I do."

"That is correct, you do. And you and your father helped to put an end to that for me. So you are more than deserving of the good will that has come your way since then. Please do not ever forget that. You found a way into our hearts quickly. But you seem to understand that a bit better now."

Loki's knees threatened to buckle, but the booming sound of his father's voice forced them back to a locked position. "Let's get something to eat and let Kenzie know we have not deserted him. Celestina, wait until you meet this new lad."

Finally, the strings that had been choking his soul loosened, freeing him from all the things that had been niggling at him for quite some time.

CHAPTER TWENTY-FOUR

Bella and Loki stood by the front door of the keep, greeting all the guests as they arrived. Alex and Maddie had decided they would have a celebration of their marriage, whether her father chose to join them or not. Bella wore a deep green gown—a perfect contrast to her red hair—along with a gold chain around her hips and a deep neckline that immediately drew Loki's attention. Once he got done staring, he scowled a bit at his mother. It was obvious enough to make Bella giggle.

Celestina simply smiled her gracious smile and found a piece of lace to cover up Bella's cleavage. "I do not know why you husbands are so jealous of your wives showing off their curves. I think it would make you proud to have such a beautiful wife."

Loki clearly could not think of an answer to that, so Brodie tried. "Because it makes it too difficult for us to keep our hands off our wives around others."

Celestina lowered her lashes at her husband. "You're so diplomatic, Brodie, but 'tis a fine answer. We shall accept it."

Word had spread through the clan about Loki's fighting skills, the trickery they had used to implant Torrian in the enemy's keep, and Kenzie's part in the rescue and discovery of the jewels. Indeed, the tales had grown to such unbelievable proportions that Loki had started to make light of what they'd done. Still, he had admitted to Bella that he was proud of the way they had been received. The same lads who used to taunt him were now congratulating him on his sword fight.

Bella had gone to see her father once, a sennight ago, but he had turned her away. Her hands trembled. A slender part of her heart still hoped he would come celebrate with them.

Kenzie was working in the stables yet, and he had become quite the popular one. She knew Loki saw much of himself in the lad. They'd all been staying with his parents—Bella and Loki in Loki's old chamber and Kenzie with Braden, but they hoped to have their own cottage soon.

Robbie and Caralyn came in with Gracie, Ashlyn, Roddy, and Padraig. Gracie had turned into quite a beauty, and now that she was ten and nine, half of the Grant guards were begging for her hand, but she was in no hurry to marry just yet.

Gracie came up to Loki and said, "I've heard you question whether or not you deserve to be here. How could you, dear Loki? You saved my life when I was no more than a wee lassie."

Her mother, Caralyn, stood behind her. "Aye, we would have all been lost without you."

His Uncle Robbie grasped his shoulder. "You are a Grant, Loki, and never think otherwise. We're all proud of you."

Bella leaned into her husband, happy to see him receiving the recognition he so deserved. Then the door opened and closed. There were a few muffled gasps of surprise, followed by silence that rippled through the crowd. Bella turned her head and stared straight into her sire's eyes.

"Papa. I'm so glad you're here!" Morna stood behind him, alone.

Bella rushed over to hug them, and to her surprise, they both returned the hugs. Her father was moving along just fine with his cane.

"Father, you are doing better?"

"Aye, daughter, I am. It seems I need to apologize to your husband for all the wrong I've done both of you. Even when you acted foolishly, he did aught he could to bring you back, and I've been told many times how hard he fought for you. Loki Grant, I hope you'll forgive an auld man. I'm proud to say you are married to my daughter. And many thanks for taking care of me when I broke my leg."

"Oh, Da." Bella's eyes misted and she hugged her sire again. It was what she had wanted to hear from him for such a long while. "Thank you for that. You know we love you."

Loki replied. "You are welcome. Your daughter is a bit willful and stubborn," he said, pausing to wink at her, "but I'm hoping she's learned not to traipse off whenever she feels like it."

"Nay, I'm staying home. I'll never go off alone again." She gave Loki a squeeze. "Morna? Why are you here?"

"I didn't get along with my betrothed. He broke the engagement and I was glad for it. So I'm home for now." Her pursed lips told Bella she didn't wish to discuss the matter, so she did not ask further questions.

"I'm glad you're home. You'll find another. Come, we'll find you seats." Soon after she got her family settled, Maddie called for the servants to begin serving the food.

Loki and Bella sat at the dais between Alex and Brodie. The meal was heavenly, and Bella ate way too much. Kenzie ate more than anyone, and they knew because he told them everything he ate.

After they had all stuffed themselves, Alex stood at the dais, his usual movement when he was about to make a speech. The large crowd settled quickly.

"As most of you are aware, our clan was once again challenged by an evil force that attempted to hurt one of our own and steal some of our wealth. We were able to easily put an end to this threat. I thank all the warriors for traveling with me, as well as their wives for supporting them in this venture.

"Fortunately, the battle was short. Loki, Bella, and Kenzie, come forward please."

Kenzie's eyes bulged, but he came forward as requested, his wee legs trembling, bending his neck as far back as he could to gaze up at Alex Grant. Bella reached down to squeeze his hand in a show of support.

"I cannot tell you how proud I am of my nephew, Loki Grant," Alex continued, "who demonstrated the value of his years of hard work and training in front of all of us. He fought hard and achieved a quick victory in a pivotal sword fight. I also wish to commend Kenzie, who helped us from start to finish, and was the person who retrieved King Alexander's jewels."

Shouts and cheers erupted from the clan, and Kenzie beamed from all the attention.

Alex raised his hands to quiet everyone. "Kenzie, we are

pleased to have you at Clan Grant, and there are two people here who are interested in adopting you if you agree. Loki and Bella would like you to be their son if you are agreeable."

Kenzie's delight and surprise told them all how he felt. He burst into tears and looked from Bella to Loki, then back again. He ran to Bella and hugged her tight, then rushed over to Loki to do the same. He stared at both of them with a tear-stained face and asked, "I do not have to live alone? I have parents and a Mama and a Papa again?"

Bella knelt in front of him, Loki right beside her, and the sight of the lad's crumpled face nearly broke her heart. She couldn't imagine what Loki must be thinking and wondered how close this was to his life. "Aye, 'tis true, Kenzie, if you wish to stay with us."

"Aye, I prayed every day, just like Father Brian and Father Francis told me. I asked for a new mama and papa, and now you are here." He hugged them again. "Many thanks. I love you both."

Bella's tears slid down her cheeks, but she wiped them away when Alex motioned for them to stand.

"This really is not finished yet, though I'm pleased to see that Kenzie Grant will officially be your son. We have taken over a small castle not far from here, and my brothers and I have decided that we wish to ask Loki to take over as chieftain of the keep."

Gasps of surprise and cheers and whistles greeted Alex's announcement. Bella's heart swelled with pride as she turned to look at Loki. He met her gaze with a question in his eyes. "What do you think?"

Bella nodded with tears in her eyes. "Aye. I'll go anywhere you wish to go, Loki. Forever."

❧

Torrian ran through the meadow, three guards following behind him as protection. He had an animal bone in his pocket as he often did.

"Come on, I know you grow old, Gertie, but you should still be able to travel out here to visit your sire." He patted the side of his leg and the dog moved closer, her tail wagging.

Gertie, the Scottish Deerhound at his side, was growing old, just as Growley had slowed down after a while. Torrian and Lily had chosen a special place for the big dog to be buried, and they had used a carved cross to mark his grave.

Torrian glanced over his shoulder and laughed. He reached down to pet one of the deerhound pups chasing him, but the runt of the litter was having a hard time keeping up in the high grass of the meadow. In fact, the very moment he turned around to look, the wee pup tripped and fell face first into the grass. Chuckling, Torrian leaned over and picked her up, holding her face directly in front of his. "Greta, it cannot be that difficult. You have to grow big and strong like your grandsire. You know all the stories about Grandpapa Growley and how he taught me how to walk. Now you must learn to walk on your own."

The pup licked his cheek in response. Torrian checked on the other two pups, Ghillie and Grizzly, who had stopped to wrestle each other in the grass.

"Come along, lads, we must go visit your grandsire." They ran along to the edge of the forest, moving closer to Growley's gravesite. He waved to the guards to tell them they need not continue to follow him.

As soon as they found the gravesite, Gertie moved over to lie down, settling her face on the ground with a groan, as if to tell Growley how much she missed him. He set Greta down and the three pups scampered across the already trampled grass as they played together. Torrian spent a long moment looking at the grave marker. He had a soft spot in his heart for the animal that had not only taught him to walk after his sickness, but had done a great deal to help him believe in himself. He'd vowed he would never be without a deerhound at his side as a tribute to his childhood best friend.

Just as he was about to set the dog bone down, he glanced up and caught a lass standing between the trees not far from him. At first glance, he thought it was his aunt, Gwyneth, because she was dressed in lad's clothing, a tunic and leggings with a bow strapped to her back, but she was much younger than his aunt. She watched him without moving. He took a few steps toward her because he was totally entranced by her. Her beauty was almost unnerving.

"Greetings. Do you need assistance? Do you live nearby?"

Rather than answer, she continued to assess him warily, looking as if she were about to bolt. Her hair was a beautiful shade of yellow with highlights of every color interwoven in it like sunlight through tree branches. When he got a little closer to her, he gasped in shock.

There was a longing in her gaze he'd not seen before, but it was something else that had caught him off-guard. She had one blue eye and one green—just like Loki.

And then she was gone.

EPILOGUE

The following summer

Loki stared at his sweet Bella lying on Celestina's bed, panting and groaning. He swore he'd never plant another babe in her belly. She'd already gone through so much carrying this bairn, and now he had to watch her in pain. He could not handle it. She'd asked him to stay because Alex always stayed with Maddie, but he could feel his knees weakening.

"Loki, you look ill. You do not have to stay," Aunt Caralyn said.

They'd come back to Clan Grant for the babe's birth to make sure Bella received the best of care. She'd helped him so much in their new keep, making it special for both of them. They'd had a wonderful first year, but this? This was too much.

"Go, Loki," Bella panted. "Do not faint in here. Caralyn has enough to do, and so do I."

His mother stood and ushered him out the door, leaving Maddie, Ashlyn, and Caralyn behind to soothe Bella through the delivery. A maid busied herself about the room, retrieving whatever was needed.

"Come, you need to relax," his mother said. "You'll have a sweet bairn soon. Perhaps you need an ale."

As they moved down the passageway, Bella let out another wail, so he rushed back inside the room. "Bella, promise me."

Bella groaned, "What, Loki? Can you not see I'm busy?"

"I cannot leave you until you promise me you will not die." He moved back to her side, suddenly changing his mind about leaving.

"I'll not die," she said through a clenched jaw as she attempted to push the babe out. "But I may wallop you with my fist if you do not stop. I warned you. This must be a laddie like you because he is too big to get out. What'll I do? He will not come out."

Caralyn spoke in a calm voice. "Aye, this bairn will come out whether 'tis a lad or a lassie. I can see the fine hairs on its head. It just takes hard work, Bella. Keep pushing. Loki, if you are determined to stay, you must help her."

Help her? What in hell could he do for her? He said the first thing that popped into his mind. "Punch me all you want, Bella, but you will not die." He leaned over her, offering her his shoulder. "Go ahead and hit me if 'twill make you better. Do you hear me, wife? You will not leave me. You must be here to help me raise our bairn." Once this fear had entered his mind, it would not leave him.

Moaning, Bella turned to him, her head falling back against the pillow. "Loki, I know you're afraid I'll do the same as your mother, but I'll not leave our bairn any sooner than I'll leave you. I'm staying. I've promised you many times that I will not abandon our son. But you must accept that we could have a wee lassie, too. Do not be upset if it is." She growled again and squeezed Loki's hand almost hard enough to break it.

"I do not care if 'tis a lass or a laddie, you just have to promise me."

Loki stared at the wee fighter he'd chosen as his wife. Bella was strong, he had to believe in her ability to do this. Why was it that he could stand tall against the worst of adversaries, but anything involving his wee wife made his gut churn and his head swirl?

"Bella's strong, she'll make it through," his adopted mother said, reading his thoughts. "You'll see she'll be a wonderful mother to your children, every one of them."

He glanced at Celestina, wondering what he would have been like without her guidance and love.

Bella broke his thoughts short when she gripped his hand to pull herself back up.

Aunt Caralyn said, "Bella, you're almost there. Push hard, lass.

I can see the bairn's head."

Helpless to do aught but encourage, Loki whispered through gritted teeth, "Push, Bella."

Bella squeezed again, and with a whoosh, out came the wee one into Caralyn's capable hands. Loki stared at the bairn, waiting to see if the babe was hale.

"What is it?" Bella said. "What is it?"

Caralyn and Celestina answered at the exact same moment, but Loki was too nervous to register what they said.

Loki turned to his wife. "Bella, you are all right? There's naught wrong with you?"

Her gaze softened. "Husband, I'm fine. I will not be running down the staircase, but I'll not be leaving you." She cupped his cheek and tugged him closer for a kiss. "We have a son."

"We do?" His eyes lit up as he stared at the small bundle being wrapped in a warm plaid. "A son? A laddie."

Bella and Loki stared at their son until Caralyn set the babe into Bella's arms. "Loki, he's beautiful," she whispered.

Loki leaned over to take in everything about this wee creature in front of him. As soon as he got near, the bairn opened his mouth and let out a bellow, startling Loki. "What's wrong with him?"

"Naught is wrong. 'Tis the sign of a strong bairn." Celestina reached over to squeeze Loki's shoulders. "Congratulations to both of you. I could not be happier."

Loki stared at the babe in his wife's arms.

"Loki, he looks like you," Bella said as the babe swung his wee fist out toward his sire.

He couldn't help but grin at the sight of his son's fist, but then the babe flexed his fingers open. Loki put his finger next to his son's, only to have him grasp on tight.

"He's strong, Bella. Just like you. You did a fine job."

Nothing would ever affect him more than this moment. This was their son, and he would do everything in his power to teach the laddie and love him the way parents should—the way his adopted parents had taught him. He leaned over to kiss his wife. "I love you, Bella."

"I love you, too." She kissed the top of their son's head and fell back against the pillows, her eyes already fluttering shut.

"Bella?"

"Do not worry, Loki," Caralyn whispered, "She had a tough labor, and she's exhausted. Why do you not take your son downstairs to show him to everyone? Have you chosen a name?"

Loki shook his head. They'd decided they wished to wait and see their bairn before they chose a name. Caralyn picked up the babe, swaddled him tight again, and placed him in his father's arms. "Go, while we clean Bella up. Your mother will help you with him. He seems quite content now."

Loki headed down to the great hall and sat near the hearth while everyone stood around admiring the bairn. His mother rushed over to his father, who was anxious to see the babe.

"What's his name, son?" Brodie asked.

"I'm not sure. We haven't chosen one yet." Loki continued to stare at the wee one's face, and then the babe opened his eyes to stare up at him.

The front door of the Grant great hall flew open with a warm gust of wind and Kenzie scurried across the floor, only to come to a skidding halt in front of Loki.

Celestina said, "I better get the wee one another plaid to help against that wind." She disappeared, presumably heading to the family's tower rooms.

Kenzie scowled when he glanced at Loki and the wiggling bundle in his arms. "Loki? Is that your bairn you are holding?"

"Aye. This is our son and your new brother. Bella just gave me the greatest gift in the world. Does he not look like the strongest, most braw laddie you've ever seen?" Loki held him up so Kenzie could get a better look at him.

"Uhhh…why is his face all red and scrunched up? And he acts as if he wants to bellow. I think he wishes to punch someone with his wee fists." He took two steps back in an apparent effort to find safety. "Are you sure he's your bairn? He looks too small to be yours."

Loki laughed at Kenzie's questions. "All bairns are much the same when they are newly born."

Brodie agreed. "But he'll be a handsome lad, I can attest to that, Kenzie. You'll see someday."

The door opened again and Robbie Grant strode across the floor of the great hall, a priest following in his wake. Loki could hardly believe what his eyes were telling him. "Father

Prestwick?"

The man hurried over to him and bowed in greeting. "I hope you do not mind, Loki, but you did issue the invitation, so I thought I would travel while the weather is warm."

Just then, Celestina emerged carrying a small plaid for the bairn. She stopped in her tracks when she saw the Blackfriar standing next to Loki.

"Father Prestwick?"

Loki's true sire turned to Celestina, who was now hurrying over to him. "Aye? May I be of assistance to you?"

Celestina's eyes widened. "Oh my goodness, Loki looks quite a bit like you. Welcome to Clan Grant. Please sit down. You must be tired from your journey. I'll find you something to drink." She covered the bairn in the plaid and headed off to the kitchens.

Loki was suddenly overcome with conflicting feelings. How did he introduce his sire to his true sire? "Da, ummm...this is my true sire, Father Francis Prestwick. This is my sire, Brodie Grant."

Kenzie jumped up and down. "Father, I'm so glad you came to visit us. On the morrow, I'll show you everything here, though we're just visiting, but 'tis late now."

"My thanks, Kenzie. I'll just sit for a spell, if you do not mind." He smiled at the group in front of him, then turned his attention back to Kenzie. "My, lad, but you've grown since I last saw you. They must have a fine cook here?"

Kenzie giggled and then froze, "Father, you must try one of Cook's fruit tarts. They are the best ever."

"You are happy here?"

Kenzie moved over and stood next to Loki, leaning in toward him. "Aye, I'm adopted now and I love my new clan."

The group clustered around the fire, all switching their attention to the bairn in Loki's hands.

Celestina returned with an ale for the priest and said, "Father, this is Loki's son, our grandson and yours. He was newly born tonight."

Loki relaxed now that he saw how accepting his parents were of the situation. "I'm glad you came, Father. I'd like to get to know you, and I'd like you to get to know your family better."

Father Prestwick beamed. "I'd like that, as well. That's a handsome babe you have in your arms there."

Loki gazed at his sire, saw his mismatched eyes, and thought of his mother and all she'd suffered. How he wished he could remember more about her. At least now, he could get to know his father better. He also noticed that his son's eyes were both blue.

Father Prestwick asked, "What have you named your bairn?"

Loki gave him a perplexed look. "We have not decided yet. I must go speak to Bella. Come with me, she would love to see you again, Father."

⸾⸾

Bella stepped cautiously, her hands on Maddie's shoulder, making her way from the chair back to the changed bed.

"There you are," Maddie said. "Do you not feel much better with a fresh gown on? We'll get you back in bed so you can rest. What a fine son you have."

"Many thanks, Lady Madeline."

"Once we get you settled, I'll get Loki to bring the bairn back up to you. Have you decided what you'd like to name him?"

Bella frowned as she thought back on all the names she and Loki had discussed. "We tried many times, but we just could not come up with the perfect name without having first seen the babe. Once he returns, we'll discuss it."

Once they had her in bed and covered with furs again, a knock sounded on the door. Loki entered carrying their bairn with Father Prestwick, Celestina, and Brodie trailing behind them. Caralyn motioned to Ashlyn and Maddie, and they all stepped out of the chamber to make room for the others.

"Good eve to you, my lady," Father Prestwick said.

"Father? What a lovely surprise." Bella glanced at her husband to see his reaction, but he seemed pleased. Brodie and Celestina both had genuine smiles on their faces, so she hoped Father Prestwick's visit was acceptable to all.

"I apologize for the surprise at such a moment. I had no idea, but I confess that I am overjoyed to see the babe."

Celestina pulled a stool out for him. "Father, please sit." She sat in the chair next to him. "Bella, we're all pleased to meet Father Prestwick, and he wished to give you his best wishes. I promise we will not tire you."

"Aye, congratulations on your new bairn." Brodie kissed her cheek.

"Father? Would you mind giving a wee blessing on our son?"

"Why, of course, lass. I'd be delighted."

He took his place beside Loki and reached for the babe's forehead, but then stopped. "What's his name?"

He glanced at Loki, then at Bella, but neither spoke. Bella nodded at Loki, because she knew her husband and could see in his gaze that he had thought of the perfect name.

He leaned down to kiss her cheek, then gazed at the beautiful babe in his arms.

"Lucas. His name is Lucas."

THE END

NOVELS BY KEIRA MONTCLAIR

Dear Readers,

I hope you enjoyed my first novel in The Highland Clan series. If you enjoyed reading about Loki and wish to read more, his story began in my Clan Grant series, LOVE LETTERS FROM LARGS.

If you haven't guessed yet, Torrian's story will be next in the series. If you haven't read about Torrian and his beloved deerhound, Growley, his story is told in HEALING A HIGHLANDER'S HEART.

If you want to know more about my novels, here are some places for you to visit.

1. Visit my website at www.keiramontclair.com and sign up for my newsletter. I'll keep you updated about my new releases without bothering you often.

2. Go to my Facebook page and 'like' me: You will get updates on any new novels, book signings, and giveaways. **https://www.facebook.com/KeiraMontclair**

3. **Stop by my Pinterest page: http://www.pinterest.com/KeiraMontclair/** You'll see how I envision Loki, Bella, Kenzie and their world.

4. Give a review on Amazon or Goodreads. Reviews help self-published authors like me and help other readers as well.

For those of you waiting for another Summerhill novel, don't worry, I have two planned for next year. But first, back to the Highlands of Scotland!

Happy reading!

Keira Montclair

www.keiramontclair.com

ABOUT THE AUTHOR

Keira Montclair is the pen name of an author who lives in Florida with her husband. She loves to write fast-paced, emotional romance, especially with children as secondary characters in her stories.

She has worked as a registered nurse in pediatrics and recovery room nursing. Teaching is another of her loves, as she has taught both high school mathematics and practical nursing.

Now she loves to spend her time writing, but there isn't enough time to write everything she wants! Her Highlander Clan Grant Series is a reader favorite and is a series of eight stand-alone novels. The Summerhill Series is a contemporary romance series set in the beautiful Finger Lakes Region in Western New York. Her third series, The Highland Clan, is set twenty years after the Clan Grant Series and will focus on the Grant/Ramsay descendants.

You may contact her through her website at **www.keiramontclair.com**. She also has a Facebook account and a twitter account through Keira Montclair. If you send her an email through her website, she promises to respond.

Made in the USA
Lexington, KY
09 October 2017